"Stand right where you are. I've got a gun, and I don't mind using it."

Tate didn't move, forcing herself to do as the man's voice commanded. The door was still open, and a man's figure was silhouetted in front of it. He was tall, and his hair and beard glinted gold in the light of the outlaw moon. He was wearing a tattered blue uniform and a gun belt, but the gun was in his hand and pointing at her chest.

She had never seen his photograph, but she knew the identity of the man standing before her.

Carl Petersen stepped forward.

Regrets flashed through her mind. She wished she had searched for her father while he was still alive. She wished she'd made more friends, done more good, made love to a man. She was twenty-one, and life had seemed endless.

He took one more step. The gun wavered.

She hurled the pile of logs just as he took step number three. Then, as the firewood slammed against his chest, she turned and fled.

Dear Reader,

The weather's getting colder, and the holidays are approaching. Why not take a little time for yourself and curl up with a few good romances? This month, we have four outstanding candidates for you.

Start things off with *Fugitive*, by popular Emilie Richards. An isolated mountain cabin, an escaped convict who is both less and more than he seems, moonshine and memories, and a woman who is just starting to make sense of her life—such are the ingredients that combine in this deliciously romantic brew. You won't want to miss a single word. Ann Williams is a relatively new author; *Haunted by the Past* is only her third book. But what a story it is! A woman on the run from a dangerous past meets up with another sort of danger: a man with revenge in mind and no time for love. But, forced to travel together, they discover that revenge is not always sweet, safety *is* within reach, and a loving future can make up for any past.

Also this month, Linda Shaw returns with *One Sweet Sin*, which will have you on the edge of your seat. There's just something about a man in uniform.... And Nikki Benjamin weaves a tale of romance and suspense in her first book for the line, *A Man To Believe In*.

There's always something going on at Silhouette Intimate Moments, so sit back, open a book and *enjoy!*

Yours,

Leslie Wainger
Senior Editor and Editorial Coordinator

EMILIE RICHARDS

Fugitive

SILHOUETTE·INTIMATE·MOMENTS®

Published by Silhouette Books New York

America's Publisher of Contemporary Romance

SILHOUETTE BOOKS
300 East 42nd St., New York, N.Y. 10017

ISBN: 0-373-07357-7

First Silhouette Books printing November 1990

Printed in the U.S.A.

EMILIE RICHARDS

believes that opposites attract, and her marriage is vivid proof. "When we met," the author says, "the *only* thing my husband and I could agree on was that we were very much in love. Fortunately, we haven't changed our minds about that in all the years we've been together."

The couple lives in Ohio with their four children, who span from toddler to teenager. Emilie has put her master's degree in family development to good use— raising her own brood, working for Head Start, counseling in a mental-health clinic and serving in VISTA.

Though her first book was written in snatches with an infant on her lap, Emilie now writes five hours a day and "rejoices in the opportunity to create, to grow and to have such a good time."

Prologue

In the forgiving embrace of rose-tinted twilight, the gun towers rising above High Ridge Penitentiary resembled the turrets of a fairy-tale castle. The man with *Petersen 94729* stenciled above the pocket of his khaki work shirt knew better. High Ridge was neither a castle nor the setting of a fairy tale. It was hell, pure and simple, where the damned learned to placate the devil or died trying.

Inmate 94729 had been a quick learner. In his three months at High Ridge, he had learned everything he had to know. The problem was that he had learned too much, and sometimes knowing too much was more dangerous than not knowing anything.

He watched as guards vacated the two closest towers. Both the prison workday and supper were over, and apparently the inmate count had just been cleared for the night. No prisoners were on this side of the vast High Ridge complex to worry about now—at least officially.

At the sound of footsteps, the tall, blond prisoner straightened and cursed softly. "Damn you, Josiah Gallagher." He thrust one hand in his pocket and ran the other over the neatly trimmed beard he sported in a prison where clean-shaven men were the rule. The beard was just one example of his exalted status at High Ridge—a status that could backfire in the worst way, if he didn't take some action.

"Talkn' to yerse'f, Petersen?" The tobacco-chewing guard stopped and leaned on the doorjamb, watching curiously as Carl Petersen walked back to the computer and away from the window that looked out over a thicket of small pine trees and neatly trimmed yews. The landscaping was part of the fairy-tale illusion, too. The trees and hedges had been planted to hide the fourteen-foot Cyclone fence behind them—not to mention the thick coils of razor wire beyond that, or the second fence rising just beyond the wire.

The prisoner spoke. "Go away, Cooney. You bother me."

The guard chortled good-naturedly. Jim Cooney was one of the few good-natured men at High Ridge. His boss, the warden, Captain Roger Shaw, was not one of the others.

"I've got work to do," Petersen said.

"Now, *you* know I can't go away. Captain Shaw likes you well enough, but he likes you here, not hoppin' away to the briar patch."

Ignoring the guard, Carl Petersen silently damned Josiah Gallagher once more. Gallagher had left him here to rot. Gallagher, his trusted friend—which just went to prove that nobody—*nobody*—could be trusted. Not ever.

Cooney chortled again when Petersen didn't answer him. "Now me, I don't think you got rabbit blood. You won't run. Too civilized, that's what I think. Too educated. Never did see no educated rabbit."

Petersen spun his chair around. The chair, like everything else in the warden's office, was state-of-the-art. "I'm not going to get this finished if you don't stop chattering. Didn't I hear you were supposed to feed me tonight? Baked chicken and fresh asparagus?"

"Don't eat like no rabbit I ever seen, neither." Cooney's gaze roamed the room. Apparently satisfied nothing was amiss, he left to retrieve the tray that had been brought over from the kitchen half an hour before.

"And don't forget to warm it in the microwave," Petersen called after him. He was out of his seat and across the room again before the words were out of his mouth. The silver letter opener with the warden's initials flashed as he wrenched it from his pocket and twisted the last bolt from the air conditioner covering the bottom half of the one window that wasn't barred. Then, as satisfied as he could be under the circumstances, he strode across the room and melted into the crack between the door and the wall. He didn't have long to wait.

"Ham hocks and turnips, tops and bottoms," Cooney called out as he entered the room. "Don't need no microwave. Still as hot as a hooker's—"

"Just set it down, nice and easy," Petersen said from behind him. He stepped forward and pressed the letter opener against Cooney's throat.

Cooney didn't move. "You got no call to hurt me, son. And you ain't got no way a'tall of gettin' out of here 'cept in a pine box."

"The way I've got it figured, some of the poor bastards who end up in this hellhole don't even *get* a pine box." Petersen slid the letter opener lightly back and forth against the guard's throat to make sure Cooney knew he meant business. He had been sharpening both sides for days, every time he was called to the warden's office. Now he drew tiny beads of blood. "Now set the tray down."

"I'm doin' it, I'm doin' it." Cooney bent over and set the tray on the floor.

As he did, Petersen slid his hand down the guard's side and took his .44 out of his holster. Then he removed Cooney's two-way radio. "Turn around slowly. Hands over your head."

Cooney did as he was told, but his fingers passed lightly over his throat as he raised his hands, as if to be certain the cut was really bleeding.

"You'll live, if you're careful," Petersen assured him. "And you'll have something to tell your grandkids."

"You ain't gonna make it. Even if you get out of the yard, they'll round you up afore daylight."

"Too bad you won't be able to watch." Petersen motioned Cooney to the closet. "Unlock the door."

"I don't carry that key."

"Yes you do. You'll unlock it right now and give me the keys. Then you've got one minute to strip."

Cooney seemed to know what was coming. "I'm three inches shorter and forty pounds heavier than you are, son."

"Fifty-four seconds."

Cooney gave up the argument. His tie came off first, then the blue shirt with the official High Ridge armpatch. Finally his pants.

Petersen stripped simultaneously, holding the guard's gun squarely on him the entire time. He pulled Cooney's clothes on as Cooney watched, cinching the holster with its rounds of ammunition in the last hole. Cooney's pants hung in folds around his narrow waist, but there was nothing to be done about it. Petersen held out his hand when he'd finished. "You forgot your hat."

Cooney's expression grew pained. "This hat's all broke in. Jus' the way I like it."

Petersen held out his hand, and a nearly naked Cooney removed the wide-brimmed felt Stetson. He watched as Petersen jammed it on his head. Petersen motioned him farther into the closet.

"The captain'll have your hide for this," Cooney said sadly.

"Tell the captain something for me, Cooney. Tell him I talk just as well as I run. And tell him I took a little present with me, will you?" Petersen lifted two five-inch computer diskettes off the warden's desk and slipped them in the neatly trimmed pocket of the uniform he now wore.

"You'll be a dead man for sure, son. Hate to see it."

Petersen slammed the door, cutting off anything else that Cooney might have wanted to say. He considered, just for a moment, taking the necessary time to shave off his identifying beard with the electric razor the warden always kept in the bathroom just off his office, but he decided against it. The time to make his escape was too short already.

In seconds he was prying the air-conditioning unit from the window using a jail-cell bar. The bar was a souvenir from another inmate's "run to the briar patch." It was one of Captain Shaw's favorite knickknacks. The inmate who had so neatly sawed it from his cell door hadn't lived to see it put on display. He had lived just long enough to see the captain lift it high and swing it toward his skull.

The air conditioner fell with a crash to the carpeted floor. Petersen waited tensely for an alarm or the clatter of footsteps in the hallway. But there was only silence.

As he lowered his legs out the window, he cleared his mind of all fears, all doubts. He would make this escape as he had made others. He was young, strong and daring enough to make this work.

There wasn't now, nor had there ever been, a building or a fence or a man who could hold him if he didn't want to be held. And he didn't want to be held at High Ridge Penitentiary any longer.

He had a score to settle with a man named Josiah Gallagher.

Chapter 1

"*When the moon rides low in the night sky, like the biggest pumpkin in October's frostbit pumpkin patch, folks here about call it an outlaw moon. I call it the same. You would, too, if you'd been lucky enough to hear the tales I've heard.*

"*Once the Ozarks were the home of many an outlaw band. The James Gang, the Daltons and the Doolins all had hideouts hereabouts or down the road a wander. Every family I know can tell you about one of them, or about Belle Starr, the outlaw queen.*

"*There are caves in these hills where fugitives could hide until the law got tired and the moon got full. Then, by nothing more than moonlight, they could find their way to freedom.*

"*There's an outlaw moon hanging on the horizon as I write this. I can almost hear the whickering of the James boys' horses as they ride along my riverbank to Missouri.*

"*I wonder how the men in prison at High Ridge feel on such a night? Does the moon stir their blood as it once stirred the blood of their brothers? Do they wish that they, too, were following the river? Or do they sit patiently in their cells counting the days until they make parole? Is the outlaw moon shining through their bars only a sign that they are one month closer to freedom?''*

''Not for one man, Millard.'' Tate Cantrell closed the leather-bound journal and spoke her thoughts out loud—although there was no one to hear them. ''Just the day before yesterday one man at High Ridge got tired of crossing off days on his cell wall and slid out a window, instead. Jesse James would have been proud to know him.''

She hugged the journal to her chest for just a moment as a shudder passed through her. Either the crisp air of autumn, the pumpkin moon just clearing the horizon, or the folk legend recorded in her father's painfully neat handwriting had precipitated the chill—not that it mattered which.

Tate set the journal on the kitchen table beside her half-eaten supper and went to look for her wool jacket. She would make a fire when she came back in from her evening chores. In the meantime she would bundle up and force the chill away. There was no one else to warm the house for. She was alone in an Ozark mountain cabin with only her father's written musings and one cinnamon-colored hound dog for company.

And that was all the company she needed—maybe too much, if she counted Cinn.

After a search of the cabin she found the red-and-black checkered jacket hanging from a wooden peg on the back porch. She remembered she had hung it there after her last trip to the outhouse. She shivered again before she could button it. The jacket had belonged to her father. She had never seen Millard Carter, hadn't even known his name until recently. Now the jacket was just one more piece in the puzzle that was the man who had sired her.

For a moment she stared at the orange moon and considered what she'd learned about him since the day three months before when she'd been told that the man she had long since ceased to wonder about had died and willed her everything he'd owned.

She knew that he had been a huge lumberjack of a fellow. The jacket she was wearing hung just inches above her knees, and the first time she'd put it on, she'd had to roll the cuffs half a dozen times to get them to her wrists. In addition to size, she had an idea of what he had looked like. There had been three photographs of him in the cabin when she arrived. One was of a young man just about her present age of twenty-one, one of a middle-aged Millard accompanying a newspaper article headlined "Ozark Folktales Kept Alive," and one of him in his coffin.

The last had given her nightmares for a week—until she realized it hadn't been left there to horrify her. Mountain Glade and the surrounding area overflowed with people who claimed to be Tate's kin. They were a silent lot—though not disapproving, exactly. "Watchful" was a better word. But although it was clear that the members of the Carter clan weren't sure how they felt about her, their feelings about her father were clear. They had respected Millard Carter, and the photograph was a mark of that respect.

Tate had put that final photo away and concentrated on the others. From them she had discovered that her black hair had come from Millard, along with her pointed chin. She wasn't sure about her features. It was difficult to look at the two-dimensional photograph and compare noses, brows and lips. Eye color was a mystery, since the photographs were black-and-white.

One thing she was sure of, however, was how her father had felt about the land stretching down from this porch to the river, a quarter mile beyond. Millard Carter's slice of the Ozarks had been his whole life. He had lived and died on his five hundred acres, and he had left them indelibly stamped with his personality.

Cinn chose that moment to howl. In the month Tate had been living on her father's land, she had never seen any real display of energy from the lop-eared hound. Yes, he breathed. And sometimes he slunk from shade tree to shade tree, when the afternoon sun changed positions. Once she had even caught him lapping at a mud puddle—as if the bucket of fresh water she provided was permanently out of reach instead of fifty yards away. But now he was howling.

"Thatta boy, Cinn. Liven the place up a bit, why don't you?" she called.

The noise, coming from somewhere in the distant shadows, ceased abruptly.

"Blew your cover, didn't you?"

Her only reply was the noise of wings as the small flock of geese that made their home in the pond behind the barn rose as one into the night sky.

Tate debated between going back in the house to finish supper or taking care of her chores so she would have the rest of the evening free. The chores were few, the meal meager. She decided to finish the first before the second. Then she could eat what was left of supper in front of a warm fire.

The outlaw moon had risen a notch. Tate thought about her father's journal entry as she walked along the path toward the barn.

The journal, begun just months before his death, was one of the only really personal things of her father's that she had found. She was reading it slowly—gleaning Ozark folklore and history, as well as a picture of Millard Carter. It was odd that she had chosen the outlaw-moon portion to read with supper. Odd because tonight's moon so closely fit his description, and odd because there really was an outlaw on the loose. A federal prisoner named Carl Petersen, computer criminal and murderer, had escaped from High Ridge Penitentiary, twenty miles away, just two days ago.

Her portable radio, Tate's only link to the world, had been full of details. Petersen was known to be armed, dangerous and wounded. He was thought to be headed back home to Houston—which was just fine with her, since Houston was far south of the prison and Mountain Glade was due east. There had been two reported sightings south of High Ridge and, this evening, one unconfirmed story that Petersen had been seen hitchhiking out of Little Rock.

Tate felt a twinge of sympathy for Petersen, who seemed to have the whole state of Arkansas on his tail. From experience, she knew what being on the run was like. And a man like Petersen, a man reported to know everything about computers and nothing about life, probably wouldn't have a prayer of staying free. High Ridge wasn't rumored to be a place where ''forgive and forget'' was a popular motto. When Petersen was returned to prison, his life would be hell. He would probably never see daylight again.

Of course, he had brought his troubles on himself. According to the radio he was a former bank official who had neatly embezzled a cool 1.2 million using a complicated wire-fraud scheme, then killed the man who tried to turn him in. And even though the murder charge had been plea-bargained to second-degree, he was still guilty of taking a life. She hoped that he wouldn't take others before he was captured.

Tate stopped just short of the barn door and took two metal buckets off a set of pegs. One of the things she *definitely* knew about her father was that he was a man who had eschewed creature comforts. ''Simple'' was itself too simple a word for the way Millard had chosen to live. The cabin had no electricity, no running water or plumbing of any kind, and no telephone. The drive leading from the unpaved country road back nearly a quarter of a mile to the cabin was nothing more than a parallel set of ruts etched from hillside and forest.

She didn't mind the austerity or the isolation, but there were times like now, when she was dead tired and needed a bath, that hauling water uphill seemed an injustice. Still, chastising a dead man was a waste of time.

Tate carried the buckets a few yards down the hill to the rock-lined basin where a galvanized pipe spurted pure mountain springwater to the rocks below. She set first one bucket, then the other, below the pipe, emptying them as they filled into a small wooden rain barrel mounted on a makeshift wagon. When the barrel was nearly full, she would trundle it up the gentle slope to her back porch, where two more buckets waited to empty it. And when she finished with that, there was still wood to bring in for the fire-

place and cookstove, as well as geese and one stupid hound
dog to feed.

As she worked Tate wondered why Millard Carter, the
father she had never known, had struggled so hard to stay
off the twentieth-century path of progress. At that moment, with the outlaw moon bearing down on her and a
day's worth of strained muscles crying out for reprieve, the
nineteenth century seemed anything but romantic.

She was halfway up the path with the rain barrel before a
more obvious question occurred to her.

Why exactly was *she* living in the middle of nowhere, following inch by inch in Millard Carter's footsteps?

Inmate 94729 regained consciousness slowly. One moment the sun had hung heavily on the horizon, refusing to
sink into oblivion, the next the sky was black except for a
huge amber moon leering behind a patch of pine and sassafras. The hours in between were a void filled with nothing but pain and thirst.

He opened his eyes wider and increased his field of vision slowly, turning his head from side to side as he tried to
remember where he was. "Why" he was there was impossible to forget. He remembered too well sliding through the
warden's window and the minutes afterward when he had
blended into the shadows, watching for the slim possibility
that someone might have returned to one of the towers.
There had been a sweet moment of victory when he had
known for certain that he wasn't being watched.

He remembered the fence he had climbed, too. Not one
of the insurmountable Cyclone fences; he wouldn't have
made it halfway up one of those without being seen. But the
grassy area outside the warden's window had led to a lower
fence, marking the entrance to a staff parking lot. There had
been no need for scrupulous security here. Every window in
the warden's wing was barred—except for the one that had
held the air conditioner. And prisoners were only allowed in
that wing under armed escort.

Good luck had run out abruptly at that point. His escape
wouldn't have been detected except that at the same mo-

ment he scaled the fence top, a guard who was either late for his shift or coming back for something he'd forgotten had driven into the lot and seen him.

After that moment of discovery, his memory was mercifully blurred. He had run toward the woods. There had been gunshots, but none from his own gun, because it would have slowed him down too much to draw. There had been a siren and searchlights. There had been the realization, after endless minutes of plunging through the forest, that his leg had been hit by a bullet some undetermined distance back, and he was losing blood at an alarming rate.

That discovery had marked the beginning of brief moments of lucidity alternating with moments when he hadn't been sure of his own name. He had bandaged his leg with a piece of his shirttail, and despite excruciating pain he had stumbled on in the direction of the river separating High Ridge property from the nearest town. He had known that come daylight trackers would be after him, if they weren't already. His best chance of remaining free was to float downriver as far as he was able, until he could be sure his scent was lost to the hounds. Then and only then could he rest and recover his strength.

He had followed his own plan, and it had almost killed him. Finding the river had taken most of the night. Once there, the water had been numbingly cold and the current faster than he had expected. With the vines of wild muscadine that he had sawed with the warden's letter opener, he had tied himself to a log he found at the water's edge. Then he had pushed himself out to the middle of the wide stretch of water and begun the long trip to freedom.

Sometime later, hours, days, years perhaps, he had washed ashore like a beached survivor of a shipwreck. The log had broken into pieces; his shoes were gone, Jim Cooney's uniform sodden and tattered. Somehow, before he had bound himself to the log, he had found the presence of mind to strap the gun belt to a branch rising high out of the water, and it had endured unharmed.

Inch by inch he had dragged himself into the shelter of the brush-covered riverbank. Shivering and half dead, he had clawed a hole in the coarse silt, pulling what he displaced back over himself, along with branches and pine needles, until he fainted from the effort.

His own moans had awakened him sometime later, followed closely by the sound of men's voices. He had been rational enough to force himself to lie quietly and wait. He had expected recapture. Instead he had gradually realized that the men were farmers, working on the far side of the slight ridge along the riverbank. As the day progressed and the sun warmed him, he had listened to the sound of their farm machinery and their occasional shouts. He had grown so hot he had dared throw off his makeshift cover; then he had grown hotter still, until the cold water yards away was a torment.

He had dragged himself to the river to wash and drink after the men had gone home and the sun had gone down. The strength he had hoped to recover was as elusive as the miles he had hoped to gain. The wound in his leg throbbed incessantly, and the flesh around it was swollen and angry.

Through sheer determination he had found a better place to sleep that night. An abandoned hay barn just over the ridge had sheltered him until the first light of his second morning of freedom. Then he had made his way to the woods behind the barn, leaning heavily on a branch he used as a cane. His first taste of food since the escape had been a handful of black walnuts, husked between two flat rocks. His stomach hadn't been able to handle them.

He had wandered, after that. The woods were thick, the land surrounding him harsh and wild. He had stopped to rest often, once in a shallow cave, once under a pile of brush. He had drunk from a shallow stream whose water tasted of decaying leaves, and his stomach had rebelled again.

He knew he had covered no more than a mile before the sun began to sink in the sky once more. And he had known, somewhere in between the chills and fever that constantly racked him, that he was going to die if he didn't find food and warm shelter. The night promised to be colder than any he had yet experienced. And the infection in his leg was raging out of control.

He had begun to find his way out of the woods, then. Where before he had stayed in the densest part of the forest, now he moved toward a section that had been recently cleared. His plan had been to find a house and wait until night to forage for food, clothes, money. He had weighed his chances and known just how slim they were. But he wasn't a man to give up. Hope just wouldn't die. There were people who could help him—Aaron could help him, if he could just get to a telephone. He still had Jim Cooney's gun. If he had to hold someone prisoner to save his own life, he would do it.

He struggled on, now using two sticks as crutches. Gauging the sun's position, he guessed it was near five o'clock when he reached the forest's edge. There were hills beyond, some planted in neat rows of evergreens. The land zigzagged like a crazy quilt of forest and field. But beyond the last stand of trees was an old log cabin with a wide front porch. Far below it was a blue ribbon of glistening water, the river that had carried him this far.

He had backed into the forest and begun to follow its edge until he found a better position for reaching the house. Then, after watching as carefully as he could for the cabin's inhabitants, he had taken a gamble and crossed the first field. The effort had cost him everything, and he had sunk into oblivion in the cradle of a leaf-filled pit. He had awakened later to watch the sun hover on the horizon.

And now the sun had been replaced by the biggest moon he had ever seen. There were details about his odyssey that he would probably never remember, but now his task was to bring it to a conclusion. Somehow he had to get into the cabin, find a change of clothing, first aid for his leg and food his body would tolerate. He would not die here, in some godforsaken hillbilly county, immersed in pine needles and fallen leaves.

He sat up slowly, pushing himself with both hands. The moon revolved in fiery comet streaks; the skeleton forms of the trees danced a bizarre tarantella. He waited, breathing slowly to force his dizziness away. His makeshift crutches lay on the ground beside him, but finally, with their aid, he was standing and moving toward the cabin.

There was no sign of life inside, only a dull glow from the back of the structure, like a night light, perhaps. There was no smoke from the chimney despite the rapidly falling temperature. There was no car or truck parked outside, no pack of dogs clustered on the porch, no farm animals begging to be fed. If he was lucky, truly lucky, the cabin's residents were away for the evening. He could break in, find what he needed, even call Aaron in Memphis, perhaps. He could give Aaron the phone number, and Aaron could find out just exactly where this place was. Then he could find a safe spot to wait until Aaron could get to him.

If he was lucky.

He used the tree line for shelter, until he came to the best spot for making a break for the cabin. He started across the clearing, his skin soaked in sweat despite the chill night air. Once his leg twisted beneath him, and only stern self-control kept him from giving in to the agony and falling. Each inch between him and the porch seemed a mile, each step a relentless torture.

He had reached the porch steps when he heard a dog's howl. He stumbled, falling forward to the bottom step, and the world went suddenly dark. Nausea gripped him, and bells seemed to clang in whirling frenzies of sound. He held onto the wooden plank and hung his head. From somewhere far away he thought he heard a shout.

It was a minute before the mists began to clear. He listened intently, but everything was silent. The shout was a mystery, perhaps real, or perhaps only a voice from his fever-riddled brain. Whichever it had been, he had to move on.

The steps seemed as numerous as the stars breaking out in the night sky. He dragged himself up them, one by one. On the porch he rested, too exhausted to continue, too relentless to quit. After a moment he clawed his way up the porch post until he was standing once more. Lurching unsteadily, he reached the door.

There wasn't a lock he couldn't pick, but he didn't relish trying this one with hands that shook like poplars in an autumn windstorm. He turned the knob, and the door swung in with a creak. Silently he blessed the trusting souls of country people.

Inside, the cabin was larger than he had expected and more rustic. There had been no attempt to cover the massive logs and mortar with wallboard. Abe Lincoln would have felt right at home.

A quick scan uncovered a doorway to his far left and told him that the cabin had at least one more room. The majority of the space wasn't divided by walls but by the placement of simple furniture. Opposite the front door was a round oak table, beside it an old-fashioned wooden icebox, a counter and sink. A cast-iron wood stove separated the kitchen from the living area to his right. A massive fieldstone fireplace covered that wall, with a sofa and chairs placed in front of it. Opposite the fireplace, above more chairs and wall-to-wall bookcases, was an open loft with stairs leading to it.

The dim glow he'd noticed from outside came from a kerosene lantern burning on the table. By its light he recognized the obvious. The cabin had no electricity. More important, a kerosene lantern needed tending. No one left a lantern burning, without staying nearby. Particularly not in a firetrap like this.

And there was food on the table beside it.

He leaned against the door and drew his gun. There was no one in this room. He was still alert enough to know that. But there was at least one room to his left, and a loft. As quietly as he could, he hobbled in that direction. He determined to try the room. Surely if anyone was in the loft he or she would have made a sound when a half-dead stranger dragged himself through the front door.

The room beyond the doorway was medium-sized, obviously a bedroom. There was a large ornate iron bed made up with a patchwork quilt. No one was in it.

He stumbled to a closet and opened it to see men's clothing, overalls, mostly, and plaid flannel shirts. He grabbed one of each, then rummaged in the chest of drawers by the bed for socks and underwear. Two of the drawers yielded only women's things, but the third produced what he needed. Encouraged that he had made progress so quickly, he searched the near-darkness for a telephone but found none. Out of the bedroom, he made his way across the room to the table.

Half a sandwich stared back at him from hand-thrown brown crockery. Most of a glass of milk sat beside it. His stomach lurched as he imagined trying either, but he forced himself to lift the sandwich and take a bite. He chewed slowly, willing his body to accept nourishment. He had to be strong, and he had to eat if he was going to survive.

He tried the milk next, but he could only manage a sip. Nausea and dizziness overwhelmed him, no matter how hard he tried to fight. He slid into the chair and used what remaining strength he had to lift the glass chimney of the lantern and blow out the flame. His head slipped to the tabletop, and he lapsed into unconsciousness.

Later—he didn't know how much—he came to again at the sound of a mournful whistle and the shuffle of footsteps. His fingers closed on the butt of his gun. With what failing strength he had, he pushed himself upright and struggled toward the back door.

The lantern had gone out. Tate stopped whistling as she glanced toward the window that had framed the outlaw moon at supper. She was surprised. She didn't think the lamp had been low on kerosene, and despite the cabin's one hundred-plus years, it was surprisingly draft-free and cozy. Still, kerosene lanterns weren't exactly high-tech. At least the preposterous pumpkin moon was high enough to light her way until she could get the wick burning once more.

Maybe she would light the other lamps, too. Kerosene wasn't expensive, not when she figured what she was saving on utility bills. There was something about this night that called out for light. She would start a fire right away, as well. She might even toast marshmallows and make s'mores. She had missed Girl Scouts and slumber parties as a teenager, but later, thanks to Kris and Jess, her adopted parents, and Stagecoach Inn, the home for runaways that they had founded, she had regained a little of those lost years.

Kris and Jess were sold on s'mores, she remembered fondly. They squashed toasted marshmallows and graham crackers and chocolate bars into sandwiches on autumn nights, as if they were a special remedy guaranteed to heal the saddest or most rebellious adolescent in Stagecoach Inn's care. And sometimes, s'mores—or maybe the love that went with them—even seemed to help.

Tate climbed the back steps, her arms filled with firewood. Some of it was from an apple tree, and she looked forward to the scent of applewood filling the old cabin. Simple pleasures, s'mores and applewood, but oddly comforting on a night such as this one.

She balanced the logs against her chest, leaning backward as she reached for the doorknob. She whistled to herself again as the knob turned. The song was one she had heard last week at a Mountain Glade hootenanny. She couldn't remember the title, but the words had told the story of the murder of a faithless wife. So many of the songs of the region had survived the trip to America from the British Isles virtually unscathed. And so many of them were about murder and mayhem. She remembered that this one had been sung by a long-faced old woman with the husky voice of a New Orleans chanteuse.

The door swung open an inch before she had to grab a falling log. She settled the wood firmly in her arms again and pushed the door with her knee. The door was heavy and handmade, and it moved only a foot. The whistled folk song changed to a softly voiced curse. She pushed the door with her elbow, and it swung a little wider.

She stepped into the cabin and started toward the fireplace. The cabin seemed colder than when she had left it, and strangely desolate. She would set her wood on the hearth and light the lamp closest to it. Then she would start a fire. By the time she returned with the next load, the room would be...

"Stand right where you are."

For just a moment Tate was too surprised to feel fear; then it set every nerve in her body twanging. She didn't move, but she wasn't sure whether it was the harshly voiced order or shock that made her stand so still.

"That's right. Now turn around slowly. Very slowly. I've got a gun, and I don't mind using it."

She forced herself to do as the man's voice commanded. She moved slowly, still clutching the load of wood. Finally she faced the door she had just entered. It was still open, and a man's figure was silhouetted in front of it. He was tall, and his hair and beard glinted gold in the light of the outlaw moon. He was wearing a tattered blue uniform and a gun belt, but the gun itself was in his hand and pointed at her chest.

She had never seen his photograph, but Tate knew the identity of the man who was standing in front of her. Carl Petersen—who had not, after all, headed straight for Houston.

"You're a woman." He sounded surprised.

"Last time I looked." Her eyes were drawn to the gun. Her life seemed to depend on its whims.

"Who else is out there?"

In fascinated horror she watched the gun barrel waver. "Nobody."

"Don't play me for a fool. You don't live here alone."

She debated the wisdom of telling the truth. Perhaps the threat of someone else would force him to leave. "You're right," she lied. "I've got family coming home any minute. If you're smart, you'll run while you can."

He gave a derisive laugh. "I'm not running so well about now."

The gun barrel did a right side step, then a left. "Take what you need and get out of here," she said as calmly as she could while she still watched the gun. "I've got no reason to report you. Whatever you've done is no concern of mine."

"This is a democracy, lady. You *are* your brother's keeper. Or didn't that lesson make it to the Ozarks?"

"I've got food and money. You can have as much of both as you can carry. But if you stay, you're going to be caught." She improvised. "My father won't take kindly to you being here."

Carl Petersen stepped forward. The gun barrel continued its unsteady dance. "Let's deal with you first, then we'll worry about your father."

Regrets flashed through Tate's mind. She wished she had been better about telling Kris and Jess that she loved them. She wished she had searched for her father while he was still alive. She wished she had made more friends, done more good, made love to a man. She was twenty-one, and life had seemed endless.

Carl Petersen took one more step. The gun wavered.

Tate hurled the pile of logs just as he took step number three. Then, as the firewood slammed against his chest, she turned and fled.

Chapter 2

Only the same will to survive that had brought him this far kept Carl Petersen from lapsing into unconsciousness when the firewood knocked him to the floor. Had he not been so ill, he would have dodged easily. As it was, he managed to protect his weapon and the arm holding it as he fell. He rolled to his stomach, propped himself on both elbows and steadied the revolver. "One more step and you're dead."

Tate stopped just inches from the door. She didn't turn.

"You try anything like that again and you won't live to see your family come home." He blinked and sweat dripped into his eyes despite the chill in the room. "Now turn around."

Tate debated. The man behind her was obviously near collapse. At best, his aim would be poor. She knew enough about guns to realize that television shoot-outs made the difficult look too simple. The room was dark, and Petersen was shaking so hard he could hardly hold the gun, if she ran and made it another twenty yards, he would never have the strength to come after her or the control to aim carefully.

If she made it another twenty yards.

She turned slowly, having calculated the odds and found them wanting. "If you kill me, there'll be a new trial. They won't call *my* death second-degree. Kill me and you'll spend the rest of your life at High Ridge…whatever life they leave you before your appeals run out," she added.

The room was revolving slowly. Petersen concentrated on the small figure of the woman wearing the oversize jacket and ignored the rest of the merry-go-round. "Do what you're told, and I won't kill you."

"And your word is good," she said, cynicism oozing from every word.

"Get over here."

Tate moved slowly back across the room. "What do you want from me?"

"Silence." Petersen slid to his knees. The pain that lanced through his leg made the room revolve faster. He concentrated on the woman as he reached inside his back pocket. Slowly, with the hand not holding the gun, he slid his hand deeper and drew out a pair of handcuffs. He debated how best to use them.

Tate had learned long ago not to show fear, but now the bravado she had been forcing wavered. "You don't have to use those. I'll do what you say."

He laughed harshly. "Yeah. You've proved that." He motioned with his gun to the bedroom. "Move, but not too fast." He staggered to his feet, trying not to put weight on the injured leg.

"My family—"

"Isn't here!" He started toward her.

Tate searched his grim face, then turned and headed slowly for the bedroom as he followed a short distance behind. "It's obvious you're a sick man. Give yourself up. Let me go for a doctor. You aren't going to make it anywhere in the shape you're in." Tate tried to sound calm, but she was afraid she was pleading. "You haven't hurt anybody, and I'll tell the authorities you didn't hurt me. They'll take you back to High Ridge, but at least you'll still be alive."

The cabin grew darker as they moved across it. There were no windows under the loft, not until the bedroom. Tate considered all her possibilities as she neared it. Petersen hadn't bothered to answer her. She suspected that the short walk was taking all his concentration and strength.

He was a sick man, and she was a healthy woman. He was holding a gun, but just barely. If she let him handcuff her to the bed—and she was certain that was his goal—she could be a dead woman. Even if he didn't shoot her, he might not make it, and then *she* could starve to death.

Two yards from the door she leaped forward, squeezing through the narrow opening between the slightly open door and the jamb, then slamming the door behind her. She searched for a lock, but there was none. Instead she jammed an old rocker beneath the knob and raced the short distance to the window, trying with all her strength to lift it.

There were sharp blows against the other side of the door, and the chair shook. Desperately she struggled with the window, but it remained firmly in place. She expected gunshots through the door, but instead the chair began to slide across the pine floor. Wildly she looked around for something, anything, to defend herself with, but the room was bare except for the iron bedstead. And the half-open closet.

She was almost to the closet when the chair skidded across the room, rocking violently. She jerked the closet door and dove inside. There was a crowbar behind her father's clothes. He had probably kept it there to pry open the window when the frame was swollen with humidity. She remembered seeing it before, a useless object she had paid little attention to because she had never needed it. Now her life depended on it.

She found it at the same moment that the bedroom door slammed against the wall. Her fingers closed around the thick metal bar, and she stood and swung when Petersen stepped into the room.

She missed him by inches, but the strength it had taken to open the door, then to dodge her blow, seemed to be his undoing. He fell forward, grasping the quilt to break his fall. His gun clattered to the floor beneath the bed.

The momentum of her swing had carried Tate forward. She fell against the wall, then braced herself and turned, the crowbar still in her hand. She swung low, but he rolled away.

This time there was no chance to reposition and try again. He grabbed her ankle and jerked, and she fell beside him, the crowbar clattering uselessly to the floor. He was on top of her in a moment, pinning her hands.

Tate twisted beneath him, frighteningly aware of the odds against her. He was exhausted and sick, but he also outweighed her by at least seventy pounds. She was in good physical condition, but his body, despite the trials of his escape, was all tough, lean muscle. She struggled, but he used his extra weight like a street fighter who wasn't afraid to use any advantage he had.

She had once been a street fighter, too. Her hands were pinned, but one leg was free. She bent her knee and brought it sharply against the leg where he had so obviously been wounded.

He grunted and sagged against her. More importantly, her hands fell free. She kicked again, and instinctively he drew himself up to protect his leg. She dragged herself out from under him and searched for the crowbar. It was just yards away, and she scurried toward it, grabbing it as she scrambled to her feet. She was moving toward him when she saw the glint of moonlight on the gun in his right hand.

"That's one too many strikes against you," he said in a voice so rough it grated along her spine. He slid to his back and held the revolver high, aiming it at her head. The safety moved under his thumb.

Instinctively Tate squeezed her eyelids shut and waited for the explosion. The sound, when it came, was as loud as a cannon shot. She heard the bullet plow into one of the huge chestnut logs from which the cabin was built. She waited for the searing pain that should follow.

She heard Petersen's voice instead. "There are more bullets in this gun. And right now there's one three inches to the side of your head. It's not there by accident."

In the mind-numbing shock of finding she was still alive, Tate felt sensitized to everything around her. She could feel the cool cabin air caress the backs of her hands, could smell the pungent odor of cedar that lined her father's closet. She opened her eyes. In the eyes of Carl Petersen she could see something that looked amazingly like regret.

"Why didn't you kill me?" She whispered the words. To her ears they sounded as loud as a scream.

"Because I'm hoping you just needed a lesson."

She nodded. In the aftermath of certain death averted, her knees began to tremble.

"What's your name?"

She moistened her lips. "Tate."

"I give one lesson per customer, Tate."

She nodded again.

"Drop the crowbar."

She did, and it clattered musically to the floor.

He sat up with a grimace, then pushed himself upright, using the bed as a prop. "Get on the bed." As if he knew her thoughts, he shook his head. "I could have killed you more times than once."

Whether or not he was telling the truth, Tate knew she had no choice but to obey him. She moved across the room and lowered herself to sit on the quilt.

"Get in the middle." He motioned with the revolver.

She slid to the middle of the bed.

"Lie down and put your hands over your head."

She didn't move.

"Now."

He was an escaped convict, filthy and undeniably hanging on to consciousness by a thread, but his voice held command, like that of a man who was used to being instantly obeyed. And her choices were limited to none. She lay on her back and slowly stretched her hands over her head until they touched the iron railing. Carl Petersen came toward her and grasped one hand. In a moment one cuff was snapped snugly on her wrist, the other on the railing.

He dropped to the edge of the bed beside her, as if his legs wouldn't hold him any longer. "Where has your family gone, and when will they be back?"

"To town, and any minute."

"You're a convincing little liar, but I've known better."

Tate didn't answer. She was all too aware of being under his control now.

"I'll ask again, and this time tell the truth. I'm not in much of a mood . . . for games."

She heard his voice waver, and saw his chin drop toward his chest. "Give yourself up, Petersen," she said, trying not to sound afraid. "Isn't it better to be alive in prison than dead on the run?"

"Your family."

"I'm telling the truth. They'll be home any minute."

With an effort he turned to look at her. There was no emotion in his voice. "Then if I leave the key to the cuffs on the table on my way out, they'll set you free sometime in the next hour?"

She didn't answer.

"It's your choice."

For the first time since moving into her father's cabin, Tate wished there really was a family coming home tonight. But she knew—and she suspected Petersen did, too—that there was no family. If he left, she would lie here for more than an hour. She would lie here until some member of the Carter clan recollected that they hadn't seen Millard's girl in town for weeks. Will Carter from the next farm over would be appointed to investigate. And what he would find would not be pretty.

"I live here alone," she admitted. "No one's coming home."

"What about the men's clothes in that closet?"

"They belonged to my father. He died almost a year ago."

"Why are they still here?"

Tate wasn't about to share the story of her life with the embezzler-murderer sitting beside her. She hadn't gotten rid of anything of Millard's yet. She was still trying to figure out who he had been, and she needed all the clues she had.

"I haven't lived here long," she answered instead. "And Mountain Glade isn't exactly brimming over with charities looking for overalls and flannel shirts."

He shrugged with an effort. "If someone did come home, it would be a simple matter for me to shoot them before they got inside."

"No one is coming."

Petersen tried to read her expression. He already knew a lot about the young woman he had cuffed to the bed. She was a survivor, just like he was, with unusual courage and a trace of foolhardiness. She was slender, but she was also strong. By anyone's standards but his, she was a good liar.

She was pretty, too, he noted dispassionately. Smooth black hair fanned out on the quilt under her head. She wore it one length, not short, not long, and with none hanging down over her forehead to mar her delicately arched brows and widely spaced blue eyes. Her nose was straight and narrow, her lips enticingly lush, and her chin the pixyish focal point of a heart-shaped face.

"You're not from here," he said. "The accent's different."

"I'm not from anywhere."

He felt a curious twinge at the words. Apparently his physical weakness was weakening him in other ways. But he wasn't from anywhere, either, and despite himself he felt a reluctant bond between them.

He turned away sharply. The movement made the room whirl again. The woman was no longer a threat. And he believed her latest story, although he could be making a mistake. Now he had to decide what to do.

Decisions floated around him. All of them seemed to hinge on one fact. "Where's your telephone?"

Tate was surprised. She had been expecting almost anything from the man beside her, but that question seemed so normal. *Where's your telephone, miss? I've got to call my mother and tell her I'm all right. Where's your telephone? The warden will be worried about me.*

"There's no telephone," she said, hoping the news wasn't going to send him into a rage. "No telephone, no electricity and no plumbing."

He didn't believe her. "You live here without a phone?"

"Why would I lie? You could find out the truth easily enough."

He let the news settle into all the corners of his mind. No family. No phone. No neighbors—at least none he had been able to see from his vantage point in the woods. "How close is the next house?"

Again this was a fact so easy to check that there was no point in lying. "A half to three quarters of a mile as the crow flies. Almost a mile if you go by the road."

He was beginning to wonder if the room's twirling dance was just the normal state of things. It had gone on so long, and amazingly he was still conscious. "How often do you get . . . visitors?"

"It depends."

He knew she could just as easily lie as tell the truth about that. "Anyone who came looking for you might get more than they bargained for," he warned. "Unless . . . I could plan ahead."

"I've got no visitors on my social calendar, if that's what you're asking."

He wondered at his luck. He couldn't seek Aaron's help, but he could stay here for a day and gather strength again. His fight with the hellcat now handcuffed to the bed had taken everything he'd had left . . . and then some. Realistically, he could go no farther until he recovered.

He was in the exact middle of nowhere. Surely there was no better place to hide until he was able to move on. "You know who I am. How?"

"I've got a radio."

"Have they . . . searched this area?"

There was no point in lying. Tate was sure he would be listening to the news soon enough. "They think you're south of here, heading for Houston."

The room no longer seemed able to decide which direction to take. The woman's voice came to him through a thick fog. "Houston . . . that's where he'd have gone, all right," he mumbled to himself.

Tate wondered if she had heard him right. Then curiosity was replaced by satisfaction as she watched his head drop forward. In a moment he had passed out beside her.

The outlaw moon had cleared the treetops before Petersen came to. He was disoriented at first, believing himself to be back at High Ridge. But the woman being over him, assessing him, was nothing like the wild-eyed gorilla who had been his cell mate. Memory layered memory until he knew who she was. "Let me guess." He licked his parched lips. "You got my gun."

"You dropped it on the floor when you passed out."

He swallowed, then lifted his head. She was still securely cuffed to the bed. "You didn't find the keys."

"Not for lack of trying," she said coldly.

He managed a dry laugh. "I've been out for an hour?"

"More like two." Tate moved as far away from him as the cuffs would allow. "My arm is getting numb."

"Then sit up." He didn't wait to see if she took his advice. He began the arduous process of trying to manage sitting up himself. The room was still whirling. And he was hot enough to set the cabin on fire. "I . . . need water."

"Uncuff me and I'll get you some."

He didn't bother to answer. The cabin seemed impossibly huge, the kitchen miles away. Still, he had no choice. He slid to his feet, holding on to the post at the foot of the bed. His leg throbbed unmercifully. He had to clean and care for it.

Tate watched him stumble toward the door. She felt a peculiar flash of pity. "There's water in the icebox."

He made it halfway across the cabin before he collapsed again.

The outlaw moon had risen so high it was no longer visible from the bedroom window. Tate had watched its climb as if her life depended on it. There had been nothing else to do. The bed was wide enough, the cuffs short enough, that she could only dangle her toes against the floor to the side of the bed. She had thoroughly examined the bed frame.

The headboard was bolted to it with four rusted bolts that wouldn't budge under the mere pressure of twisting fingers. After an hour of concentrated effort she had given up the hope of marching her body, headboard and all, out of the cabin and over to Cousin Will's.

The cuffs themselves gave no quarter. Carl Petersen had snapped them on like a pro. They were just tight enough to keep her trapped, just loose enough to keep her blood circulating. And if the cabin had been warm enough, her blood probably would have moved right along like it was supposed to. Unfortunately, though, the cabin wasn't warm. The temperature was dropping quickly. And even under the quilt, she was freezing.

"Petersen," she yelled. She was beginning to get hoarse. She had been shouting for him since the moment she had admitted that escape from the bed was hopeless. She had heard him fall; then there had been silence. Her worst fear was that he had died. If that were true, she envied him the ease of it. Her death, chained to the bed frame, wouldn't be as quick or as painless.

"Petersen!"

Tate thought she heard a moan. It was the first positive sign since he had fallen. "Petersen!"

She heard a series of thumps and what sounded like something being dragged across the floor. There was silence, then more thumps. Silence, the swish of something dragging. Silence.

Just as she was about to call out to him again, she heard a click. He had made it as far as the icebox. Relieved tears sprang to her eyes. He wasn't dead yet, and neither was she. Her life depended on his now. "Petersen, you've got to uncuff me! If you die, I'll die here. Let me go and I'll see what I can do to help you."

There was no answer.

She repeated her plea into the silence. Just as she had decided he had fainted again, she heard the slam of a cabinet door. He was rummaging for food. Sometime later she heard the dragging sound again, the the unmistakable sounds of retching. Finally she heard his voice. "Where do you keep... medical supplies."

She was irrationally glad to be communicating. "There's a first-aid kit in the loft."

His answer was a mumbled curse. She thought she knew why. "Look, unlock these cuffs and I'll get you what you need. We both know you'll never make it up there and back."

"I'm... not crazy."

"Maybe not, but you are half dead." Tate watched the doorway. His voice had sounded close. As she watched, he materialized out of the darkness. She was surprised to see he was standing. "Look, you're not going to make it much longer like this." The pity she'd felt earlier sounded in her voice. "You've put up a great fight, but it's over now. If you die and I die with you, you haven't won anything. Uncuff me. You can hold the gun on me, if you want, while I take care of your leg and fix you some soup."

"And when I go under again... you'll go for the sheriff."

It would be foolish to deny it. "It's your only chance. Maybe you'll stay conscious long enough to chain me up again."

"I just need... rest." He lurched toward the bed. When he reached it, he shoved something toward her. It was the package of graham crackers that she would have used for s'mores. She couldn't believe he had given any thought to whether she was hungry or not.

His hands shook so badly that he could hardly unbuckle his gun belt, but after repeated fumbling, he managed. It hit the floor by the door, followed by everything in his pockets, including the set of keys that she guessed would unlock the cuffs.

He didn't stop there. He unbuttoned his filthy shirt, agonizing over each button. In the moonlight his chest was a warm golden tan brushed by hair a darker gold. He slipped the shirt over his shoulders.

"What are you doing?"

"I think . . . s'obvious." He pulled at his pants as if to unbutton them, but they remained fastened. He tried again and succeeded. They slid only as low as the scrap of cloth tied around his wounded leg. Fumbling badly, he loosened the shirttail bandage, and the pants slid to the ground over his shoeless feet. He stepped out of them, one foot at a time, pulling the bandage back over his leg and tightening it once more with a groan. In the moment he stood that way, Tate got a clear picture of why he was such a formidable opponent—even with infection raging through his body. Then, clad only in cheap cotton briefs and the filthy bandage, he fell to the bed and struggled to get under the quilt.

"Petersen. Listen," Tate said frantically. "You're dying. Are you too much of a fool to realize it? People don't get over gunshot wounds without treatment. This isn't the flu! For God's sake, get the damn keys and let me go! I'll do what I can for you, I promise."

He sounded halfway to hell when he spoke. "Not . . . going back . . . kill me."

"This is the twentieth century! They don't kill prisoners for escaping! You might get a year or two added to your sentence, that's all. And you'll probably still be eligible for parole about the same time, anyway!"

"They'll kill . . ." The rest of the sentence died away.

Tate slid as far to the other side of the bed as she could. The man beside her was unconscious again.

The sun hadn't risen, but the sky was growing lighter. Carl Petersen slept on, but Tate had not slept at all. Her eyes hadn't flickered shut; her body hadn't relaxed for even a second. The keys that could free her were on the floor by the door, but Petersen was between her and them.

Tate knew she could eventually slide the bed in that direction with a combination of bouncing and pushing against the wall. Then, with the help of a sheet or pillowcase, she might be able to fish successfully for the keys. It could take hours, but every inch would bring her closer to freedom. The problem was that Petersen might come to as she bounced and pushed. Gauging her intent, he might find the strength to rise and throw the keys into the next room.

As the night had progressed she had realized her only chance was to wait until he died.

"God, no!" The horror of it overwhelmed her. She could not bear even a few minutes of being chained in bed next to a dead man. And once she was sure he was dead, she would have to crawl over him for the keys....

He was still alive now. Tate turned so she was facing the outlaw beside her. Jesse James in the flesh wasn't nearly as romantic as the legend. Would an Ozark tale grow up around this? In a hundred years would the locals tell their children bedtime stories about Carl Petersen and the woman he chained up to die of terror in bed beside him?

"Petersen!" Tate stretched her arm toward him, swallowing hard as she forced herself to touch his shoulder. "Petersen, wake up."

He mumbled something. His shoulder felt as if it was on fire. He had tossed restlessly, mumbling incoherently for the last hour. Did people survive fevers of this magnitude without brain damage? He was a human being, and he was suffering. But whatever pity she would normally have felt was eclipsed by her need to be free.

She shook him. "You've got to uncuff me!"

He tossed his head from side to side, then turned and gripped her hand. "Double-cross..."

"Wake up!" Tate tried to free her hand, but he wouldn't allow it.

"Bastard...you bastard. Said a month. No more..."

Tate was only half listening, her concentration fixed on waking him. "Petersen, please! Wake up. You've got to get up and uncuff me while you still can!"

"You'll pay... Gallagher.... No wall could hold..."

"Petersen!" When he didn't respond, she tried his first name, hoping he might believe she was a friend. "Carl. Carl, wake up. You've got to let me go before I have to lie here with a corpse!"

His eyelids opened. His eyes moved back and forth as if he were watching a movie. "Gallagher...you bastard...a month. No more!'' He gripped Tate's hand harder, and she winced in pain. ''Left me there to die!''

''Petersen. Carl. Carl!'' She was nearly weeping in frustration. ''Please wake up!''

''Simon.'' He turned toward her. ''Simon. My name...''

''Please. Get the keys! Carl, can you hear me?'' She wrenched her hand from his and shook him.

''Not Carl...Simon.''

She was in no position to argue. Whatever reason his fevered brain had concocted for the identity switch didn't matter. ''Simon, then. Please, I'm begging you. Try to wake up. You've got to wake up and get the damn keys! If you don't, I won't be able to help either you or me! You're going to die.''

''Die.'' The mumbled word seemed to penetrate his delirium. His eyes opened wider. ''Die. No justice in justice.''

''Yes, die! Your fever will kill you, if nothing else does first. Look, Car—Simon, whatever you call yourself. I don't want to rot here beside you. Understand? I don't want to be a damn folktale.''

''Folk...''

''The keys. Get the keys. You're going to die if you don't!''

He raised his head from the pillow. His eyes seemed to struggle to focus for the first time. ''You don't quit....''

''No, I don't. Please. Get the keys. It's over. You're not going to survive this unless you get help. And you can't leave me chained beside a dead man!''

His head fell back to the pillow and his eyes closed. ''I'm not...die...''

''Just because you never *have* doesn't mean you're not going to!'' Tate wondered if he was weakening enough to believe a lie. ''I won't go for help. I'll take care of you myself.''

''Accomplished...liar.''

''I mean it.''

''D'like you on my...side.''

''I'll be permanently at your side, if you don't get me the keys!''

He managed the ghost of a smile.

"Please. Simon, let me go."

His eyes opened. "How'd you know...Simon?"

"You told me to call you that."

"Damn!"

"Look, I just want you to let me go. I don't care who you are, or anything else. Just let me go. If you've got any shred of humanity, do it."

He lay very still.

"I'll beg, if you want," she said.

"Listen..."

Tate instinctively drew nearer. His voice had wavered and become less than a whisper. "I'm listening."

"I'll be killed...if I go back. Innocent. I have to prove...That's why..."

Tate leaned over him. "Simon?"

"Escaped. To prove..."

Tate suspected that ninety-nine murderers out of one hundred at High Ridge would stubbornly proclaim their innocence, even if their victims came back to identify them wearing angel wings and halos. "Why will you be killed?" she probed.

"Captain Shaw...I've got something.... Look in my shirt."

"I can't look in anything! I'm handcuffed here beside you!"

He lay very still. Tate waited, uncertain whether he was lapsing into delirium again—or just considering. Then, just as she was about to shake him once more, his eyes opened. With what seemed a superhuman effort, he pushed himself to a sitting position. He slid off the bed and crashed to the floor beside it. Tate heard a sharply indrawn breath.

Despite herself, she felt sympathy. "Are you all right?"

There was no answer. She slid as close as she could to the side, hoping to get a look at him. "Simon?"

As she squinted into the darkness, he began to inch his way to the door. She knew the movement was agonizing, but he continued. Inch...stop...inch...stop.

Finally his arm stretched as far as the door. She held her breath as he grabbed his clothes and pulled them toward him. The keys were on top of his pants. At last they were in his hand. Slowly he propped himself with his back against the wall and tossed the keys to the bed. His eyes closed.

Tate wasted no time finding the smallest key on the ring. Unlocking the cuffs took longer than she wanted, and she fumbled repeatedly, sure that any second he would change his mind.

"I didn't . . . kill you," Simon said from the floor.

The cuff fell from Tate's wrist. She was surprised at the tears of relief that formed. "Thanks, I guess."

"I could have."

"I know."

"If you go . . . for help, you'll be killing . . . me."

Tate's eyes flicked to the gun. It was within his reach, although she imagined that in his weakened state it would take him so long to get it, she might have a chance to get past him first.

"You were tried and convicted by a jury of your peers, weren't you?" she asked, slowly lowering her feet to the floor.

"I'm not what you think.... I let you go . . . saved your life. Save mine." His head slid to the side. His lips parted, and his breathing grew shallower.

Tate realized her chance to escape had arrived. She could get past him now and grab the gun on the way. She stood and started toward him. His head lifted, and his eyes opened. As she watched in horror, he reached for the gun. Then, with a hand that shook so badly he almost couldn't lift it, he held it out to her.

"Take it.... Shoot me.... Turn me in.... Either way, I'm a dead man." The gun fell from his hand before she could take it. Then the man who called himself Simon sagged to the floor.

Chapter 3

The unconscious man on the cabin floor was an escaped convict. He had threatened her life repeatedly through the long night, and once he had even fired his gun to terrify and subdue her. So why, Tate asked herself, couldn't she just drag him a foot closer to the bed frame and handcuff him there until she could alert the sheriff?

Because he was suffering. Because the floor was freezing cold, and he was exhausted and wounded. Because he had spared her life, when a desperate criminal should not have. Because, damn all sound reasoning, she wasn't convinced he was lying about his innocence.

Because the law and the people who enforced it had never unduly impressed her.

Tate held the revolver in both hands, aiming it at Simon's head. She could fire if she had to. She *would* fire. She had learned much of what she knew in ghetto classrooms, in overburdened child-care institutions, on the streets. She had learned the hard way how to protect herself, and those lessons had never been forgotten.

So she would fire the gun if she was forced to, but as she stared at the fallen heap of masculinity on the floor, she knew she didn't have to worry. Simon—or Carl Petersen, or whoever he was—wasn't going to fight her anymore. He had come to the end of his strength, and he had realized it. He had offered her the gun, and by so doing he had offered her his future.

She didn't want his future. She didn't want any part of him. But he was conveniently unconscious, and she was stuck with him for a while, at least. Now she had to decide what to do.

One thing was certain. She couldn't leave him on the floor. She had to get him on her bed, if only to wait for the sheriff. The cold floor would kill him quicker than his wounded leg.

She considered how best to work this miracle. He outweighed her by seventy pounds, at least, and unless he came to and helped, he would be deadweight. He was also nearly naked. Getting a grip on him was going to be difficult, but she had to try.

Tate set the gun on a closet shelf so she wouldn't tempt Simon to grab it from her. She knelt beside him and shook his shoulder. "Simon, can you hear me?"

He groaned, then lapsed into silence.

"Simon?"

She got behind him, and using her own body as a lever, she grasped his broad shoulders and began to push him to a sitting position. His skin was hot to the touch and surprisingly slippery. With dawn breaking and the room growing lighter, she could see how dirty he was.

"Come on, Simon," she said, trying to encourage him. "If we can get you sitting up, maybe we can get you back in bed."

He groaned again, but he seemed to be trying to help. At least he wasn't fighting her. She pushed, straining hard until he was propped against the wall. It was still too dark to get a good look at him, but she could see how pale he was. His whole body looked drained of color, like the white-marble statue of a Greek god. Despite everything that had happened, she felt a pang of concern. People died from gunshot wounds. *He* could die.

Tate gauged the short distance from the wall where he was propped to the bed. She could not move him that far without his help. She shook him, her fingers biting into his flesh. "Simon. Can you hear me?"

He groaned in answer.

She raised one hand to his cheek, slapping it lightly. "Look, you've got to get in bed. You'll die here. I can't get you there without help."

His eyelids flicked open, but he seemed unable to focus.

"I'm going to put your arm around my shoulder. Lean on me as much as you need to. Once you're standing it will only be a few steps to the bed." Tate crouched beside him and slung his arm across her shoulders. For all its muscled length, it flopped there uselessly. For a moment she considered abandoning him. He was a fugitive, and only hours ago he had threatened her life. What was she doing with her arm around his naked back, her fingertips lightly brushing the mat of golden hair on his chest?

He shook his head as if he were trying to clear it. She felt his body contract uselessly against hers. He was struggling to help because he didn't want to die. He was a human being, just like she was. She hugged him tighter and lectured him. "You've got to help. You're going to die if you don't."

"Die...if you turn me...in."

She was relieved to find he was conscious enough to speak. She tightened her arm still further. "Right now we just have to worry about getting you in bed. I'm going to stand on the count of three. You've got to help. Do you understand?"

His head fell forward. She wasn't sure if it was a nod or if he was lapsing into unconsciousness again. She began to count. "One...two...three." With all her strength she hauled him upward, bracing her hip snugly against his. "Come on, Simon!"

They struggled together. He was so weak he was little help, but at least he wasn't deadweight. Tate strained and pushed. Then, when he was almost standing, she began to move across the floor, half dragging him as she took the required steps. "Come on, Simon! We're almost there. Don't faint now."

At the bedside, he fell forward. "Can't . . ." he muttered.

"You're there already. Just lie there. I'll help you lift your legs. Just don't slide off! Understand?"

He didn't answer, but she didn't waste time asking again. Before he could slide off, she grabbed his good leg and a mighty effort lifted it to the bed. She was gentler but equally resolute with the other. He lay across the quilt at an angle, but at least he was no longer on the floor.

Tate rested for a moment, viewing her handiwork. The man on the bed was still drained of all natural color. She had a well-grounded suspicion that the dirty rag wrapped around his leg covered more than a scratch.

Holding her breath, she eased the rag to his ankle until the wound on his leg was in full view. It was an obscenely gaping flaw on something so otherwise perfect. The place where a bullet had entered his calf wasn't large, but it was ripped unevenly, and the skin around it was red and swollen. The swelling was rising toward his knee, and the wound still trickled blood.

She swallowed hard. She was no stranger to injuries and illness. In college she had trained as a medic at the local free clinic. Under the supervision of whatever physician happened to be on duty, she had helped with any problems that were presented. Once she had even assisted with a minor gunshot wound. But nothing she had ever seen had been this serious. A case like this would have been transported immediately to the local hospital emergency room.

And the emergency room was where Simon belonged. Except that if he went, it would be under police escort. And when he was well, he would go back to High Ridge. To be murdered?

The possibility nagged at her. This was the twentieth century, but like her father's cabin, High Ridge was said to be a nineteenth-century sort of place. She'd heard talk about it on her infrequent trips to town. A number of Mountain Glade residents worked at the prison, since it was one of the few employment possibilities in the region. Those she'd spoken to didn't say much—saying anything to strangers wasn't the style here—but what they did say indicated that High Ridge was the last place a convict wanted to end up.

But a tough prison and a prison where inmates were murdered were two different things, weren't they?

Tate went to the dresser and took out a clean bandanna. Wincing at the pain she must be causing, she bandaged Simon's leg, then worked the quilt out from under his body. He didn't move. She noted that his breathing was rapid and shallow. With her hands at his shoulders he was easy enough to turn, and she positioned his legs so that she could draw the quilt over him, tucking him in like a small child.

The handcuffs swung from the iron headboard where he had anchored them. Tate considered them carefully, then lifted his wrist and snapped the cuff over it. He was her prisoner now, just as she had been his.

As she was leaving the room she stumbled over the clothes he had discarded. She stooped and picked them up. The guard he had stolen them from wouldn't want them back, that was for sure. The clothes smelled worse than the prisoner himself, and they were in tatters.

Tate searched the pant's pockets as she walked through the cabin. There was a letter opener, engraved with the initials RS, but nothing else. She dropped the pants by the back door. Just as she was about to toss the shirt on top, she remembered that Simon had said something about looking in his shirt pocket.

Frowning, she lifted the flap and reached inside to pull out a small, plastic computer diskette. The label was blank. Unless the diskette was, too, it was probably a copy of a program. What was Simon doing with a computer diskette? The man the papers called Carl Petersen had been imprisoned for a computer crime, but why was this diskette in the pocket of the uniform he'd stolen from the guard?

Unless it really did have something to do with his escape.

The diskette was wet. As she lifted it to the light, water seeped from it. Whatever information it had contained was probably lost. But its mere presence made the mystery of the man in her bed that much more complicated.

After setting the diskette in the kitchen, she busied herself gathering the logs from the floor where she had thrown them the night before. As the sun began to rise in the sky, she lit fires in the fireplace and stove to hasten heating the cabin.

When she returned to check on her prisoner, she discovered that he hadn't changed positions. Briefly she monitored his pulse. He was still as hot as he had been, and his pulse was rapid, but strong. She knew she had to be concerned about blood poisoning and shock. The first was certainly a possibility, although she thought the wound would look worse if blood poisoning was developing. The second would be heralded by a drop in blood pressure.

She left the room, returning a few minutes later with the first-aid kit she had told him about. The kit contained more than the usual bandages and disinfectant. She had purchased her own equipment to use at the clinic, and she had a stethoscope and sphygmomanometer for measuring blood pressure. She lifted his arm and wrapped the cuff around it. Then she put the stethoscope to her ears and inflated the cuff.

His pressure was on the low edge of normal, not yet in a danger zone. He had certainly lost blood from his wound, and he was exhausted, both possible reasons for the low pressure. She pulled the quilt lower and listened to his heart. The beat was even, if too rapid.

He was a sick man, but she guessed—accurately, she hoped—that the major portion of his illness was caused by exhaustion, blood loss and dehydration. The wound itself looked serious but not life-threatening. With luck it would respond to good care.

She put her instruments back in her kit and covered her prisoner once again, adding an extra blanket from the closet. She would have to boil water to tend to his infected leg. She didn't want to disturb him now, nor did she want to take the time to care for it properly. Not until she knew what she was going to do with him. Whatever decision she made, she had to make soon. She didn't think he was in immediate danger, but without treatment in the near future, Simon Carl Petersen could die chained to her bed.

Mountains weren't new to Tate. Stagecoach Inn was in the Virginia Blue Ridge. She had gone to live there when she was fourteen, and despite a childhood spent in the flatlands, the mountains had seemed like home. Maybe that was because Stagecoach Inn was the first place she'd lived as a teenager that had *been* a home. Whatever the reason, though, coming to the Ozarks hadn't seemed strange, although the mountains themselves were subtly different, rockier and rougher hewn.

Now, as her Ford Bronco churned up a red dust cloud behind her, she sped around once more in the series of Kalix Road curves that would take her into town.

Kalix Road was a study in contrasts. The houses closest to Tate's cabin were modest, but the yards were neatly kept, and pride was evident in fresh paint and flower gardens. Farther along the road, the houses turned into shacks, and the children playing in front of them were dirtier. It was almost as if Kalix Road was divided into the have-nots who had quit trying and the have-nots who hadn't given quitting a thought.

The land in this section of the Ozarks was too rocky for lucrative farming, and the countryside was too inhospitable and remote for industry. But some of the families along Kalix Road fought the odds. They farmed, and they worked at any job they could find, no matter how dirty. They educated their children and supported their churches, showing a stubborn pride and intelligence.

When Tate turned, and the clay road changed into blacktop highway, the houses changed again. These home owners, the town merchants and professionals, were not wealthy by city standards, but the closer to town Tate drove, the larger and more modern their houses became. If she had just been a tourist passing through, she might never have known about the poverty that existed in these beautiful mountains or the people's day-to-day struggle to maintain their pride.

And of course if Millard's cabin had been anywhere else, she never would have been introduced to Simon Carl Petersen.

Mountain Glade was so small it would have been easy to miss, except that by now she knew every inch, every shop, every café. It was a picturesque little mountain town with brick and frame buildings, wooden sidewalks and a character or two in constant residence. She had learned where to buy groceries, and where to park if she was attending the Friday evening hootenanny. She knew the bank's hours and policies, and where to get change for the laundromat.

She knew where the sheriff's office was.

Tate slowed to the required twenty-five miles an hour as she crossed the town boundaries. Mountain Glade was a sleepy town by anyone's standards, but it was no sleepier at eight in the morning than at high noon. The best parking places on Main Street were already taken, mostly by pickups. The largest number of vehicles were clustered in front of the Sassafras Café.

She parked in front of Allen's Pharmacy, but she didn't get out for a moment. Instead she reviewed the decision she had reached as the morning sun finally broke free of the horizon. She had decided *not* to decide her prisoner's fate—at least not by herself. There was too much she didn't know, but there was one person who might be able to enlighten her.

Her adopted father, Jess Cantrell.

Jess was an extraordinary resource. Not only did he direct Stagecoach Inn along with Krista, but he was also a journalist who'd written best-sellers. Jess always had his ear to the ground. And if there was something he didn't know, he knew someone who did. Jess was the perfect person to provide information about Simon, if she could just nudge him past the fact that she had a dangerous criminal handcuffed to the bed in her peaceful mountain retreat.

Tate grimaced as she silently practiced framing the bad news. Neither Jess nor Krista had been thrilled about her decision to spend several months alone in the Ozarks. They had been concerned about her isolation here. Nothing they'd said had been discouraging, but Tate had known them both too well not to understand their real feelings. Now they were going to be sure their concern had been justified.

She was no longer the fourteen-year-old waif they had rescued from the streets, but she supposed that, like parents everywhere, they were having trouble coming to grips with her maturity.

Still, even if this set them back a decade, she had to ask Jess to find out what he could about the man who had escaped from High Ridge. Consulting Jess was the adult thing to do. She just hoped he and Krista realized it.

There were two public phones in Mountain Glade. The one in front of the gas station had been out of order since she arrived. The second was inside Allen's Pharmacy. It was a wall phone, installed just inches from the counter where pharmacist and customers traded prescriptions, medication and gossip.

Wally Allen, the owner and sole dispenser of advice and medicine, was middle-aged, red-headed and the nosiest human being Tate had ever encountered. The telephone's proximity to his listening ear was no accident. Wally kept a willing finger on Mountain Glade's pulse. At a moment's notice he could tell you who was doing what with whom and where they were doing it. Tate sometimes wondered if Wally kept a diary, readying himself for an early retirement funded by Mountain Glade residents willing to trade cash for pages.

Today Wally seemed in rare form, performing happily for a dour-faced old woman. In a county with only two overburdened physicians, Wally functioned as the third. To his credit, Tate had never heard him give bad advice. He had filled a local doctor's prescription for her once when she'd had a sore throat, and his helpful hints had been useful.

He was expounding on the merits of fiber therapy when she approached his counter. Tate had overheard this particular lecture before. She guessed she might have as much as five full minutes on the phone before Wally would stop long enough to listen to her conversation.

She guessed wrong.

"Morning, Miss Tate."

Tate reminded herself that someday she might have to get a prescription filled again, and she smiled pleasantly. "Good morning, Mr. Wally."

He grinned, showing every tooth he had. "Still enjoying your stay?"

She wasn't about to tell him that her stay had suddenly become something less than enjoyable. "The fall colors are lovely, aren't they?"

"Nothing like them in the city." Wally watched Tate lift the receiver. "Need a phone book?"

She forced another smile before she turned away. "No thanks." There was silence behind her as she dropped her quarter in the phone. Pretending to fumble in her handbag for a phone number, she shifted so that she could see Wally and the old woman in front of the counter. Both of them were staring openly at her. There was no way she could call Jess now to ask him for information about an escaped convict. In ten minutes, everyone in town would know about the call. In twenty, the sheriff would be at her door.

Instead she consulted a blank memo pad, then dialed a string of ones. As she had expected, a recorded message told her to try again. She hung up as if no one had answered and retrieved her quarter. "I guess I'll have to try later," she muttered.

"Early bird catches the worm," the old lady said, as if she had just coined the phrase.

Hoping that Wally would be busy filling prescriptions soon, Tate nodded and left the pharmacy.

How long could Petersen go without treatment? He was obviously a strong man, but even strong men died. She decided to wait half an hour, then return to use the telephone again. If Wally was still eavesdropping, she would have to rule out getting additional information from Jess and make a decision on her own. In the meantime, she would force herself to join the crowd at the Sassafras Café and have some coffee. She hoped her stomach, which was clutching convulsively in anxiety, could handle it.

There was nothing extraordinary about the café. There were several others in town with similar menus and prices.

The building itself was just one of a connecting string, with a plate-glass view of Main Street. Apparently, however, Mountain Glade residents knew their country cuisine and had given the Sassafras a five-star rating. And to give the residents their due, the few times Tate had eaten there, she'd had to admit the food, though simple, was tasty and plentiful.

With her mind whirling with thoughts of Simon, she opened the door. She scanned the room before entering, to be sure that there would be space for her. But it wasn't until she was inside that she realized a sizable portion of the vehicles parked in front belonged to her relatives.

The room didn't grow silent, but it did grow quieter. Since it was too late to leave, Tate walked to the large table holding six of the Carter clan to dutifully say her good mornings. She had never felt less like a family reunion.

Will, a gaunt string bean of a man, stood as she approached. As her closest neighbor, Will had seen more of Tate than the other Carters had. It had been Will who had shown her around her father's property and cabin when she first arrived in town. Unfortunately, it had also been Will who had suffered the greatest loss at her sudden appearance. Had she not been located and told of her inheritance, Will would eventually have owned her father's acreage.

Tate tried to sound glad to see them. "It looks like everyone's enjoying breakfast." She scanned the table. Will's wife, Dovey, more than pleasingly plump, sat beside him like an illustration for the nursery rhyme "Jack Spratt." Beside her was Dovey's mother, Zeddie, who resembled a bulldog more than an old woman.

Across the table and closer to Tate were three more Carters: Canna, Andy and Esther. They were older than Tate, but of her generation. Canna, an attractive blonde, worked as a teller at the bank. Andy and Esther were married and owned their own broiler house about two miles from Tate's cabin. They were all related to Tate, but she wasn't clear how.

"Pull up a chair and join us." Before Tate could refuse, Will was beckoning the one harried waitress toward the table. "Don't worry about me. I don't want to interrupt," Tate protested, but the waitress was at her elbow before she could continue.

"Coffee?" The waitress, who looked a bit like Zeddie, held out the pot as if she were waiting for Tate to cup her hands. Will had already dragged another chair up to the table. He took the paper place mat and silverware that had been in front of it and set them in front of Tate, along with a clean cup and saucer.

Aware that she'd been bullied into submission, Tate nodded. She was relieved when the coffee was directed into the cup.

"Want the special like everybody else?" the waitress asked. She left before Tate could respond.

"I guess I'm having the special," Tate said. She hoped she could choke it down.

Zeddie scrunched her face into even more wrinkles. "You need it."

Tate tried to think of something to say, but a sleepless night and a problem she hadn't yet solved kept her mute.

"So what do you think of Mountain Glade?" Canna asked.

Tate wished she could really tell them. *I think it's a little close to High Ridge for comfort.* "I like the mountains," she said instead.

"Are you makin' out all right at Millard's place?"

Notwithstanding the fact that a convict was sleeping in her bed at that very moment, Tate wasn't sure how to answer. If she pointed out that it was a little rough, she might be stepping on toes. For all she knew, the entire Carter clan lived as simply as her father had. "I've got everything I need," she said. *And one living, breathing thing I don't.*

"Winter's comin'," Will said.

Tate expected him to say more, until she realized everyone was waiting for her to answer. "Indisputably," she agreed.

"Gonna be a bad 'un."

Tate wondered if Will predicted the weather with the help of woolly worms and the breastbones of geese. Her father's journal had been specific about weather-forecasting superstitions. "How can you tell?"

"Oh, Will keeps charts," Dovey said breezily. "Got charts of all the weather for years back. Knows more than a weatherman."

Despite her preoccupation, Tate was impressed. Will looked embarrassed. "You can't know what a winter's like here, 'less you been through 'un."

Tate sipped her coffee. "What should I know?"

"Roads get so thick with snow, only a truck'll pass. And you've gotta have wood cut. Lots of it. Or I reckon you'll freeze. And you gotta have food stored by. Don't have it, you'll go hungry, that's for sure."

Tate realized she was being warned away. She hardly knew these people, and she felt no kinship to them. But somehow, the warning rankled. She had as much right to be here as they did. She wasn't going to let them scare her back to Virginia.

God knows, if she could be easily scared, she would be out on the highway right now hightailing it for Stagecoach Inn.

She finished half her coffee before she spoke. "Well, you don't have to worry about me. My car has four-wheel drive and all-weather tires, so I'll be able to get around. Millard cut enough wood before he died to keep me warm for three winters. But thanks for the tip about storing some food. I guess I'd better be sure to lay in a couple of bags of canned goods in case I can't get out to the store for a week or two."

No one smiled. Every eye at the table looked right through her. Tate thought about all the years of her childhood, when she had yearned for a big family, for grandparents and cousins, aunts and uncles. Krista often told the girls at Stagecoach Inn to be careful what they wished for, they might just get it. Tate wished someone had warned her earlier.

Breakfast came, to Tate's relief. The special turned out to be beaten biscuits with gravy, eggs and hickory-smoked bacon. She steeled herself and ate it quickly, not pausing once to savor the wonderful flavors. She was acutely aware that enough time had passed that she could reasonably try to use the telephone at the pharmacy again. The man handcuffed to her bed could wait no longer.

Conversation went on around her, but just as she was about to excuse herself, Will addressed her again.

"Noticed you put in trees."

Tate knew "noticed" was the wrong word. She and Will were next-door neighbors, but their houses were almost a mile apart. The only way Will could notice anything was to come on her property and spy. The thought sent a chill through her. If he was going to spy, he couldn't have picked a worse time.

"That's right." She didn't elaborate.

"Wondered why."

"I guess I was just finishing what my father started," she said, stressing the word "father," in case they needed a reminder of her right to do anything she wanted with the property. "I know from his journal that he wanted to plant the acres in front of the cabin with white-pine seedlings. The world can always use more Christmas trees."

"They take tending," Dovey said.

Tate wondered why they didn't just come out and ask her how long she was going to stay. "Yes, I know." She stood and lied, "I hate to rush right off, but I've got to get back. I need to use every bit of daylight if I'm going to get the rest of the seedlings in by the end of the week." She nodded pleasantly. "Thanks for inviting me to eat with you."

Will stood. "You know there's a man on the run from High Ridge, don't ya?"

Tate wondered if this was more scare tactics. She made herself nod, as if it were no concern of hers. As if the man in question wasn't handcuffed to her bed, dying.

Will nodded, too. "You need me, just give a holler."

She was surprised. For a moment Will had almost sounded as if he were concerned. But his face showed no expression. She wondered if her father had ever smiled. "Thank you," she said. She lifted her hand in goodbye to everyone else and went to the front counter to pay her bill.

There was more traffic, both foot and vehicle, when she emerged from the restaurant and headed quickly for Allen's. Silently she prayed that Wally would be busy filling prescriptions now that the town was waking up. Amazingly, he wasn't even behind the counter when she reached the telephone.

She deposited her quarter, then spoke in low tones to the operator, giving the Stagecoach Inn credit-card number to pay for the call. The phone rang repeatedly. Since Virginia was an hour behind Arkansas, Tate could just imagine Jess grumbling as he came awake enough to answer it.

But it wasn't Jess who answered. "Hello."

Tate recognized Krista's voice. "Hey, Kris," she said. "Did I get you up?"

Krista laughed huskily. "Hey, sweetheart. Everything all right?"

Tate hesitated, but she decided not to answer honestly. Krista was much more her best friend than her mother. Still, the fact that less than a decade separated them didn't stop Krista from worrying like a mother. Jess, on the other hand, was capable of a bit more objectivity. She would let him break the news about Carl Petersen to Krista. "Everything's fine. I was in town, so I just thought I'd call."

"It's wonderful to hear your voice."

They chatted for a few minutes, catching up on gossip, before Tate came to the real reason for the call. "Is Jess there?"

"You haven't gotten his letter?"

Tate frowned. There was no mail service on Kalix Road. And she hadn't been to the post office in a week. "I guess not. It's probably waiting in my box."

"He's out of the country, Tate. He wrote you before he left. It was pretty sudden. An old friend of his phoned from Lebanon—"

"Lebanon!"

"There's a group there that claims to have three American hostages. They're promising to let them go if they get the publicity they want. They chose Jess as their publicist."

Tate tried to fathom all the implications of what Krista was saying. "Why?"

"Because of the work he's done in the past and because of his reputation. He's been promised safe passage and return."

"And what are their promises worth?"

Krista's concern for her husband seeped into her voice. "I can only hope they're worth what they say they are."

Tate wished she were there to offer comfort...and receive it. "How long is he going to be gone?"

"Two weeks...three at most. He'll be home for Thanksgiving. Will you be here, too?"

Tate wanted to say that Thanksgiving was the last thing on her mind, but one thing was for certain: Krista had enough to worry about now. Tate couldn't add to her troubles.

She was on her own, and a man's life was in her hands.

"Don't worry about Jess," Krista said, when Tate didn't answer. "He knows how to take care of himself. You will think about coming home for Thanksgiving, won't you?"

"Sure. Look, you can send telegrams here. I'm sure you can. I mean, Mountain Glade isn't that isolated. You send a telegram if you need me. Okay? And I'll call you soon."

They exchanged warm goodbyes before Tate hung up.

She stood staring at the telephone until a voice sounded behind her. "Waitin' for it to ring, Miss Tate?"

She turned to see Wally behind the counter again. She sucked her bottom lip between her teeth as she considered him. Considered all the things she didn't know. Considered the state of her life. Considered that she might be making a terrible mistake.

"Wally," she said at last, "I've got a problem."

He looked delighted to hear it.

"I've got this cut on my leg." She pointed high on her thigh so he wouldn't ask to see it. "I got it when I was splitting firewood, and I think it's getting infected. Now, I don't have all day to spend in town waiting for Dr. Monson to see me, but when I had that bad throat after I first got here, he prescribed penicillin and put a refill on it. Do you think if I get that refilled now, it'll take care of the infection?''

"Had a tetanus shot lately?"

Tate prayed that High Ridge routinely inoculated its prisoners. "Yeah."

Wally rubbed his hands together in satisfaction and began a lecture. Tate left Allen's Pharmacy half an hour later with enough advice, first-aid supplies and medication to care for a battalion of war heroes.

Chapter 4

Tate had carefully banked both the fire in the fireplace and the one in the cookstove before leaving for town. By the time she returned, however, both the glowing coals and hours of sunlight had heated the cabin. She quickly dumped new logs on the fire before going to check on Simon.

He was in the same position he had been in before she left. His eyes were closed, his breathing too rapid. His skin was still hot to the touch, but he shivered when she laid her hand on his forehead, as if he were chilled.

Briefly Tate considered her plan. This was a very sick man, and her ability to heal him was laughable. But if what he said was true, sending him back to High Ridge would mean sure death. Her own life experiences had taught her that things were often not what they seemed. What if he was telling the truth? Sure, the odds were against it, but what if he was?

He had spared her life, and he had turned himself over to her keeping. What could she do except give him a chance? She would give herself twenty-four hours with him. If he took a turn for the worse during that time, she would go right for the sheriff. If he didn't, and she was able to reduce the fever and the infection in his leg, she could take her time deciding. He was handcuffed to her bed, and she had his gun. Even if he improved rapidly and regained his strength, he wouldn't be able to harm her.

With her decision made and a timetable in place to review it, she set to work. Before she even touched Simon's leg, she had to get water, aspirin and a double dose of antibiotics down him. She was sure he was dehydrated. With a fever the magnitude of his, she doubted he could even drink enough liquid to keep dehydration at bay. Intravenous fluids were a better answer, but impossible under the circumstances, so she was going to have to make do with dribbling medication-laced liquids in his mouth.

She decided to try plain water first. She knew he had experienced some nausea, and she wanted to be certain water stayed down before she added the precious antibiotics. First water, then water with liquid Tylenol added to it, then water with antibiotics. She calculated that the process would take an hour.

She bypassed the water on the back porch and went straight to the spring for fresh. Surprisingly, Cinn, who had never gotten remotely close to the house, was on the porch when she returned. He lumbered inside when she opened the door and parked his red-brown bulk by the bedroom doorway. Shaking her head, she added ice to the water from the bag of cubes she had bought on the way out of town, then resolutely strode past the self-appointed guard dog.

Simon still hadn't moved. With the cabin filled with light, she could examine him closely. His hair and beard were ragged and dirt-encrusted, his skin waxy. Simon Carl Petersen would win no beauty prizes right now, but she wasn't so sure about his potential once he was well again. His features were purely masculine, yet refined... elegant, she decided. Intelligent. Of course, he was no commonplace liquor-store bandit. He was an outlaw of a higher order. A computer criminal, which obviously took intelligence, or at least a good education.

Tate set the glass of water beside the bed and left, then came back a few minutes later with a washcloth and a basin of water. The water was warm, taken from the cast-iron kettle she always kept heating on the wood stove. She sat down on the edge of the bed, dipped the washcloth into the basin, wrung it out, then began to smooth it over his cheeks.

At first he made no noise or movement. Then, after she had dipped, rinsed and wrung several times, he arched his neck, as if trying to avoid torture.

"That's right," she said softly. "Show me you're still alive."

She continued smoothing the cloth over his face, over his beard and mustache and down under his chin. Clean, the beard was a dark gold, a shade or two darker than his hair, or so she guessed. His hair was too dirty to be sure. She worked on his face until it was as clean as a washcloth could get it, then set the basin beside the bed and picked up the ice water.

She had decided on an eyedropper instead of a spoon because it was more difficult to avoid. "Simon," she said gently, "this is just ice water. You've got a high fever, and I've got to give you liquids. All you have to do is swallow." She accompanied her words with action, drawing water into the dropper and sliding it into the corner of his mouth. Drop by drop she dribbled water between his teeth, speaking reassuringly as she did.

The first two droppers went in with no difficulty, but then he balked, locking his jaw tight and refusing to part his teeth. Rather than fight him, she went into the kitchen and emptied the basin of water into the sink. Then she refilled it with soapy water and carried it back to the bedroom, stopping momentarily to add another log to the fire.

He was still, but as soon as she joined him on the bed, his head tossed restlessly on the pillow.

"That water probably steamed away before you could even swallow it," she lectured. "If we don't get more inside you, you'll dry up and the wind will blow you back to High Ridge."

Surprisingly, his eyes opened. But they stared straight ahead, as if he were watching something she couldn't see.

"Simon?" She touched the washcloth to his cheek. "Do you know where you are?"

His eyelids drifted shut.

Sighing, she continued to wash his face with the cool cloth. At least he wasn't trying to avoid it anymore. After a few minutes she began feeding him water with the eyedropper again and managed to give him the equivalent of a cup.

She waited to see if the water was going to stay down. As she waited, she smoothed the cloth over his cheeks again. Thanks to her diligence, he seemed cooler. Since the cabin was now a comfortable temperature, she decided to take the blanket off completely and fold the quilt down to his waist. Then, allowing herself only a brief thought about the strange intimacy of this, she began to wash his chest, shoulders and arms.

He was a tall man, but not heavy. He had the body of a runner or a major-leaguer, slender but muscular. She wasn't sure how long he had been in the penitentiary, but whatever the length of his stay, he had remained in shape...or gotten into it. She could almost picture him down on the floor of his cell doing push-ups. Had he spent that time planning his escape? Had he become obsessed with fitness because he knew that he had to be ready to break out of High Ridge?

She guessed that his superb conditioning had kept him alive. From the shape he was in now, she could only guess at what he had been through. A weaker man would have stopped when the bullet plowed into his calf. This man had kept going.

It felt odd to think of him as a strong man, when he was lying unconscious and burning up with fever. It felt odd to be caring for him so intimately. She owed him nothing, certainly not tender, loving care. But he was a human being, and so was she. He was a fine specimen of the human male—at least physically. And even if she didn't owe him anything exactly, wasn't it her human duty to keep him alive?

Tate smoothed the cloth over her prisoner's arms. Even relaxed, they were ridged with muscle. His forearms were covered with golden hair and tanned—apparently he had made good use of the prison yard while sojourning at High Ridge. She pictured him pacing its perimeter, plotting just how he was going to make his escape. Had someone helped him? The radio had been fuzzy on details. Had he escaped from High Ridge alone when, according to the news, no other prisoner in the penitentiary's history had managed the same feat?

She rinsed the cloth and began to wash a hand. It was broad, his fingers long and shapely. They were capable hands, hands that had held a gun and fired it three inches past her head despite a debilitating fever.

Silently she made a guess that the escape had been attempted without help. This was not a man who wanted to rely on anyone. Last night, he had believed until the bitter end that he was just going to sleep off the effects of the infection raging through his body. Only when he'd realized that he had really lost, that not a shred of hope was in sight, had he asked for her help.

She moved to the other side of the bed to wash his other arm. Maybe she was tired—missing a night's sleep did that to people. Or maybe she was just crazy—after all, this was an escaped prisoner she was treating so gently. But whatever the cause, she was becoming increasingly aware of the bond that was forming as she washed him.

She was twenty-one years old, and there had been men in her life. But she had always called a halt to relationships before they built to a natural conclusion. She wasn't sure why. She liked to believe it was because she had never fallen in love. The alternative—because she was unfeeling, cold, even frigid, perhaps—was less appealing.

And yet considering her background, considering where she had come from and what she had come through, it seemed understandable that she would have trouble giving herself to anyone. She was cautious. Life had insisted on it. Maybe she would always be too cautious to fall in love or make love to a man.

Of course, a truly cautious woman would have run screaming into the night when Simon Carl Petersen, escaped convict and murderer, asked for her help.

Gently she stroked the washcloth over Simon's chest. There were scratches covering him that she hadn't been aware of until she'd begun to clean him up. The one deep groove on his side near his waist looked as if a bullet had grazed him. Had it been directed only inches to the left, he never would have made it to the cabin.

He was badly bruised, too. Sympathy grew as she tried to imagine his ordeal in the woods before he'd found her cabin. The past few nights had dropped to near-freezing, and the tattered uniform he'd arrived in would have done nothing to keep him warm. She felt compassion and just a trace of some other indefinable emotion as she brushed the washcloth over his chest once more. It seemed almost a shame that a man as physically perfect as this one should spend the best years of his life locked away in an Arkansas prison.

She realized just exactly where her thoughts were taking her and dropped the washcloth back into the basin. He was much cleaner, and the water had briefly helped cool his skin. She left the room, then returned with one more basin of water to rinse off the soap. She worked efficiently and quickly, trying not to notice anything else about him.

When she'd finished, she diluted the correct dose of Tylenol in half a glass of ice water. Luckily he'd had no trouble with nausea since she'd given him the plain water. She just hoped that would hold.

"Come on, Simon. Cooperate just a little longer. Let's see if we can get that fever down." With absolutely no intention of taking no for an answer, she set to work.

He was in the tropics somewhere. He should know where; he was never lost. Madagascar, maybe. Or Brazil. Somewhere hotter than the hinges of Hades.

And he was in a jungle. Running, except that he could barely move. Cutting his way through rain forest, green everywhere, everything green. The machete they'd given him was dull and growing duller. He slashed, and the machete bounced against green, then ricocheted toward him, covered with green, dripping green. Blood. Green blood. A forest bleeding green.

He was bleeding.

Where was Josiah? Josiah had brought him to this forest, hadn't he? Left him here to find something, but what? The heat was dissolving his brain. Green everywhere. And something...something he was supposed to find. He chopped uselessly. His machete slid against the trunks of trees like the bow of a Stradivarius, searching for the perfect symphony. But there was no music here, only green. And something he was supposed to find.

Thirst swelled his tongue and narrowed his throat. Rain forest all around him, yet there was no rain. Living, breathing heat. Rain forest withering in sun, and sun that seemed to radiate from the ground at his feet. And where was Josiah?

He swallowed convulsively, and something cool trickled past the thirst knot in his throat. He raised his eyes to the heavens. In prayer? He hadn't prayed in a century. But there were clouds forming. He opened his mouth and rain, sweet, sweet rain, poured in.

He was afraid he could not swallow fast enough.

The Tylenol was gone. Tate knew Simon would take more water if she offered it. Toward the end of the dose he had seemed eager to swallow. He had even turned his head, making her job easier.

She knew better than to rush things, though. She would wait half an hour, then try the antibiotics. They wouldn't taste so pleasant, even though she intended to mix them with half a can of cola. If he couldn't keep that down, she would have no choice but to go to Will's and make a call to the sheriff. Simon had to have antibiotics, even if they were administered in the prison hospital.

In the meantime, she had to take a good look at his leg. She didn't know if the bullet was still embedded in his calf or whether the wound would conceivably heal without stitches. Now seemed a good time to make an assessment. He was still, as if too exhausted to toss and turn. Later her might be a worse patient.

Steeling herself for what was to come, she pulled the quilt and blanket from under the mattress and folded them back so that Simon's legs were exposed. Her eyes traveled the long length of them. Like the rest of him, they didn't seem to belong to a man the radio newscaster had dismissed as a paper-pusher. They were an athlete's legs, long and lean, and his thighs were muscular.

Her eyes flicked higher. His briefs were cheap, prison-issue cotton riding low on narrow, thoroughly masculine hips. The fabric stretched tightly across his abdomen and below, leaving no curve or bulge to her imagination. The girls at Stagecoach Inn would have glowing praise for a man endowed like this one.

She forced her thoughts back to the job at hand. Her first task was to clean the uninjured part of his leg, then strip off the bandanna and clean the infected area. To prepare for the chore ahead, she left the room to fire up the cookstove and begin boiling water. She thoroughly washed her hands and took a clean basin of soapy water back with her to begin the process.

Half an hour later she had already discovered good news. There were two wounds on his leg. The first and nastier was the entrance wound; the second—a smaller, neater hole— the exit. The bullet had gone through at an angle, apparently missing the bone, since his leg didn't appear to be broken, but badly injuring muscle and tissue. She knew little about such things, but she guessed that without physical therapy, Simon might never regain full use of the leg.

First and foremost, however, was to get rid of the infection so that no more injury could result. The area around the wound was hot to the touch and swollen, but it had stopped bleeding. She wondered what havoc her efforts might wreak. Might she be responsible for causing the wound to bleed again if she cleaned it and packed hot cloths around it to drain the infection?

The risk was certain, but she saw no other choice. Something had to be done or blood poisoning would be the result. Steeling herself for the task ahead, she sat so that she could take Simon's leg in her lap and hold it still as she worked. She only hoped he would remain unconscious until she was finished.

There was a house in the jungle ahead. No, not a house. A shack built into the towering, menacing green. It was constructed of bamboo and held together by crudely crafted jute rope. A parrot, with plumage so brilliant it seemed to undulate in waves of color, flew back and forth in front of the door, barring entrance.

He would find safety inside. There was shelter here, food and drink. And rest. He had never been so tired. His eyes were heavy with sleep, and as he shaded them against the glare of the bird's feathers, they grew heavier still.

Shelter. He hacked a path, but his arms were as rubbery as the trees he tried to cut away. For each tree he felled, two took its place after he passed. He could feel the jungle pushing him, propelling him toward the shack even as the trees in front of him barred his way.

He could die here, with the jungle closing in around him. Die here to nourish the trees, become yet another layer on the spongy rain-forest floor. He forced himself to strike one more blow, then one more, but as he tried to move forward, something gripped his leg. A vine, perhaps. His head dropped forward. Slowly, slowly. His gaze drifted downward.

The vine moved sinuously, stretching and contracting as it twisted around his leg. Gleaming reptile eyes smiled up at him. Scales glistened along the vine's surface.

He struggled to lift his leg, struggled to dislodge the vine-turned-python. Only when he no longer found the strength to struggle did the python slither away.

Tate hung her head over the kitchen sink and took deep breaths. During her years at the free clinic she had considered becoming a physician. Then an old man, a homeless wanderer who was regularly treated there, came in one morning, sat down in the waiting room and died.

She had known the man for months, traded stories with him, made him sandwiches and coffee, then more sandwiches to take with him when he left. She had done some volunteer social work, introducing him to a sympathetic counselor at the local welfare department, going with him to meet the owner of a boarding home for recovering alcoholics. But nothing she had done had helped. He had died, anyway, in the one place where he could be sure someone would mourn him.

She had taken weeks to master her grief. And when it was a tolerable ache inside her, she had realized that becoming a physician was out of the question. She had never thought of herself as a particularly emotional person, but the loss of the old man had nearly devastated her. How could she possibly handle the endless losses a doctor experienced? She knew of no specialty or position where she could be guaranteed that none of her patients would die.

Now she knew she had another reason for finding a profession other than medicine. She didn't have the stomach for it. She had cleaned and treated Simon's wound, but the memory of the pain he had suffered would haunt her forever.

She took another deep breath, then slowly lifted her head. Her nausea was passing, and her head was no longer whirling. At least she hadn't allowed her squeamishness to overwhelm her. And though her experience and knowledge were less than ideal, she thought there was a good chance that with the help of antibiotics he could fight the infection now, although he still needed stitches.

A moan echoed through the cabin. She splashed some water on her face from a jug by the sink and went to check on her patient.

Only his head moved, tossing from side to side on the pillow. She wondered if she dared try to give him the antibiotics now. Surely if treating his leg had sickened her, it had done more serious damage to him. She perched on the side of the bed and put her hand on his forehead. If the Tylenol had begun to work, it hadn't yet touched his fever. She soothed her hand along his brow.

It was a funny thing, how the intensity of caring for him was affecting her emotions. She felt bonded to him. He was totally at her mercy, and it felt strange to be so responsible for another human being's life. Too, it was particularly strange that the human being so dependent on her was an escaped convict.

Her hand halted on its gentle path. Was this the sort of relationship that sometimes developed between a kidnapper and his victim? Was she beginning to convince herself that he was really good, when all the evidence pointed to the opposite? She had always been a rebel. Was she making the ultimate statement now? Wasn't living in an old log cabin in the middle of nowhere good enough for her? Or did she have to go a step further and prove to the world that she honored none of its conventions?

She stood, trying to shake off the sympathy she was developing for the murderer, embezzler, escape artist, gun-toting terrorizer of isolated women. He probably didn't deserve her help; he most certainly did not deserve her sympathy. She was going to have to be careful. She obviously had a soft spot in her heart for people who were alone and in need. She'd better be careful that the soft spot didn't ooze right into her good sense.

With that thought to guide her, she went back to the kitchen to prepare the antibiotics.

Somehow, he made it to the shack. The parrot flew toward him in an agonizing flash of color, all wings and exquisite rainbow torture. He ducked, and the parrot soared into the jungle, where it was lost in relentless green.

He stumbled to the door and peered inside. The shack was dark, a deep, velvet black that sucked at him until he entered. It was cool inside, enticingly, insidiously cool. Cool, then cold. Cold as the jungle had been hot. His heated flesh contracted against the thick, frostbitten air. He tried to wrap his arms around his chest for warmth, but he remained statue-still.

He would die here, in the cold, just as he would have died of the jungle heat. He had struggled so hard, only to come to the same ending.

His eyes began to close. Slowly, slowly.

At first there was silence; not even his own thoughts could penetrate its shell. Then he heard a voice. He forced his eyelids apart. A woman was staring at him. He saw her, but he could not see her face. In the frozen darkness, he could only see all that made her human.

She stretched her hand toward his. "Come," she said. "I'll give you comfort."

His fingers began to warm. He moved them as his hand warmed, too. With growing strength, he stretched his hand toward her. The movement took time that wasn't. He was moving toward her, and she waited.

When their fingers touched, in whatever millenium they walked together, she led him back to the jungle. The trees burst with rainbow foliage and bent in quiet greeting as they passed. And then, beside a forest glade, they lifted their heads and tasted the sweet, sweet rain together.

Simon had swallowed the antibiotics and cola without incident, although twice he had opened his eyes and mumbled incoherently. Tate felt drained of everything inside her, but her prisoner was looking better. Peaceful, at least. He seemed to have fallen into a quieter sleep, now that she was finished.

She felt the satisfaction of a job well done. Was this the way a mother felt after caring for her new infant? The answer was obvious, if humiliating. She felt no spark of maternal pride. Even depleted and unconscious, this was not a man to stir that kind of emotion. She felt something entirely different. The man lying in her bed had roused some darker feeling, although she couldn't or wouldn't name it. She had touched him in ways and in places she had never touched a man before. And she had made a commitment to him that was more serious than any other she had ever made.

She had no resources left to question either the feeling or the commitment now. It would take time for the antibiotics to make a difference, but she was encouraged by his response to her care. He was certainly no worse. If he could continue to tolerate the liquids and medication, he had a good chance for recovery. On the other hand, she was going to hit the skids if she didn't get some sleep.

There was a bed in the loft; in fact, that was where she usually preferred to sleep, but now that was out of the question. She couldn't be that far from her patient. The next twenty-four hours were going to be crucial. She had to be alert to any changes for the worse. She contemplated the alternatives and realized there was only one. She had to make a bed on the floor for herself. Never mind that it was fast approaching an Ozark winter and the floor was the worst place in the cabin to be.

She climbed up to the loft and stripped the bed, returning to the bedroom with two blankets and a pillow. Then she went out to her car to retrieve an old sleeping bag that she always kept in the back. A few minutes later she had made a tolerable pallet on the floor, with the aid of three sofa cushions. She left the room, pulling the door only half closed in case Simon called for her.

She considered going to bed without taking a bath, but decided against it. Once Simon was alert again, bathing might be a problem; certainly it would be an inconvenience. She balked at the idea of hauling bucket after bucket and splashing them into the round washtub that was propped beside the fireplace. But a sponge bath just wouldn't do. She needed a real bath. For just a moment she let herself fantasize about the luxury of going into a bathroom and turning on faucets, from which would pour clear, steaming water. Mumbling insults to the father she had never seen, she opened the back door and set to work.

The jungle heaven faded, to be replaced by thick, ancient logs. For a moment Simon believed he was in a fortress. Pictures formed slowly, the truth settling over him at so torturous a pace that he could only grasp its end—its beginning was already out of reach.

He was in a cabin. He couldn't remember why. He was in a bed, but he was too tired to have slept. And he was bound to the bed, although he couldn't see how.

He was both hot and cold, but something told him that his suffering was less than it had been. His leg throbbed until each heartbeat was a torment, but the pain was confined to one place. Some intuition told him that was good, but he was too tired to explore just why.

His eyelids kept drifting closed, but he forced them open. He focused on a wall, a chair, then a door. It was ajar. He narrowed his eyes, like an old man squinting at the newspaper. Light floated in from the window. And through the crack in the door he saw puddles of sunshine on the cabin floor.

He seemed to be alone. He yearned for the jungle and the woman's hand in his. He knew that he was a man who never reached for anyone, yet he had in the rain forest, and reaching had been good.

His eyelids drifted shut once more until he heard a noise. He was in no hurry to respond. He listened. The noise was a song, a whistle that seemed somehow familiar. He opened his eyes and saw the woman from his dream. She was as far from him as she had been then, as strangely undefined. He could see only her outline, could only experience, somehow, all that made her human.

As he watched, her figure began to take shape, shimmering against leaping flames until, even with her back to him, she was flesh and blood and sweetly curving femininity. He saw that she was naked, that her skin was the color of snow against the blazing fire. Like a dancer she stretched her arms over her head and piled her black hair on top of it, holding the inky mass with one hand as she poised at the edge of a round metal tub. Then with infinite grace, she lowered herself into the water.

He saw the silhouette of a breast, small and firm, the perfect curve of a hip, the slender length of a leg. She merged with the water until all he could see was the smooth white breadth of her back and the coal-black length of her hair spilling over the side of the tub.

He knew what it would be like to touch her, to stroke his fingers through the silk of her hair, to brush them over the satin of her body. He yearned to reach for her, but he could not move. He yearned to call to her, but his lips made no sound.

He stared until she grew dim, and even then he struggled to see more, fought not to lose her. At last his eyes closed unwillingly. At once he fell into a dreamless sleep.

Tate came back into the bedroom after her bath. She straightened the quilt and felt Simon's forehead. He seemed cooler, and he was no longer fidgeting. He seemed to be sleeping deeply.

She reached for his wrist and wrapped her fingers around it to check his pulse. The beat was strong, still too fast, but slower than it had been an hour before.

She stood gazing down at him. There was something between them now. She could deny it, could chastise herself for caring, but a bond had formed. Later she would have to face what to do about him. Now she could only be glad that he seemed to have improved.

Gently she laid his arm back across his chest. Her fingers brushed his hand as she began to move away, and in the briefest of moments, her hand was captured in his.

The pressure of his fingers was slight; his skin was fever-coarse and dry. But he held her hand, not in protest or plea, but as if in gratitude. As she stood there, holding her breath in surprise, his fingers tightened around hers . . . only for a second, for so brief a time that she might have imagined it. Then abruptly her hand was released. His lay on the quilt, fingers curled.

She was so moved that for a moment she could not turn away. Fugitive, murderer, the same man who had fired a gun to terrify her. Yet even unconscious, he had found a way to show her he was more than that. He was a human being, and he was grateful.

And she was a woman who was in danger of giving in to emotion and exhaustion.

Tate turned away and forced herself to stare at the scar in the cabin wall made by a bullet that could have lodged in her brain. She stared at it until she felt everything but exhaustion drain away. Then she found her way to the cushions she had lined up at the foot of the bed and crawled under the blankets.

Chapter 5

By the next afternoon Simon's fever had soared and plummeted as often as a skydiving stunt team. Through the hours of sweats and chills he had never regained consciousness. He slept more easily when his fever dropped and tossed restlessly when it spiked, but he never opened his eyes and asked where he was. Tate was certain of that, because she hardly left his side.

When his fever had climbed the first time, she had considered, yet again, going for the sheriff. She had even decided on an arbitrary number of degrees that would signal the need for a trip into town, and she had taken his temperature faithfully, hour after hour. The thermometer, anchored tightly under his arm, had never quite climbed to the point where her decision would be made. His fever had hovered near crisis point but never exceeded it.

Tate had slept in the periods when Simon's temperature dropped and, depleted by his body's struggles, he no longer tossed and turned. When she was awake she did the most cursory of survival chores, hauling wood for the fireplace, cooking and heating water, putting out food for Cinn, who watched her every movement from his post at the bedroom door. But she never left Simon alone for more than a few minutes. By deciding not to turn him in, she had made a commitment to watch over him.

Now, more than twenty-four hours after deciding to care for him, she was exhausted and discouraged. His fever was rising once more, after hovering just two degrees above normal all morning. She knew fevers often rose in the afternoon, and that if this one wasn't accompanied by other symptoms, it might not be as bad as it seemed. But she also knew that if she didn't see a definite improvement soon, she was going to have to seek help. Eyedroppers of liquids were inadequate to stop dehydration, and antibiotic capsules weren't nearly as effective as injections and intravenous medication.

She was losing the battle.

Tate sank to the edge of the bed, too tired to stand any longer. Beside her, Simon tossed his head. Despite her efforts to keep the pillow plumped, he had worn a deep valley in its center. She knew he must be suffering, although she doubted that his mind registered it. Hours ago she had unlocked the handcuff, then snapped it to the bedsprings to give them both more freedom as she washed him once more. He was certainly in no shape to escape or to threaten her. At the first sign of returning strength she intended to lock him to the bed frame again.

She laid her hand on his forehead, brushing the lock of freshly washed blond hair away. She didn't need a thermometer to determine the obvious. Even though she had given him the maximum dosage of Tylenol half an hour before, he was not responding. Faithful Nurse Cantrell was going to have to bathe his skin again and force more fluids down him.

Telling herself that she would find the strength somewhere, she rose and went to the back porch for the water she had hauled earlier that day. The ice she had bought in town was gone, but the spring water was still cool, since the porch was in shade. She filled the basin and a pitcher and went back into the cabin, where she poured powdered lemonade in a glass and mixed it with water from the pitcher. It was the closest thing to glucose that she had.

She began with the eyedropper and told herself she was lucky he wasn't so deeply unconscious he couldn't swallow. Of course, if he had been, her decision whether to notify the sheriff or not would have been easy. He would be back at High Ridge now, and she would be in bed asleep.

Of course, if what he had claimed was true, he might be back at High Ridge in a coffin.

The small jolt of adrenaline that followed that thought got her through the next fifteen minutes and Simon through an entire glass of lemonade. With that behind them, she squeezed a washcloth out over the basin and began to wipe his cheeks and forehead.

Her movements were rote. She had done this so often over the past twenty-four hours that she knew all the contours of his face by memory. He was almost as familiar as an old friend, although to her knowledge none of her old friends was a fugitive from justice.

A dry chuckle squeezed from a body she had believed too tired to ever laugh again. The truth was that if she went far enough back in her life, plenty of the people she had once considered friends could be fugitives from justice. For all she knew, some of them could have ended up in prison like Simon—which was probably why she was sitting here sponging him off.

She moved down to his neck and began to smooth the cloth over it, then down to his chest. If any of the runaways she had met before going to live at Stagecoach Inn were criminals now, they would not have been convicted for anything as white-collar as computer crime. And though her memory of those years was fuzzy, she doubted that anyone with whom she had raided Dumpsters or fleeced tourists had grown up to look like Simon Carl Petersen.

In fact, very few males indeed grew up to look like Simon.

She was cooling the arm closer to her when he moaned. It was another sign that his fever was climbing. Unless she could keep it from climbing higher, he would probably begin to thrash about and mutter. That had happened on two other occasions, but both times she had been able to give him Tylenol almost immediately. Now she had hours to wait before that was an option.

She wondered if he would say anything she could understand. None of the words she had been able to decipher before had made any sense. He called for someone named Josiah, but not as if he expected rescue. And she thought once he had said the name "Erin."

She wondered if Erin was a girlfriend. She didn't think he was married. The radio had never mentioned a wife, and since they had no hard news to report, they dredged up details of his past life at every newscast, just to keep the story before the public.

She had heard his story told time and time again, but never once had a Josiah or an Erin been mentioned. Odder still was the lack of detail about his escape. Apparently no one at High Ridge was willing to talk about that.

Tate knew all about the 1.2 million dollars Petersen had stolen, though. He had been an officer with the highest security clearance at a Houston bank. With his good reputation, access to computer codes and electronic fund-transfer lines, and the help of a banking system so complicated that it made wire fraud nearly impossible to detect, he had coolly embezzled his small fortune over a period of three months.

And he wouldn't have been caught and convicted, wouldn't be lying in her bed, if an unlucky surprise audit hadn't uncovered his scheme.

The auditor, a man named Joe Masters, had been even unluckier. Thanks to his own careful investigation, he was now lying in his grave. According to testimony at the trial, Masters had decided that *he* didn't make nearly enough money for all the work he did and offered to relieve Carl Petersen of his newfound wealth in exchange for his silence. Petersen hadn't thought the swap a fair one, and instead he had bought Masters's silence with one perfectly placed bullet.

And Tate knew just how perfectly the man lying in her bed could place a bullet.

Petersen had almost gotten away with his crime. It had taken months before the police had zeroed in on him for either embezzlement or murder; then the trial itself had taken more months. The jury hadn't taken quite that long to make a decision, but there had been doubts that Petersen had killed Masters. No weapon was ever found; no evidence that Petersen had ever owned a gun or shot one had been presented.

In the end he had been convicted because of the testimony of the accountant who took over for Joe Masters and discovered the embezzlement, too. Petersen's motive was ironclad; his alibi was not. The aunt he had supposedly visited on the night of the murder admitted, when pressured in court, that she had not seen her wayward nephew for more than a year.

So, although there were some significant gaps in what Tate knew about her own personal fugitive, there was much she did know. One other important detail was muddy, however. Never, in any of the news reports, had the name "Simon" been mentioned. Fellow bank employees, neighbors, the grocer at the store he had patronized, had all been given a chance to spout their two cents worth about him. He had been Carl to all of them. Never Simon.

He was a man of mystery, a man of contradictions. He was a man lying in her bed and possibly dying, and she was a woman who should know better than to help him.

Tate sponged his chest, observing the way the golden hair swirled into plastered curls. If Erin was his girlfriend, was she worried about him now? How had she felt when he had been sentenced to High Ridge? How had he felt knowing that he wouldn't kiss her, touch her or make love to her again until he was old and worn out from his years in prison? Had his desperate escape been motivated by a love so strong he would risk his life for it?

Tate realized how sentimental her thoughts had become, spurred, she was sure, by the intimacy of stroking his body so tenderly. She wrung out her washcloth and hardened her heart. It was more likely that greed had motivated the man in her bed. None of the money he had embezzled had ever been recovered. It was probably squirreled away in a foreign country gathering interest. Was Erin there, too, watching it grow and waiting for her fugitive lover?

Simon moaned again, and his lips moved as if he were trying to speak. Tate leaned closer.

"Josiah . . . bastard."

"Who is Josiah, Simon?" she asked softly.

"Gallagher . . . bastard . . . get you."

"Mighty unchristian of you," she said, moving the cloth back to his cheeks.

A hand captured her wrist. His grip was surprisingly strong. "Why? Friends . . . You saved . . ."

Tate felt a spurt of fear. She wished she hadn't gotten so close. "I'm nobody you know," she said soothingly. "I'm not Josiah."

"Bastard."

"Bastardess." Tate jerked her arm free. "I'm a woman," she said. "A woman taking care of you while you get better. You've got to rest. You've been shot."

He turned his head away. "Kill me. They'll kill . . ."

"Nobody's going to kill you. Nobody even knows where you are. You're safe."

His head turned, and his eyes opened. He stared at her, but she knew he didn't see her. "Why?"

She couldn't answer a question she didn't understand. "You've got to rest. You're very sick, and if you don't get better soon, I'm going to have to get the sheriff to take you to the hospital."

He stared at her; she wondered whom he saw. He stared until his eyes glazed over and his lids drooped shut.

She pulled the sheet over his chest and racked her brain for something she could do to calm him. His eyes were closed, but he was so fitful she was afraid he might reopen the wound on his leg if he began to struggle. His fever was worse, but the wound looked better to her. If she could just keep him still as his fever peaked, he might weather this.

She wished she could sing, but her rough alto was guaranteed to send him back on the run. Talking to him didn't seem to help. No matter what she said, he seemed to suspect she was this Josiah person. She settled on whistling. She couldn't sing, but she remembered melodies, and her whistle was clear and accurate. She started on tunes she had heard at the last hootenanny. They were mournful and melodic, tailor-made for a whistler.

He grew calm almost immediately.

Someone had weighted Simon's eyelids. Hadn't physicians once put copper pennies on the eyelids of the dead? The reason for the bizarre practice escaped him, but the possibility he was dead did not. He could not open his eyes. Surely that indicated something out of the ordinary. And although death was an ordinary occurrence, it had never happened to him. At least, not while he was paying attention.

His head spun as he tried to order his thoughts. They were like waves washing over a beach. He couldn't catch them; he couldn't depend on them to do what he wanted. They surged through his head, and there was no rhyme or reason to any of them.

He forced himself to concentrate on his eyelids. He realized that they weren't open because he was just too tired to push them apart. But why was he so exhausted? He had never been this tired before, not even when he had been lost in the jungle, fighting his way to...

But that had been a dream. Hadn't it? And this wasn't. At least, he didn't think so. He tried to concentrate on what he knew. He was lying down, and something covered him loosely, like a sheet or blanket.

Or a shroud.

Surely he wasn't dead. Death was final. Kaput. You didn't think and you didn't feel. He was doing both. And in a minute he was going to open his eyes. Just as soon as he summoned the energy and the focus.

In the meantime, he listened intently. Someone was breathing. It could be him, and if it was, that was an excellent sign.

There were no other noises that he could hear. No cars rushing by, no crickets chirping, no jungle squawks and squeals. But then, the jungle had been a dream. Hadn't it? And what else had he dreamed?

A woman. And a haunting, twine-around-the-gut whistle.

He summoned all his strength and pried his eyelids apart.

At first he thought he had been unsuccessful. There was still nothing but darkness surrounding him. How could anything but death be this black? Then, slowly, images formed. A window with glimmers of light filtering through gossamer curtains. The footboard of an iron bedstead. A closet door, slightly ajar.

Not dead. By why was he in bed? And why did he feel as if every bone in his body was made of rubber?

Something moved beside him. He knew he should respond. Some instinct told him to be wary, but the best he could do was begin to turn his head to the side. Once past a certain point, gravity finished the job.

His neck was stiff, but his view was better, although better was a matter of opinion. Something *had* moved—or rather, someone. There was a woman beside him, a lovely young woman, sleeping deeply with her head on his pillow. It was probably her breathing he had heard.

She wasn't a stranger. That much he knew. Who she was danced somewhere at the edge of his consciousness. Why she was in his bed was a total mystery.

He considered his choices. But until he could remember who she was and why she was here, there was nothing he could do.

He was beginning to remember faces and scenes, although he couldn't sift through them yet to order them. He remembered prison and running. He remembered a searing pain in his leg, pain that was seated in the same location as the distant throb somewhere below the sheet covering him. He remembered woods and a river. He remembered a cabin.

He forced himself to concentrate. Flashes of memory tantalized him. Firewood flying through the air. The woman running. A gun in his hands and a bullet splintering ancient logs.

Lord, had he really shot at her? And if so, what was she doing breathing so softly beside him? Was she wounded? Dying? Had all this happened just minutes before?

She didn't look as if she were dying. She looked as if she was asleep. Deeply asleep. So deeply that he could push himself off the bed and steal away without her knowing. Of course, a man who had to summon all his resources to open his eyelids didn't have much of a chance of stealing anywhere.

Why was she sleeping beside him? Surely she knew who he was. He was wearing a prison guard's uniform.... He wiggled the fingers of one hand against his leg and contacted bare skin. He *had* been wearing a uniform. How long had he been here? And why hadn't she called the police?

As he watched her sleep, he listened intently for movement elsewhere in the cabin. The deep silence was broken only by the woman's breathing.

She was remarkably lovely. With light stealing across the room and touching her face, he could see the milk-and-roses complexion, the straight black silk of her hair, the delicate features. He couldn't guess her age, but she was younger than he had ever been.

So what did he do now? And where was Jim Cooney's gun? The light breaking through the window was sunshine, not the obscene gold of the moon that had guided him here. Broad daylight was no time to run anywhere, and it was doubtful he could crawl, anyway. Somehow he had to force her to let him stay and recover. Then, if he had even ordinary luck, he could find his way to Memphis and Aaron. He was sure that Aaron could be trusted. Of course, once he had trusted Josiah, too.

His plan hinged on knowing why she hadn't turned him in. He couldn't think of one conceivable reason. He had threatened her, shot at her and...handcuffed her to the bed! That was why she was sleeping beside him. She must still be cuffed there. And what if he had died? Could she have found a way to escape?

He tried to struggle to one elbow to see if he was right, but something held him to the mattress. At first he thought it was his own lack of strength; then he realized the truth.

He stared at the woman, and as if his struggles had wakened her, her eyes opened sleepily and she stared back.

"I've been told I'm good in bed...but no one's ever chained me up...to keep me there," he said. The words were halting. To his own ears his voice sounded as if it was coming from a tunnel.

Tate sat up immediately and moved away from him. She finger-combed her hair away from her face as she stared groggily. "You're talking."

"Have been for years."

"You haven't been, not for days," she corrected. She couldn't begin to deal with the fact that she had fallen asleep beside him. Close beside him! The last thing she remembered, she had been whistling "John Riley" for the fifth time, perched on the edge of the bed. With horror she realized she had probably fallen asleep in the middle of a chorus and just keeled over. And when had she snuggled up to him like her favorite teddy bear?

"Days?" he croaked.

She struggled for objectivity. "How do you feel?"

He didn't answer. Tate thought he looked like a man who was searching for his past.

She filled him in. "Do you remember coming here?"

He gave a curt nod.

"After you so sweetly introduced yourself, shot at me and chained me to the bed, you finally relented and gave me the gun and the key to the cuffs."

He grunted.

She could tell he was wondering about his sanity. She knew the signs. She was wondering about her own. "I've been taking care of you ever since. Your leg was badly infected, and you've had a high fever."

"How long?"

"Two days." Tate wondered if she dared feel his forehead. She decided against it.

Simon stared at her. Two days and she hadn't called the sheriff. By all rights he should be waking up at High Ridge right now. Waking up so that Captain Shaw could kill him with his own bare hands. "Why am I still here?"

Tate stood, brushing nonexistent lint off her jeans so she wouldn't have to look at him. She wasn't sure why he was still there herself. And to give him a truly good answer, she would have to tell him the story of her life. "Let's just say I'm probably a nut case and let it go at that."

"Nobody knows?"

"Nobody but me." She lifted her head. "I should have turned you in. We both know I should have."

"Why didn't you?"

She could almost see him trying to make sense of her answers. "Do you remember anything you said before you passed out?"

He shook his head, making a deeper well in the pillow.

She smiled a little. "Good. Then let's see if your story is the same this morning. Sort of an informal lie-detector test."

He shut his eyes and wondered just how many secrets he had spilled, when he was out of his head with fever and pain. The thought wasn't pleasant. He felt something touch his forehead, and his eyes flew open.

Tate backed away. "You actually feel cool. I think the antibiotics must have kicked in. Since you're awake, let's get some liquids down you. Feel up to swallowing?"

"Yeah. Just unlock the cuff and I'll sit up and drink a gallon."

"If you feel up to it, I'll help you sit up. And you can drink one-handed."

He didn't answer, although Tate wasn't surprised. He was beginning to look like a man who was about to fall asleep again. She watched his lashes droop over eyes that were an icy gray. His color was better now that his fever was down.

"Go ahead and get some sleep," she said. "I'll wake you up when I've something ready for you. Any chance you could handle some food?"

The last thing on earth he wanted to do was eat. But food was energy, and God knew he would need energy if he was going to get out of here. He managed a nod.

He knew when she was gone, even though she made no sound. He thought of the woman in his dream.

In the kitchen Tate leaned against the sink and closed her eyes. He was real. *This* was real. Lying in the bed only yards away was a fugitive, and she had been lying with him! She could no longer pretend to be Nurse Nancy tending to the wounded. There was a name for someone who hid a fugitive, and that name was "accomplice."

Simon Carl Petersen didn't look half so heart-wrenching, now that he was awake. He looked dangerous, even though he could barely keep his eyes open. He looked amazingly like the man who had blasted a bullet past her right ear.

Weren't there stories about women who fell in love with prisoners? Stories about death-row brides hopelessly infatuated by serial killers? She was a far cry from being in love with the man chained to her bed, but was she somehow connected to all those crazy women who liked their men best when they were dressed in orange jumpsuits stamping out license plates?

She opened her eyes and looked around the cabin. She had lived alone for weeks, making meaning from hauling water and chopping wood. Had she really lost her mind in the process? Had even a fugitive looked like promising company?

Tate pushed away from the sink. She would feed him and make sure he got enough to drink. Then she would question him. His answers would determine what she did next. It would be more than interesting to see what he told her. His future would depend on it.

And hers might, too.

It took her only minutes to assemble a light breakfast of poached eggs and toast. To finish off the meal she made hot tea to serve along with a glass of canned orange juice. She knew that even if he could take just a few bites, the food would do him good.

Back in the bedroom she watched him sleeping. He was no longer restless. Even if he began to run another fever she suspected it would only climb a few degrees. She knew that when she checked his leg she could find it much improved. He was a strong man; from this point on he would probably recover quickly.

"Wake up," she called softly. She waited, but he slept on.

"Wake up," she repeated. "Simon, wake up!"

His eyes opened, and he stared at her. "What?"

"I said wake up."

"What did you call me?"

She didn't answer. It appeared that the test had begun.

He continued to stare at her. She would have given anything to read his thoughts. "I must have thought you were worth trusting," he said at last, "to tell you that."

"Why do the papers call you Carl?" Tate set the tray on the edge of the bed, but she didn't move any closer.

His hesitation was so brief that it would have been nonexistent to a less wary eye. "Simon is my middle name. Only the people I'm closest to call me that."

"People like Josiah and Erin?"

"People like that."

His eyes were such a frostbitten flint that they were impossible to read. Tate had thought that after years of practice she could read anybody. How unfortunate to find at such a crucial moment that she had been wrong.

"Here poor Josiah calls you Simon and all you can call him is 'bastard.'" She folded her arms.

"You're entitled to the story." He took a deep breath, and the aroma of the breakfast almost overwhelmed him. Nausea played around the edges of hunger, then disappeared. "Could I eat something first?" he asked.

She almost refused, but she had cared for him too long to deny him something that would make him stronger.

"First, there are some rules," she said, "and some things you should know. Number one, both your gun and the key to the handcuff aren't in this room and certainly not anywhere on me. If you grab me, you'll be wasting your time. I couldn't free you even if I wanted to, which I don't. Second, if you grab me for any other reason, eventually you'll have to let me go. When you do, you'll still be cuffed to the bed and I'll be at the sheriff's office giving directions to this cabin.''

"I see."

"Do you?"

"I promise on my word of honor..." He took a breath and rested for a moment, "...that I won't grab you."

Other than the absurdity of his having any honor, something else about his words struck her. He had just the slightest accent. There was something about he way he clipped his words that was distinctly European. She wondered if she was imagining it.

"Besides, if I grabbed you right now," he concluded, "I wouldn't have the...strength to hold on."

"That won't wash with me. I've observed firsthand what a fighter you are. You'd hold on, if you thought it would do you any good. I'm telling you it won't."

"I'm hearing you."

She believed him. "Good. Are you strong enough to hold a glass?"

He started to say "of course," but he realized it might not be true. He wanted to be strong enough to yank the handcuffs into half a dozen pieces, but he wasn't even sure he could tear a newspaper.

Tate watched his brief struggle. She was surprised he had allowed it to show. "On second thought, I'll hold it," she decided for him. "You need to save whatever strength you've got."

The chain between the cuffs was long enough that she calculated he could be propped up in a semi-sitting position. She took the second pillow from the other side of the bed and stood over him. "Can you lift yourself up enough for me to slip this under you?"

He did, with maximum effort and minimum gain. She considered helping him get into a better position, then decided against it. She still wasn't sure he wouldn't try something, and she didn't want to take any chances.

When he had propped himself as much as he was able, she sat on the edge of the bed and put the tray on her lap. "Let's start with the juice." She lifted the glass, turning so she was facing him. "This should be quicker than an eyedropper."

"Eyedropper?"

"That's how I got liquids in you. Slow but foolproof."

He looked disgusted, as if a real man should never need something so ridiculous. She almost laughed. "Quarts and quarts of liquid. Lemonade, water, cola. You burned it right off with that fever. I'd guess you're still a couple of quarts low."

"Like somebody's old jalopy."

A sense of humor, even a cynical one, was something she hadn't expected. She lifted the glass to his lips, keeping a wary eye on him as she did. Any sudden moves and she would be on the other side of the cabin in a flash. His first few sips were clumsy, almost as if his lips and tongue had forgotten how to coordinate, but he improved quickly.

When the juice was half gone, Tate set the glass on the tray and picked up the plate. "You can talk between bites. You shouldn't eat too fast, anyway."

Simon was grateful he had been given a chance to plan his story. His head still wasn't completely clear. He had the peculiar feeling he was floating somewhere just out of reach of good sense and caution. He knew one thing, though. He wasn't going to tell this woman any more of the truth than he had to. His life depended on lies. And increasingly, as his thoughts began to gel, he knew that her life might, too. There were times when telling the truth was nothing less than immoral. And stupid.

"What have I told you...so far?" he asked between nibbles of toast.

"Nice try, Simon."

The room was filled with sunlight now. He could see the woman as clearly as he had in his dreams, only now she had form and features and the softest mouth he had ever seen—even when it was twisted in a cynical smile. He wondered what gods or lack of them had brought him to this cabin.

"What's your name?" he asked.

"You asked me that before."

He shifted through his memories, then shook his head.

"Try this one. Do you remember almost blasting my head off?"

"'Almost' is the operative word, isn't it?"

She noticed the precise way he said "operative." "Were you trying to miss?"

"Would any rational man answer no?"

She considered that. "Tate."

He worked hard and finally found the proper thread of their conversation. "Odd."

She wasn't sure why she bothered to explain. "My grandmother named me Kate. As a child I could only manage Tate. It stuck."

"It suits you."

She was angry at herself for getting even *that* personal. "But at least *everyone* calls me Tate. The newspapers don't call me Elizabeth or Mary Jane."

"I'm Carl Simon Petersen. I suppose, in my way, I was letting you know I trusted you."

"I *don't* trust you."

"A wise move." He let her feed him bites of egg before he continued. "But even if you didn't trust me...you took me in and took care of me. Why?"

"This *is* story time, only it's your story we're listening to. Not mine."

He decided the rumors he had heard about Arkansas hill folk had highly underrated their intelligence. "How much do you know...about my reason for being sent to High Ridge?"

She decided that was a question it wouldn't hurt to answer. As she fed him more egg she told him what she had heard on the radio, since that was undisputed fact.

"I'm innocent," he said, when she had finished. "I didn't kill Joe Masters...and I didn't embezzle the money." He rested and cursed himself for not even having the strength to put two sentences together. "I was set up...and I can prove it if I can just get to Memphis."

Tate's fork stopped halfway to his mouth. "Memphis? You're supposed to be heading back to Houston."

"Does this look like the way to Houston?"

"It doesn't look like the way to anywhere."

He grimaced and closed his eyes. For a moment desolation washed over him. Never once in all his years had he believed he couldn't defeat whatever was blocking him. Now, for the first time, he realized how totally at this woman's mercy he was. His story had better be good, superlative in fact, or the next place he would be heading was High Ridge. And that would be his last stop.

"A man named Josiah Gallagher killed Masters," he said, admiring the irony of his own life. "Gallagher and I worked in the same department." He rested, then continued. "He worked for me, but as it turned out, he worked me over good. He . . . he embezzled the money, but he manipulated the records so it would look like I did it. Then he tipped off Masters so . . . he could do a surprise audit."

"And you didn't know any of this?"

"Not then, no."

"Funny. You don't seem like a man who would be easily taken by surprise."

He wished she weren't so perceptive. "I've learned a lot since then." He opened his eyes and accepted more food.

"So just suppose what you're telling me is true. Why didn't any of this come out at the trial?"

"My attorney swore I'd go free. There wasn't any concrete evidence to prove . . . either the embezzlement or the murder. And he said there was nothing to link Gallagher. It would just . . . be his word against mine."

"Why did Gallagher murder Masters, if Masters believed you were the embezzler?"

"Because Masters didn't . . . believe it. Not after I showed him how Gallagher could have done it himself. He went to Gallagher . . . and Gallagher killed him. But he set it up to look like I did."

Tate fed him the last of the egg. He looked as if the explanation had completely worn him out. "And I suppose Gallagher set up your aunt, too."

Simon swallowed. The food felt strange on a stomach that had been empty for so long. His head felt strange, too. Too strange to think fast enough. "I'm not sure what you mean," he said at last.

"I suppose you think I don't know anything about the trial." Tate lifted the tea. It had cooled to lukewarm.

He tried desperately to remember what *he* knew. Then it came to him. "I wasn't with my aunt, and I made a...mistake when I tried to get her to back up my story. But I couldn't...tell the truth in court."

"How inconvenient."

"I was with...a woman."

Tate nodded. "Erin. You've been calling for her." She tilted the cup so he could drink.

It took him a moment to understand. "Right. Erin...Gallagher's wife." He liked the twist. It was too bad Gallagher wasn't there to appreciate it, too.

"But why would that matter? If you had an alibi, you would have been set free. And if Erin was your alibi, she couldn't have been Gallagher's alibi, too."

He scowled. "You should have been my attorney. He...convinced me that I had nothing to...worry about and that when my trial ended, the district attorney would go after...Gallagher next." He paused in frustration. Neither his tongue nor his brain was working fast enough. And he had to convince Tate of his innocence or he could die.

He struggled to go on. "Only I didn't realize that some of Gallagher's new wealth was...lining my attorney's pocket. Erin disappeared...after I was convicted, but I know where she is. If I can just get to her...talk to her, I can convince her...to come back and tell her story. But I have to do it myself. She's afraid...of Gallagher, and...she has a right to be."

Tate weighed his story while she finished giving him the tea. He looked completely worn out, and she knew she couldn't continue to drill him for information much longer. The story made some sense, but that meant nothing. A clever psychopath could talk his way past St. Peter. What was a lie or two to a murderer? Could Simon really be expected to tell her he had killed Joe Masters and would do so again if given the chance?

She set the teacup on the tray and stood. "Even if all this is true, why was your life in danger at High Ridge? Gallagher got what he wanted, didn't he? You were safely behind bars."

"I could still talk. There...was a reporter looking into...the case. I found out last week that Gallagher paid an inmate...to kill me before the reporter...could interview me."

"Couldn't you go to the warden?"

"No."

She was surprised that one word could be so filled with contempt.

"Tate?"

She faced him.

"I didn't kill Joe Masters."

His story sounded too much like a television movie of the week to be believable. But for some crazy reason she couldn't accept the fact that he had murdered someone in cold blood. She didn't know why. Most of the time they had spent together, he had been unconscious. What did she know of him? What did she really know?

"Are you going to turn me in?"

She considered the question, just as she had been considering it for days. "I don't know."

"That's more...than I have a right to expect."

She nodded; then taking the tray, she started toward the door. "Get some more sleep. After you've had a nap, I'll have to change the bandage on your leg."

To his ears those didn't sound like the words of a woman expecting to make a visit to the sheriff. Simon thought how easy it would be to pick the lock on his handcuff. Surprisingly easy. But what would be the point? He was too weak to run, and Memphis and Aaron were light years away. He could think of no better, safer place to stay and regain his strength than this.

And if he was truthful with himself, he could think of no place he would rather be. Just why eluded him, though. It was just one more of those facts—or feelings—swirling in a mind too exhausted to grab and hold on to it.

Chapter 6

The next morning Simon was still sleeping when Tate appeared in his room, rattling a length of rusty chain like the Ghost of Christmas Past. She stood in the doorway observing her prisoner. The day before he had been awake several times after their breakfast conversation, but only long enough to exchange a few words and swallow more liquids. What little fever he'd had that afternoon had dropped by evening. The wound in his leg still looked as if it badly needed a physician's attention, but signs of infection were receding.

His color was better now. The gray, waxy hue that had worried her was gone, although he was still too pale. Under the patchwork quilt stretched over his lanky frame, his chest rose and fell in a natural sleep. He was recovering, as much because he was a strong man as because of the dedicated nursing care he had received.

Tate wondered what kind of nurse chained her patient to the bed? Simon's story had been going round and round in her head since he had told it to her. She was far from convinced he was telling the truth, but until she could decide, she was going to have to keep him a prisoner.

For the past few days he had been too weak to move. Now that he was feeling better, she knew he would be more restless, and being cuffed to the bed would be a prime frustration. She had finally thought of a way to resolve the dilemma. She had removed an old chain from the barn and a padlock from the smokehouse door. She would lock the chain to the bed frame, then lock his cuffs to the chain. That way he would have more freedom of movement. Whatever personal needs he had would be easier to take care of, too.

Now she just hoped she could rig the chain and cuffs before he woke up. There would be a second or two when he could get free. And although she had insisted she would not get near him with the handcuff keys, she had to have them to make the switch.

Dream on, she pleaded silently.

She walked softly toward the side of the bed by the window, the chain creaking ominously as she moved. Simon still seemed to be sleeping deeply. His breathing was even and slow, and not a muscle in his face twitched as she drew closer. She had given this decision a lot of thought, and she knew just where she wanted to lock the chain so he would have the most freedom. The corner of the bed was ideal. She could wrap the chain around the frame and through the metal headboard so that even if Simon was able to unscrew the bolts, the chain would still restrain him.

She reached the corner without waking him. Carefully, moving slower than she'd known she could, she began to wrap the chain. Iron scraped iron; the chain protested, creaking as it was forced to twist in ways it had forgotten. Simon slept on.

Satisfied, at last, that the chain was positioned correctly, she reached for the padlock, which she had set on the floor by the bed, and slipped it through two meshed links of chain.

Tate guessed that the padlock had hung on the smokehouse door for decades. Undoubtedly it was older than she was, and if there had once been a key, it had gone to key heaven. In her father's heyday the smokehouse had probably held treasures such as ham and bacon, and the padlock had been secured. Since the farm had become hers, the padlock had merely served to keep the door closed and had never been locked.

Now she struggled to snap it shut. It squealed like Cinderella's stepsister squeezing into the glass slipper, but each time Tate released her pressure, the lock popped apart. Finally, after she mustered every bit of strength she had, the lock held.

Simon slept on. Tate brushed back the fall of hair caressing her cheek. How could he sleep so soundly? She stared at him, but there was no flicker of awareness she was there. Sleep was the great healer; at the rate Simon was indulging in it, he would be well by noon.

Well, by noon or noon tomorrow or noon next week. Ready to hit the road again—if she let him. She pushed that thought out of her mind to concentrate on the trickiest part of her maneuver. Still watching Simon's face, she inched the handcuff key out of the back pocket of her jeans. Something tugged at her memory as she stared at him. She thought she remembered hearing his age on one of the radio newscasts. He was supposed to be thirty-seven.

He didn't look that old. With his face in repose he seemed younger, hardly more than thirty. Even after everything he had been through.

Of course, it was hard to tell what was behind the beard and mustache. Funny the way his face could be distorted by all that luxuriant golden hair. She had to admit the beard fascinated her. She knew its feel. It was surprisingly soft, even though it was not long. And it was as thick and sensuous as a golden ermine pelt, thick enough to fill in the contours of his cheeks. Perhaps even thick enough to make a thirty-seven-year-old man look younger.

Sleep made people look younger, too, because you couldn't see their eyes. Tate remembered clearly what Simon's eyes looked like. Frostbitten flint. Opaque. Impossible to read. Old eyes, generations older than thirty-seven, even if the face was younger.

His eyes remained closed, as she held the key in front of her and engaged in final debate. Should she risk unclasping the cuffs even for the moment it would take to snap them to the chain? She decided that it had to be now or never.

The key pinged against the cuffs as she inserted it. When the cuff opened the snap seemed as loud as a gunshot. Instantly, at almost the same second the cuff was free, Tate felt fingers form an iron band around her wrist.

The eyes she stared into weren't opaque this morning. They sparkled.

"So, you're going to let me go."

She echoed the words she'd thought earlier. "Dream on."

"The matter seems to be out of your hands." Simon yanked the cuffs toward him. Tate grabbed them and hung on.

They remained at an impasse for a moment; then Simon gave a fierce jerk, and the cuffs went flying from Tate's grasp. Simon's fingers bit into her wrist. He pulled her down to the bed beside him. She struggled, but his grip was a vise she couldn't escape.

"Let go of me!"

Simon's voice was calm. "I'm not going to hurt you."

"Damn right you're not!"

"Stop fighting me and listen."

She aimed an elbow at his ribs, but he rolled to one side, taking her with him. She sprawled awkwardly, half across the mattress and half across his chest.

He pressed his cuffed arm across her back and held tightly to her wrist. Tate didn't know where he had found the strength. She lifted her head and found her face was only inches from his.

He was looking at her strangely, almost as if he was seeing her for the first time.

"Let go of me!"

He didn't. "I've never known a woman with so much courage."

She glared at him.

"Or compassion."

"Stupidity!" Tate struggled once more, but he had her restrained, at least until his strength ran out.

"You saved my life. Do you think I'd hurt you now?"

"I think it's a distinct possibility!"

"Stop fighting me. Hear me out."

"You're going to get tired in a few minutes. How long do you think you can keep me here like this?"

He smiled, just the ghost of one, but a smile nonetheless. "As long as it takes to make you listen. Do us both a favor, okay? Shut up."

She pressed her lips together and let her eyes talk for her.

Simon admired the thickly lashed blue eyes spitting icy fire at him. She always brought with her the autumn fragrance of piney woods and clear mountain air, and he wondered if her finely textured skin would taste the same. Or would it taste of something more exotic, something even darker and more elemental?

Something passed through him. In another lifetime, before his months at High Ridge, he might have called it desire. Now he called it aftershock. Desire was a human emotion. Whatever had been human in him had disintegrated and died in Cellblock A.

What he felt now was a life trying to heal itself after being torn asunder. And the woman lying half across him, her delicate curves a growing, pleasurable torture, was a healer.

"I have to get out of here." Simon spoke softly. "I have to know if you're going to let me go. I'm not going to wait here like a sitting duck. I don't have much of a life left, but I plan to hang on to what's still there, if I can."

Tate wished she could lie with more aplomb, but Jess and Krista had loved the lies right out of her. She had learned to be brutally honest with herself, and somehow, in the process, she had forgotten how to be anything but honest with everyone else.

"I don't know what I'm going to do." She stared at Simon and knew lying to him wouldn't have done any good, anyway.

"Do you believe what I told you yesterday?"

"No."

"Then why haven't you gone for the sheriff?"

"Because there's one chance in a hundred it could be true."

"I didn't kill Joe Masters."

"So you say."

As she watched, fatigue seemed almost to crawl along his features. The arm clasping her to his chest trembled. "I have to get out of here." With a supreme effort he sat up and pushed her back to the bed, quickly pinning her with the weight of his body. He could feel her soft breasts flatten against his chest as she struggled. His head swam with the effort to restrain her.

"You couldn't make it to the next farm!" Tate felt panic well in her, but she stopped resisting. She knew if she didn't panic, she would be all right. She only had to wait for the right moment. One kick to the leg she had so tenderly cared for would buy her freedom.

Surprisingly, he nodded. "But I won't be your problem any more. I've got a fighting chance out there. Cuffed to this bed, the only chance I've got lies with you. I've asked you to be judge and jury. It's not your fault you can't be."

"You're concerned about my moral dilemma?"

"I'm concerned about staying alive."

Tate stared up at him. He loomed above her, very male, very dangerous, but surprisingly, she felt no fear. Before, his cold gray eyes had only been shadows of the man. Now she saw feeling there, although she couldn't name it.

"Let me up," she said at last. It was not a command.

Simon rolled away from her and shut his eyes.

She wasn't surprised he had freed her.

She sat up and turned to watch him. He was drained of what color he'd gained. "There's no easy way to Memphis from here. You'll die trying to get there."

Grim lips turned up in a mock smile. "Then your moral dilemma would be eased."

Tate knew the next move was hers. "Why my cabin, Petersen?" she asked wearily.

"Fate."

"It was that damn moon!"

"Will you give me a head start before you go for the sheriff?" He opened his eyes and turned them to hers. She saw defeat and determination there—a curious mixture. Tate knew he would go down fighting.

"I'm a fool," she said at last, "but not so big a one that I'd let you continue to stay here until you're stronger—not unless you're back in cuffs."

"And if I let you snap this cuff on the chain, you could waltz into town and get the sheriff."

"I guess you'll have to decide if you trust me."

"You're saying you won't turn me in?"

Tate had avoided making a commitment, hoping that something would come along to make her decision for her. Now she knew she wasn't going to be that lucky. Nothing in her life had ever been easy. This wasn't going to be an exception.

"If you want to stay here till you're stronger, you'll have to do it with the cuffs on. If you're leaving instead, go now. Either way, I'm not going to tell anyone about you."

He considered his choices, because he knew she would want him to make a decision quickly. His answer had to depend on whether he believed her, just as hers had depended on believing him. The similarity was ironic.

The pulse beating too loudly in his ears made his decision. He was still terribly weak. Just the brief tussle with her had worn him out. He wouldn't make it to Memphis this way. Not with the woods and highways teeming with men searching for him.

With the last of the strength that had carried him this far, he leaned behind her and reached for the chain. He felt along its length. Then, with the cuff still dangling from his wrist, he reached down and snapped it through a link.

Tate stood. He was her prisoner again. She hadn't expected to feel relieved that he was staying, but she did, even though she would have been better off if he was gone. "I'll make you breakfast. We've got to build up your strength so you can be somebody else's problem."

Surprisingly, he managed to smile. "I hope someday you'll know you made the right decision."

"I hope someday I'll forgive myself for being a fool."

* * *

Like a computer programmed for limited functions, Simon simply slept and ate for the next two days. As a result, Tate could almost watch him grow stronger. He sat up and fed himself completely now, and the hands that at first had trembled grew steady. As soon as his fever broke she had given up bathing him, but after breakfast each morning she brought him a pan of water, and with much muttering he managed the job himself.

On the third morning she came back too soon to retrieve the pan. He was sitting up with the sheet pushed low along his hips, taking a thorough sponge bath. His chest gleamed with a fine haze of water, and the golden hair arrowing toward his navel was plastered in swirls to his tanned skin.

He was no longer the desperately ill fugitive who had found his way to her cabin. The image of a lion caged and lying in wait for his keeper came to mind instead.

Other thoughts came to mind, too, thoughts like: why was she staring at him? Why hadn't she turned and left the moment she realized he wasn't finished? Why had she come back so soon in the first place?

All were thoughts to consider in the other room. She turned to go, but Simon stopped her.

"It's all right. I'm finished. There's not much I can do with a basin of dirty water."

She noted the broad *A* in "water" and the cleanly uttered *T*. She also noted his disgruntled tone. "Getting tired of being an invalid, Petersen?"

He wiped his chest with the towel she had provided. "Tired of being a cur on a chain."

She felt a pang of sympathy as she crossed the room. "Are you ready to let me change your bandage?"

He shrugged on one of her father's soft flannel shirts. She couldn't shake the feeling that he would look more at home in a custom-tailored tux. "It's about to drive me crazy."

She gathered the supplies she kept on a closet shelf. "Itching?"

He gave a curt nod. "It's healing."

"Maybe that's true, but it's a long way from being healed." She peeled the covers back, exposing his leg. "If you put any weight on it, it'll rip back open."

"I've been moving it as much as I can."

"Take it easy. You don't want to put yourself back where you started."

"I don't want to end up walking like a kangaroo, either."

"Kangaroos don't walk."

"My point exactly."

She glanced at him to see if the joke was a sign that his mood had improved, but there was no smile on his face. "As soon as you're able, you've got to see a doctor and start physical therapy."

"Sure. I'll just look somebody up in the phone book and walk right in."

He could be a murderer—probably was, in fact—but she still felt another surge of sympathy. He was a dangerous man to feel anything for, and all her best instincts told her so. But if he *was* innocent, his life had been turned upside down for nothing, and he still had a long road to travel before it was put to rights.

She snipped off the old bandage, but there was nothing she could do about the adhesive tape still clinging to his leg. She stripped it off, and although he didn't even grimace, she knew she had caused him pain.

The wound *was* healing. With a physician's care it might already have formed scar tissue. As it was, the most that had happened was that the infection had almost disappeared. He still needed time before he began to use the leg. She washed the area and smoothed an antibiotic ointment over it before covering it with a clean bandage.

She started to stand, but she felt a hand on her shoulder. Every separate finger seemed to make an impression, although he was applying no pressure. "What have you heard about the search?"

She lifted her head and stared a warning. "You're old news. There haven't been any bulletins."

He lifted his head. "What about the regular newscasts?"

"When you're even mentioned, they just say that the search is continuing. I don't sit around and listen. I know more about where you are then anyone, don't I?"

"I have to get out of here."

"I couldn't agree more." She stood. "But you're in no shape to go yet. Walk a hundred yards on that leg and you'll end up crawling."

"I don't plan to walk."

"There aren't any trains into this county, and the nearest airport is Memphis, where you're going, or Little Rock, where your picture will be on every wall."

He didn't answer.

"What are your plans?" When he still didn't speak, she hypothesized out loud. "Kill me and take my car?"

"It's a temptation. Except for one thing."

She stared at him.

"I don't kill people."

She remembered the light of an outlaw moon glinting off the barrel of his revolver. The night he had handed his gun to her, he could just as easily have killed her.

"So where does that leave you?" she asked.

"Do you really want to know?" He didn't quite smile as she made a face. "I won't touch your car."

"You won't touch anybody's anything. You're still my prisoner."

"You're going to have to let me go sometime."

She couldn't argue with that. She turned to leave.

"Tate?" There was a hesitation as he phrased his next words. "I haven't said thank you."

"Don't. I can't believe I'm doing this, anyway."

She felt his hand enclose hers. She was more than surprised; she was stunned. She had touched almost every part of his body, but this was different. Her hand fit in his as if it had been created to be there. He held it with the gentle firmness of a man sheltering a frightened bird.

Before she could pull away, she felt him lift her hand to his lips. They were warm and moist against her palm, and the impact of the kiss traveled like lightning to every nerve center. Then, as quickly as it had happened, it was over. He dropped her hand. "I won't say thanks," he promised. "I'll just say I've never met anyone quite like you before."

She was away from the bed like a shot. "I'm going into town. I've got to pick up some more supplies." She turned at the doorway. He was staring after her, his expression unreadable. "For what it's worth, I've never met anyone quite like you, either," she said.

"And you hope you never do again."

"I might not live through it the second time."

On a sunny day, Kalix Road could almost be considered picturesque. Today, with storm clouds menacing, it looked like what it was: a poor road in a poor county.

Of course, as Tate sped back home, she knew that her mood might be distorting what she got from the scenery. After everything she had just learned in town, heaven itself would have no appeal.

She had bought groceries and ice in Mountain Glade; then she had gone to the pharmacy. She had shopped there, waiting and watching for Wally to launch into a lecture to another customer, so that she could call Krista. She hadn't expected miracles, hadn't expected to find that Jess was safely home and able to find out about Carl Petersen for her, but it would have been nice. Instead she had discovered that Krista hadn't heard a word from Jess since she and Tate had last talked.

On the way out of Allen's she had stopped to buy the Sunday edition of the *Arkansas Gazette*, even though it was four days old. She was starved for some contact with the outside world besides her radio. At times, in the past few days, it had seemed that she and Simon were the only people in the universe, two eccentric pioneers in the wilderness, *Little House on the Prairie* run amok.

She had turned immediately to the section with state news, to find that the entire front page was about Carl Petersen's escape from prison. One article described High Ridge and alleged that conditions there were deplorable. Another hypothesized how the escape had been made and where Petersen might have gone. The third and most interesting was Carl Petersen's history. Carl *William* Petersen's history.

Even more upsetting than the discovery that Petersen's middle name wasn't Simon had been the photographs. The man in them was fifty pounds heavier than the man in her bed. True, the pictures had been taken at the trial. True, High Ridge was probably a foolproof weight-loss program. But even with fifty pounds of fat on the man she knew as Simon, that man wouldn't look like the man in the newspaper. That Carl Petersen had a rounder baby face. Tate couldn't picture him with Simon's elegantly sculpted bone structure, even if he lost a hundred pounds.

There was something soft, almost effeminate, about the photos in the paper. The man she knew as Simon was all rock-hard masculinity. Even when he had been dependent on her for survival, he had never lost his swift, almost feral responses. Two days ago he had struggled with her over the handcuffs, despite debilitating weakness. He had struggled for days alone in the forest, and Lord knew where else, before finding his way to her cabin. The man in the photographs looked as if he would give himself up without a fight. The man in her bed would never give up. Period.

Yet she couldn't dispute the obvious. Simon had shown up at her cabin wearing the tattered uniform of a High Ridge prison guard. He had held her at gunpoint, and somewhere on his journey he had sustained a gunshot wound in his leg. He had told her that he was Carl Petersen. He was blond and bearded like the man in the papers, and there was a resemblance.

And the man in the papers was missing from High Ridge.

Tate gripped the wheel harder as she hugged one of Kalix Road's narrow curves. A hairy black tarantula scurried along the roadside, just at the edge of her vision. It was a living pipe-cleaner monster from some child's Halloween fantasy, and she shuddered. The world was filled with things she would rather ignore. But those were the things that always seemed to parade before her. Simon was one of them. She hadn't asked for him, and now that she had made an

uncomfortable truce with his existence, she hadn't asked to
have the truce blown to smithereens.

But whether she liked it or not, Simon was very real and
very much a problem. And if her eyes and her instincts were
even slightly accurate, he was also very much a liar.

She pushed the accelerator to the floor on the last straight
stretch before her house. She wanted to get the confronta-
tion over with. She was going to give Simon one chance to
explain himself. Then, if she wasn't satisfied, she was going
to turn him in—or out.

She was almost to the road leading up to the cabin when
she got the first premonition that something was wrong. She
slowed until she was barely crawling, and used all her senses
to try to discover what was out of place. At first she couldn't
discern any changes. There was no one on the road, and although the sky was growing darker, no rain had yet fallen.

She came to a halt at the cabin road and rolled her window down, sniffing the air. But there was no strange scent
on the rising wind. No smoke from a forest fire, no hint of
pollution from the charcoal factory two counties to the west.

The cold air rushing into the car brought with it another
clue, however. She listened intently and finally pegged what
had alerted her to danger in the first place.

Dogs. A pack of them, somewhere in the distance, baying like the hound of the Baskervilles.

Will's dogs? She knew he had several, at least. Sometimes late at night, when it had still been warm enough to
sleep with an open window, she had heard them barking.
Noise carried in strange ways on mountain nights, and at
times the dogs had almost sounded as if they were under her
window. Cinn would join in for a bark or two when he was
feeling especially energetic, and rather than annoying her,
she had found the ruckus comforting.

This ruckus wasn't comforting, at all.

She shifted into first and started up the cabin road. The
barking could mean anything. The mountains were full of
strays. Sometimes they banded together and threatened
livestock, until the local farmers hunted them down. Perhaps there was a pack wandering somewhere nearby.

But perhaps there was a pack nearby that wasn't wandering, at all. Perhaps they were doing what good bloodhounds were trained to do.

She shifted into second and sped up the road. Her Bronco bounced and shuddered like its namesake, but she didn't care. She wanted to reach Simon before the dogs did—if they did.

At the crest of the hill looking over her cabin, she slammed on her brakes. There was a white van parked in front. Beside it was a sheriff's car.

A man chained to my bed? You're kidding. I wonder how that could have happened.

She knew what it was like to be terrified; once, as a fourteen-year-old runaway, she had found herself in the clutches of a New Orleans pimp. Now she felt the same ballooning of fear as she looked down at the Arkansas law. What was she going to tell them, if they went inside and found Simon? Suddenly none of her reasons for not reporting him sounded good enough. Despite the fact that he was cuffed to the bed, who would believe she was anything but an accomplice to his escape? An accomplice with strange preferences, perhaps, but an accomplice, nonetheless.

She said a silent prayer of gratitude that the bedroom window was so high above the ground. The ground fell away on that side of the cabin, exposing a cobweb-ridden root cellar, and the window was almost two stories up. Maybe they hadn't tried—or been able—to peek inside. Maybe she could just talk to them and send them on their way.

It was obviously too late to back up and head for Virginia. The man who, even at this distance, she recognized as Sheriff Monroe Howard was pointing in her direction. She started down the slope toward her cabin. As she drew nearer, she realized that the other two men were High Ridge officials. She recognized their uniforms, although they weren't as tattered as the one Simon had arrived in.

She pulled in beside the van and turned off the ignition. She noted that the cabin door was closed. Cinn was lying in front of it, looking deceptively dead. She hoped his presence there had discouraged snooping.

Forcing herself to appear calm, she opened her door and swung slowly to her feet. "Sort of a gray day for a social call, isn't it, gentlemen?"

The sheriff approached. He was silver-haired but still built like a football player in training. Tate knew they were related, although how escaped her.

"Afternoon, Miss Cantrell."

"Afternoon." She paused, but he didn't say anything more. "Is there a problem?" she asked politely.

"You might say so."

One of the prison officials started toward her. Tate noted that the other one was working his way around the cabin.

"Afternoon, ma'am. I'm Jim Cooney, from over at High Ridge. We're searchin' the area for a man who escaped jus' about a week back. You heard anything 'bout it?"

Tate knew better than to play stupid. These men were slow-moving and slow-talking, but they were a long way from slow-witted.

"Petersen?" she asked. "I was just reading about him in the Sunday paper I picked up in town. Not exactly a tourist attraction, is he?"

Jim Cooney chortled.

She continued. "The paper said you were searching south of here." The paper had also said the search would probably be called off soon, but obviously that wasn't true.

"We was. Looks like we been wrong, though. Now we're thinkin' he might have come this way."

"Why? We're sort of off the beaten path, aren't we?"

"Some think he might've floated down the river. Found a scrap or two of cloth 'bout half a mile back yonder, when we was searchin' with the dogs. It looks like it come from a uniform." He laughed again. "He was wearin' a uniform. *My* uniform, to be exact."

So this was the man Simon had overtaken. She was surprised he could be so good-humored. "It seems strange he could escape, at all. How did he? The paper said he slid out a window, but aren't prison windows barred?"

Cooney began to look uncomfortable. "Most are. He found one that wasn't. What we need to know now, ma'am, is if we can search yer house and the other buildin's. We're coverin' the area with our dogs, but it takes time. If we find anything suspicious-like, we'll bring them right over to sniff it out.''

Tate could think of nothing she wanted less. "Well, sure you're welcome to search, but I can save you the trouble of bothering with the cabin. I hardly ever leave it. There's not much chance anybody's in there.''

"Well, sure, ma'am. But how long you been gone today? Since this morning? Someone could have gotten in while you weren't here.''

She forced a light laugh. "With Cinn guarding the door? He's a killer.''

"We'd feel better, ma'am.''

And she was going to feel much, much worse.

Tate played her last card. "Well, I'm going to go on inside while you search the outbuildings. If I see anything strange, I'll give a yell.'' She slammed the car door, then turned to start toward the house.

Sheriff Howard was right beside her. "I'm not letting Millard's girl go inside that house alone. You may not think we're much of a family, but we watch out for our own.''

She didn't have time to think about his words. She was searching for some way to discourage him. If she could just get to Simon and take off the handcuffs, she would have a fighting chance to help him hide. As it was, Simon was going to be a bit conspicuous.

Cinn was still sprawled across the doorway when they got to the front porch. Sheriff Howard looked as if he'd had dealings with Cinn before. With the toe of his boot he prodded the dog until his eyes opened a slit. "Go!''

Cinn's tail thumped against the porch, but he didn't move.

"He misses Millard," the sheriff said.

"How can you tell?''

"We all miss him.'' He opened the door, but waved Tate back when she started after him. "Let me check around.''

"There's absolutely no need for all this," she insisted, as loudly as she dared. "I'm sure you're all exaggerating. A few bits of cloth don't prove anything, do they?"

"Might. They're being analyzed right now." Sheriff Howard moved inside, his gun drawn, now. Before Tate could stop Cinn, he pried himself off the porch and followed the sheriff inside.

The sheriff surveyed the room, his gun moving with his gaze. Then his head tipped back as he looked up at the loft. Most of it was visible from the doorway, but the corners farthest back were not. He signaled his intention to climb up and investigate, then crossed the room, Cinn right behind him. When she started to follow, hoping to get to the bedroom while he explored the loft, he motioned her back.

Her possibilities had narrowed to none. She could only wait now for Simon to be discovered.

The sheriff climbed down after just seconds upstairs. Then he started toward the bedroom, where Cinn was standing by the door. Tate disregarded him when he waved her back. She followed a distance behind.

He hesitated, then flung the door open, jumping back as he did, as if to avoid gunfire.

The cabin was silent. He leaned forward and peered into the bedroom, then moved inside, where the dog had already disappeared. Tate could do nothing but follow them.

From the doorway she saw an empty bed. It was neatly made, and the room was tidy. Nothing remained to show that a man had once been chained there. Cinn was lying on the floor beside it, nose on paws, looking forlorn.

The sheriff dropped down beside Cinn and peered under the bed, then crossed to the closet and opened the door. Stunned, Tate saw that even the basin and packet of medical supplies were gone.

As was Jim Cooney's .44.

"Well, you were right," he said. "Nobody's here. But it doesn't pay to take chances."

"I guess not."

"I don't like you being here without a phone, not while this High Ridger's on the loose. You're welcome to come stay with Jo Ann and me until he's been caught. I know Will and Dovey would have you, too."

Tate stared at him. She could hardly comprehend what he was saying. Finally she shook her head. "Thanks for the offer. But I've got a lot to do before winter hits."

"You're Millard's kid, all right. Just be careful." He tipped his hat and strode across the room, disappearing into the front room. The outside door slammed a few moments later.

She went through the motions of making and offering coffee when their search of the grounds was completed, and appeared to listen as all the men lapsed into guessing where Carl Petersen had disappeared to. She even waved goodbye as they drove away.

And through it all, she had only one real thought. Where in the world had Simon gone, and how had he managed it?

Chapter 7

Was it worse to have Simon in the cabin, a prisoner in the bedroom? Or was it worse to have him loose again, his presence lurking in every corner, behind every tree?

Tate wasn't sure. She only knew she didn't like surprises, especially when they involved armed fugitives. And Simon was obviously armed now.

The sun was sinking toward the ridge of trees on the western edge of her property, when she left the relative safety of her cabin to get a load of firewood. Cinn stared at her from the lengthening shadow of the smokehouse. She shook off the feeling that another pair of eyes was following her movements. Surely Simon—if that name had anything to do with the man who had inhabited her bed—was hobbling toward Memphis.

"What kind of a guard dog are you, anyway?" she called to the hound. Cinn's droopy eyes followed every movement, though he didn't move. As soon as he had sensed there was no longer a masculine presence in the cabin, he had deserted.

"Somebody could shoot me and you'd supervise the burial!" She realized she was taking out her frustrations on an extremely dumb animal, although it didn't appear to worry him.

At the woodpile she peeled off her father's plaid jacket and set to work splitting logs. It was backbreaking labor. The first time she had tried it, the ax had bounced off the log and headed straight for her foot. And if it hadn't missed, she might have died here alone. Just as she might have died the night Simon had come to visit, if he had been a different sort of man.

What was she doing in the middle of nowhere, with a murderer on the loose? What was she doing in the middle of nowhere, period? Had she inherited hermit blood from the man she'd never known? Insanity?

She poured her frustrations into her work, and had an armload of wood in minutes. She was practiced with an ax now. And she was an expert at making fires. She had learned how to plant pine seedlings and use her father's old hand plow to dig up the expansive garden plot for next spring's garden. She had learned the habits of geese and the names of the wild birds inhabiting the forest.

For what?

She carried the firewood toward the house. The sun still hadn't touched the ridge. The day seemed endless; the night would seem longer. Every sound, every shadow and movement outdoors, would be Simon haunting her.

And where was he now? His leg wasn't well enough to bear his weight. There were no freight trains to hop, no eighteen-wheeler outlaws to hitch a ride with. He would have to leave the county on foot. One foot. Hopping like a kangaroo.

She remembered his joke. She remembered lots of things about him, like the feeling she'd had from the beginning that he was more than he was supposed to be. Wasn't that why she had risked her own safety to care for him? Because she had believed, despite all the evidence, that he was an innocent man?

At the back door she balanced the load of firewood against her chest and slipped one arm from beneath it to turn the doorknob. Not too many days ago she had gotten a landmark surprise when she walked through the same door. She would be reliving that moment, and all the ones following it, for days to come. For better or worse, Simon had escaped from prison into her life. And along the way he had forced her to face the fact that she, too, was a fugitive from the life that others lived without question.

"I wondered where you'd gone."

Tate stood with the open door to her back. Two logs slipped from the pile in her arms and rolled across the floor to Simon's feet.

She momentarily closed her eyes in shock, but the picture of Simon standing before her, gun belt slung casually around his hips, danced along her eyelids.

"Sorry to startle you," he said.

"Hey, I'm getting used to it." Tate opened her eyes. The picture hadn't changed.

"Company gone?"

"I tried to get them to stay for tea, but you know how law-enforcement types are."

The flicker of a smile softened his face. "Better than almost anybody."

"You don't mind if I set these logs down, do you?" She walked across the room and deposited the logs at the side of the hearth. She reached for a poker and used it to stir up a few coals still glowing from the morning's fire. When she straightened, the poker was still in her hand.

She hadn't heard Simon come up behind her, but when she turned he was right there. He held out the two logs she had dropped.

She couldn't easily reach for them with the poker in her hand. She knew he saw her dilemma.

He tossed the logs to the hearth. "Tate, if I wanted to harm you, I've already had a hundred chances. Forget what you think you know about me, and concentrate on what you really know."

"I *really* know your middle name isn't Simon. And I know the photograph of the man who was on trial in Little Rock doesn't look as much like you as it should."

"Put down the poker and let me explain."

"You explained once. Remember?"

"I lied."

"Terrific. I feel better already."

"I've got to get off my feet." Simon turned, leaving himself vulnerable to attack if she dared.

Tate clenched the poker in her hands, but she could not make herself swing it. She watched as he limped to the sofa facing the fireplace. Before he sat, he unbuckled the gun belt and laid it on a nearby chair. Once he was settled, the gun was out of his reach.

She stood with her side toward the fireplace and threw crumpled newspaper and pine kindling on the coals. Then, when the pine was burning, she added the smallest log. Her thoughts raced in circles, as she watched the log catch. By the time she added another, she felt as if she were captive on the Indianapolis Speedway.

When there was nothing left to do, she chose the chair opposite the one where Simon had placed his gun belt. The poker leaned against the hearth, beyond reach.

"I give up," she said, when it was clear he was waiting for her to ask questions. "Where were you, and how did you get free?"

"I was under the bed."

"Don't give me that. Cinn and the sheriff looked under the bed. I was there."

"You don't know what's under there, do you?"

"Outer space? A new dimension in time?" she asked sarcastically.

"A museum."

Tate watched pain flash across Simon's face as he shifted. In the shock of finding him in her cabin again, she had almost forgotten his leg. She was up and across the space separating them before she thought about what she was doing. "Let me look at that." She knelt beside him and began to roll up the cuff of the overalls he had apparently taken from the closet.

"Aren't you afraid?"

She didn't spare the time for a retort. The bandage she had so carefully changed that morning was streaked with blood. "I told you not to put any weight on this! Now you're in for it."

"I would really have been in for it, if Jim Cooney had found me chained to your bed."

Tate sat back and put her hands around her knees. "How did you get away?"

"I heard the dogs barking about twenty minutes after you left." Simon leaned his head back against the sofa and shut his eyes in exhaustion. He was disgusted that the simple things he'd done that day had tired him so much. "I'd already picked the locks on the cuff and padlock with the inside of the ballpoint pen I found in your father's shirt."

She wasn't sure if she was more surprised that he had picked the lock, or that her father had used something as modern as a ballpoint. "Did you pick up that little tidbit at High Ridge?"

"There aren't any locks I can't pick."

"What did you mean about a museum under the bed?"

"There's a trapdoor. I wouldn't have found it, but after I'd dressed and gathered up the evidence that I'd been here, I heard the dog barking."

"Cinn doesn't bark."

"He did this time. I looked out the window and saw the prison van coming up your road. I knew I didn't have time to get away, so I started looking for a place to lose the chain and cuffs."

"And yourself."

"I was going to shinny up your chimney."

"Sort of Santa in reverse."

He smiled. It was the first real smile Tate had ever seen from him, and for a moment she forgot everything else in the wake of its captivating brilliance. But just for a moment.

"You are truly one of a kind." Simon opened his eyes and let his gaze rest on her. It wasn't a tiring task. Even in jeans, she was a lovely woman. This morning he had thought he would never see her again. He had *planned* to never see her again. Now, despite his frustration with the way the day had evolved, he almost felt like a reprieve had been issued.

"Why didn't you tell the sheriff about me?" he asked, when she didn't respond.

"What makes you think I didn't?"

He studied her some more as he explained. "You lost the chance a couple of days ago. Taking care of me would have been too hard to explain. But why didn't you turn me in, when you could have?"

"Your story's more interesting than my motives."

"I doubt it." He raised a hand to stave off her denials. "I was going to thread the chains and cuff up through the springs so no one could see them. Before I could, I noticed that all the boards for about three feet across met in the same place. When I looked closer, I realized it was a door going down to a cellar. It's very well hidden."

Tate frowned. "There's a root cellar, but it's not much deeper than a long closet. It doesn't extend that far over, and the one time I was in it I didn't see any trapdoor."

"It probably shares a wall with the museum."

"What museum?" she asked in exasperation.

"You're going to have to see it. I don't think I can explain."

She knew they had come to a dead-end. But as interesting as the subject was, there was one of greater interest. And much greater importance.

"Why did you lie to me before? And who are you?"

He was still studying her—almost, she thought, as if he were deciding what to tell her. "Don't lie to me again," she warned him. "I'm not in the mood."

Slowly he shook his head. "It'll be safer for you, if I make up another lie."

"But not safer for you."

"You may wish you didn't know." He paused. "And you may not believe it, anyway."

"You're probably right."

He was quiet for a full minute. Just as Tate was about to give him an ultimatum, he spoke. "I'm not Carl Petersen, although I look a little like he might if he was deprived of food for a month or two. My real name *is* Simon."

"So how come no one noticed?"

"No one at High Ridge had any reason to follow the Petersen trial, and there was limited coverage, anyway. The bank didn't want to broadcast the fact someone punched a few buttons and made off with over a million dollars of their account holders' money. After the trial Petersen was held in Texas for a couple of months. Then, as far as the world knows, he was shifted to High Ridge as a federal prisoner."

"Back up."

His eyes sparked in the firelight, although the rest of him looked as if he were in pain. "Petersen's under lock and key somewhere else right now. When this is over he'll be transferred to Leavenworth, where he'll be serving a shorter sentence because he cooperated with us."

"Us?"

"The Justice Department."

She stared at him. "Right," she said finally. "You're one of the good guys."

He grimaced. "A matter of opinion. Prison officials are supposed to be good guys, too, only sometimes they're not. Sometimes they murder inmates and embezzle funds, just like the cons they're supposed to be watching."

Tate let his story filter into all the corners of her mind. "So you're an F.B.I. agent, and you were put in High Ridge under an assumed name to nail some official there?"

He smiled at her cynical tone. "No."

"No to what?"

"I'm not an agent. I work for myself, and sometimes the Justice Department pays my fee."

"They don't have enough employees of their own?"

"Not like me."

She let that pass for the moment. "Why were you in High Ridge?"

"That's what I don't know."

Tate pushed herself to her feet and went to the fireplace. She was careful not to turn her back to him, as she chose another log for the fire. "You're not making any sense."

"There's not much sense to be made. A man named Josiah Gallagher, a Justice Department official, asked me to impersonate Petersen. Gallagher's an old friend." He laughed bitterly. "*Was*, I guess I should say. I owed him a favor, and he decided to collect. I agreed to go to High Ridge as Petersen. Justice wanted somebody on the inside to investigate allegations of poor conditions there. Gallagher also wanted me to get close to a couple of cons from Oklahoma City who were on their way to making parole. He needed some information about their plans after release. The theory was the Carl Petersen would be the kind of guy these two would talk to."

"Why?"

"Because Petersen is a computer criminal, and these guys needed advice to take their penny-ante smuggling operation into the twenty-first century."

"Seems like a long shot."

"Gallagher never misses."

Tate stood with her back to the fire. "Just supposing this isn't another one of your lies, what happened at High Ridge to make you escape? Why didn't you just give this Gallagher person a phone call?"

"I was supposed to be there a month, at most. It stretched to two, then three, without a word from Gallagher or anybody at Justice. Nobody at High Ridge knew I was a plant. I got plenty of information for them, but nobody came to collect it. About the second week I was there, Captain Shaw took a shine to me."

As improbable as his story was, she was beginning to believe him. No mere actor could have uttered the last sentence with such restrained venom.

"Captain Shaw's the warden?"

"The same. He's also a murderer and a thief."

"You say."

"I have proof—or I did."

"You lost it, of course."

"There's something about floating downriver at midnight, half dead and dying another inch a minute that does that."

"What are we talking about here?"

His gaze was steady, locked with hers. Tate thought that if he was lying, he was far beyond accomplished—he was a master. "The good captain moved me into the prison office just as soon as he decently could. He said I ought to put my computer skills to good use. I wasn't there for more than a day before he moved me into *his* office, only not so anyone would know. Officially he signed me to use the law library every night between six and eight. Then a guard would march me down to Shaw's office, feed me supper and watch while I juggled the prison records."

"Juggled the records?"

"Accounts received, accounts payable, accounts going straight into Shaw's personal account." He nodded, when it was clear by her expression that she understood. "It's easy enough to do if you understand computers. And I do."

"You said he was a murderer."

"I'd been doing his dirty work for him for about a month, when he told me to start editing inmate files. Editing was his word for changing facts he didn't want in the permanent records, facts like number of escape attempts, cause of death, etc. I had to break codes, find passwords to get into the state system and sometimes the federal computers. It took an expert to do it. Nobody in his pay was good enough to do it for him. And an inmate was the perfect person for the job, because when he finished, he could just disappear." He snapped his fingers.

Tate felt chilled, despite her proximity to the fire. "'Disappear' as in murder?"

"I wouldn't have been the first. Two guys jailed for computer crime were supposedly killed by inmates, after working for the captain. Shaw thought their prison records had been appropriately adjusted so that no one would connect them with him, but I found a secret file. The second man had figured out what was coming, and he left data Shaw didn't know enough to erase. There's other information, too, that could nail Shaw."

"That's what was on the diskette I found in your pocket?"

He was silent. His eyes said it all.

"I found it," she acknowledged. "Did you think you'd lost it in the river?"

"I had two diskettes. Apparently I did lose one. And now you have the other."

"Would it be any use after soaking in the river?"

"Probably not. But Captain Shaw doesn't know that."

"Which is why such a massive search was mounted."

He nodded. "Petersen committed a white-collar crime. He shot the bank auditor when his own back was against the wall, but he's not a dangerous criminal. If men like Petersen escape, they usually get caught a few weeks afterward, anyway, even if no one is looking for them. They're stopped for traffic violations, or they try to cash a bum check. Nobody has anything to fear from a man like Petersen."

"Nobody but Shaw."

Simon stood, and Tate repressed the urge to tell him to stay off his feet. She had no control over him now. And she felt that piece of the truth dead center inside her. He started toward her, limping noticeably, and she toyed with the idea of reaching for the poker.

"I was next." Simon stopped just yards from her. "I had just about outlived my usefulness. Shaw would have arranged a convenient accident for me, and I would have been a memory."

"You still haven't said why you didn't just get in touch with somebody from the Justice Department."

"Phone calls at High Ridge are monitored and numbers are traced. After I started working for the captain, I wasn't allowed phone calls, anyway."

"Then why not by computer? Surely you could have contacted a Justice Department computer and sent Gallagher a message."

"Think about it. I was supposed to be there less than a month. I was there three, with no word from Gallagher."

"Maybe there was a mistake—"

"No mistake."

She tried to put the facts together, but it was too confusing.

"I'll make it easy," Simon said, limping closer to the fire to warm his hands. "Gallagher left me there to rot or be murdered. I don't know which, and I don't know why, but

I do know I couldn't go to Gallagher then and I can't go to him now. He wanted me dead. I've no doubt some of the men out there searching these hills are on his payroll.''

It was a preposterous story, yet unlike his last one, all the pieces fit. There was only one he hadn't addressed. "What about Erin?"

Simon leaned against the wall and lifted his foot to the hearth, so his weight wasn't on it. "Erin is Aaron, not Erin."

Tate exhaled in exasperation. "You're not making any sense."

"Aaron. With an *A*. Aaron Reynolds, of the male persuasion. He was an agent. Josiah, Aaron and I worked on a case that exposed a Mafia family forming in the Northwest. I was almost killed. Josiah saved my life, and Aaron's, too. That's what I meant about owing him a favor. Aaron retired after that. He's living in Memphis now. Runs a security-systems business and fishes every weekend, but if I know Aaron he's still got his finger on the pulse of Washington. If anyone can find out why Gallagher tried to put me away for good, it'll be Aaron."

If there were more questions that needed to be asked, Tate couldn't think of them. She stood watching him in silence.

Simon knew how his story sounded. And he knew he had used up his credibility by lying before. There were only a few people in his life whose opinion of him mattered. Surprisingly, he found he had added another, and she had gone directly to the top of the list. But there was no way to force her to believe him. She was a woman beyond force, anyway, which was part of her considerable appeal.

"This is where you pick up the poker and swing it over my head," Simon said at last. "It's now or never, Tate. Believe me or don't believe me, but now's the moment of decision. Now you know that chaining me up won't do you any good." He smiled a little. "Never did, in fact."

"Why did you stay here this evening? You could have gone out the front door when I went out the back a little while ago. You could have gone and never had to tell me any of this."

His answer was more painful than anything he had endured since his escape. "Because I can't get out of here on my own. Damn it, that's all I want, but it's impossible. I thought I could. I heard you drive away this morning, and I thought you wouldn't have to be involved anymore. I was going to shave off this beard, find my way to the next county and hitch a ride to Memphis. You never would have had to know the truth."

"Why didn't you tell me the truth in the first place? What good did it do to lie?"

"The truth could get you killed!" He ran his hand through his hair in frustration. "I've got God knows who after me, and eventually they may trace me this far. You'll be questioned by some of the best if they do. And who's to care if a young woman in some remote cabin in the Ozarks disappears after she's been found to know some things she shouldn't?"

Tate forced herself to ignore the shudder passing through her at the thought. "Jess Cantrell would care. And when Jess cares, the world tends to find out about it."

"Cantrell, the journalist? The one who writes the book-length exposés?"

"My father."

"I thought your father was dead!"

"It's a long story. Good old Uncle Grady would care, too. That's Grady Clayton, state attorney in southern Florida, about to run for the House, or so I hear. And then there's the Mountain Glade sheriff. He's some relative or other. He doesn't have Grady or Jess's clout, but he wouldn't be too lightweight to flash around if I needed him."

"How much family do you have?"

"More than I ever thought," she said with a tiny smile.

He assessed her, but he didn't ask what she meant. She was as private a person as he was, and until she trusted him she wasn't going to reveal anything. "These hills are full of men who want to kill me. You're vulnerable."

"You need my help."

"Yeah." He spat out the word as if it tasted bad.

"You don't ask for it very nicely."

"I haven't had any practice."

In the fading light of day tickling the cabin's interior, she saw his face grow paler, but he didn't move, didn't attempt to sit. She knew enough about him to understand that he would never show weakness until it completely overcame him. "What do you want me to do?" she asked.

"As I see it, you've got a couple of choices. You can use the poker and put me out of my misery, or you can hide me a little longer, until my leg is stronger and they aren't searching the immediate area."

"At least you've got the sense to see that you'd get caught if you left now."

"Oh, I've got plenty of sense. I just don't have plenty of options."

Her instincts told her to help him. She was no human lie detector, but everything she had learned about people told her that this time he was telling the real story.

But what if he wasn't? What if this was another tale, embroidered to make him look like a good guy when he wasn't?

As she contemplated his words and her choices, a third option occurred to her. "What if you didn't have to go to Memphis, at all? What if I went into town and called Aaron for you?"

"Then you'd know I was telling the truth."

She nodded. "And you'd have Aaron to help you."

"Good idea. Only you can't do it."

She lifted an eyebrow in question.

"If I could have gotten to Aaron right after my escape, that might have worked. But his phone will be tapped now. Gallagher will know Aaron is the first person I'd try to contact."

"But would that matter? If I'm calling from a public phone?"

"They'd trace me to this area. It would be a small matter to get a record of who used the phone and run them down."

"You sound like you know."

He gave a humorless laugh. "I know."

"There goes my chance to find out if this is a lie."

"Maybe not." He winced as he shifted his weight and damned himself when he realized he had shown his pain. "There's another call you can make. Go into town and call the number I'm going to give you. Don't say anything. Listen closely. With any luck what you hear might convince you."

She shrugged when he didn't explain further. "You're saying you'll be here when I get back?"

"I'm saying that."

She hesitated. "And you're saying I can take the gun with me, just to be sure I don't get shot coming back through the door?"

"There's an agency or two in the Washington area that could use your talents."

"I'd never survive the background check."

Simon reached across the space separating them and laid his hand on her shoulder. His fingers were a light caress. There was nothing in the movement to restrain her. "I don't want you hurt. If you decide not to help me anymore, I'll understand." He didn't drop his hand. He flipped it, then caressed the length of her neck with his knuckles.

Her breath caught, and for a moment she was completely vulnerable. If Simon was who he said he was, then he was highly skilled at getting what he wanted.

She wasn't Jess Cantrell's adopted daughter for nothing. Like Jess, she knew how to listen. Amidst the ambiguity of Simon's story had been an admission that he lived his life somewhere other than in full sunlight. He had told her he wasn't an F.B.I. agent, as if to reassure her. But she knew better than to feel comforted. This man would never submit himself to the restrictions an agency would impose. He wouldn't follow anyone's rules and regulations, not when it didn't suit him.

He had said it best. He worked for himself. And he made his own rules. What did the rules say about seduction?

He withdrew his hand. "Go. Make the call." He bent and tore off the corner of a sheet of newspaper beside the hearth, scribbling a phone number on it with a pen he took from his pocket. She wondered if it was the one he had used to pick the lock on the handcuffs. He straightened and held the number out to her. "If you want me gone when you come back, I'll be packed."

She took the paper, stopped for the gun and left.

Outside, the distant baying of hounds rose to meet the descent of evening.

THE JOKER GOES WILD!

Play
this
card
right!

See
inside!

SILHOUETTE®
WANTS TO <u>GIVE</u> YOU
- 4 free books
- A free gold-plated chain
- A free mystery gift

IT'S NO JOKE!

MAIL THE POSTPAID CARD AND GET FREE GIFTS AND $11.80 WORTH OF SILHOUETTE NOVELS—FREE!

If offer card is missing, write to:
Silhouette Reader Service, P.O. Box 1867, Buffalo, NY 14269-1867

Chapter 8

Allen's Pharmacy stayed open most nights until seven, although there wasn't much call for evening hours in a county where almost nobody punched a time clock. Tate figured that Wally stayed open because he was afraid he would miss some good gossip if he didn't.

Now she was glad he liked to keep his ear to the ground. One glance into the phone booth at the gas station told her that repairs still hadn't been made there. She was going to have to use the phone at Allen's.

Two little boys with candy sticks were coming out as Tate went in. One little boy wiped his hands against her jeans as they passed, and the other giggled. The Living Strings selection playing over the loudspeaker sounded as if it were winding through the tape deck at half the normal speed. Tate envisioned elderly couples waltzing to a tempo that gave "slow dancing" a new meaning.

In the back of the store, Wally was holding court with two of his cronies. One, a pot-bellied man with a long neck, reminded her of the central fixture of an old-time general store.

"Evening, Miss Tate."

She had hoped to escape Wally's eye, but she had known it was unlikely.

"Feeling better?" he called. "Leg better?"

"Lots better. You fixed me right up."

"You know, I been thinking. How could you chop your leg that high up, and all?"

She wondered how many conversations she had been the center of since Wally had filled the prescription for her. *Far as I can see, nobody could cut their thigh with an ax. A foot, maybe, or even a shin. Course there was a time that old Sam Turnbull down on Goose Creek Road . . .*

"I was swinging it," she demonstrated, making up her explanation as she went along. "And I picked it up like this. Then I brought it down too fast and lost control." She grimaced, as if she had just reopened a wound. "I guess I'm just not as good with an ax as I thought I was."

"You could kill yourself," the pot-bellied man said with enthusiasm. "Kill yourself and the buzzards would pick your bones before anybody would find you out there at Millard's place."

"What a story that would make."

The man nodded solemnly. "Too bad Millard wouldn't be around to tell it. Nobody could tell a story like Millard."

Tate couldn't respond to that, since Millard's stories were as much a mystery to her as the man himself. She forced a smile—it was a major effort, since all she really wanted to do was make the phone call—then she began to examine the aisle of shampoos and hair conditioners. It took a few minutes, but eventually the men lost interest in chatting with her. When Wally had launched into a hunting story and the other men were jumping in to add their own insights, she sidled toward the telephone.

The number Simon had asked her to call had an unfamiliar area code. She dialed the operator and gave the Stagecoach Inn credit-card number, then the phone number Simon had given her.

The number rang four times. As it did she debated what she would say. Simon had said she was to listen only, but she knew she would feel like a junior-high-school prankster if she hung up without speaking. She had settled on telling the party who answered that she had gotten a wrong number when the fifth ring was interrupted. There was a brief moment of silence; then a voice began to speak.

"Simon Vandergriff here. I'm not in at the moment, but if you leave a message, I'll get back to you at the first opportunity."

There was another pause, then a beep.

It had all happened so quickly that it took Tate a second or two to put together what she'd heard. She listened to the ensuing silence even though she certainly had no message to leave. The man belonging to the recorded voice was living in her cabin. The merest trace of an accent was unmistakable.

Simon Vandergriff. She tried to think of a reason, any reason, why Carl Petersen would have an answering machine somewhere to tell callers that he was Simon Vandergriff. If there had been any lingering question in her mind whether Simon and Carl Petersen were the same man, it disappeared.

But who was he? Was he the man he claimed to be, a man set up by one of his trusted friends to die in High Ridge prison?

She knew from experience that sometimes the most incredible stories were true. Simon's story was incredible, but he had delivered it without hesitation and with sincerity. Of course, he could be a liar. But if he was, he was superlative.

Again, she had come to a turning point. There was no restraining the man now, no false sense of security to be had from keeping him in handcuffs. If she went home to him, it would be a sign of good faith. She would be telling him that she believed him. Even more, that she trusted him. She would *have* to trust him to go back.

She realized she was still holding the telephone receiver against her ear. There was nothing else to be learned here. Simon had offered her proof—of a kind. Now she only had to decide whether to believe it.

There was a faint rustle on the line just as she was about to hang up. At first she thought she had imagined it. Then she heard voices, the same type of remote conversation that sometimes occurred on the long-distance line when wires were crossed somewhere.

"Did you get the trace?"

"Not yet. But the connection hasn't been broken."

She let a second pass, then another, before she realized what was happening. As if she could no longer hold its weight, she flung the receiver into its cradle.

Simon's telephone was tapped.

By why? Wouldn't anyone who was *that* interested know he was on the run? Surely his escape from High Ridge was no secret.

An answer occurred to her almost immediately. The phone was tapped because someone was hoping his incoming calls might provide a clue to his escape. Perhaps even because someone hoped that Simon himself would call in for his messages!

"Never got your party, did you, Miss Tate?" Wally called from behind the counter.

Tate turned around to face the men. "'Fraid not." She thought it was too bad she couldn't tell them about Simon. If she could, nobody in Mountain Glade would ever doubt that Millard's daughter had a few good folktales of her own.

The cabin appeared uninhabited when Tate parked her Bronco in front of it. Before leaving Allen's she had made several additional calls and discovered three more pieces of information. One was that the area code Simon had told her to dial belonged to Washington, D.C. The second was that directory assistance did have a listing for an Aaron Reynolds in Memphis. The third was that Jess was still out of the country, but Krista had heard from him and he was safe, although it would be at least three weeks before he returned to the U.S.

Tate wondered what Jess could have uncovered that she didn't already know. Not much, she supposed, although she knew she would have been in for a great deal of advice.

But she didn't need advice. She was a woman. Wary, worried, rebellious, still, but a woman capable of making a decision.

And she *had* made a decision.

Inside the cabin she scanned the main room. There was no sign of Simon, although she suspected he wanted to be sure she was alone before he showed himself.

"Simon," she called. "I'm back. By myself."

The door to the bedroom opened, and a man appeared.

For a moment she wasn't sure who he was. Then she knew. "You've shaved off your beard."

Simon watched her from the doorway. Moonlight struck her hair with a silver gleam and caressed the defiant cast of her head. She hadn't taken the time to change for her trip into town, but she had tied the tails of her black flannel shirt into a knot at her waist, pulling the fabric tight across her breasts. The shirt only accentuated how slender she was, and how perfectly proportioned. Without shirttails hanging over her jeans he could see their snug fit, the taper of her hips, the flawless curve of her bottom and length of her legs.

Something inside him tried to break free, some long-restrained, threatening part of himself. He leashed it with difficulty.

She had been gone more than an hour. He could remember no time when he had waited that long for someone else to decide his fate. Fifteen minutes into his wait, he realized that he trusted Tate as he had trusted few people. Half an hour into it, he had realized that he cared what she decided. She was not a stranger, whose opinion would have been worth less than yesterday's newspaper. In some ways he knew her better than he had ever known anyone.

He had found that realization disconcerting. Now he was more disconcerted, still.

He walked toward her, a towel dangling from his shoulders. His progress was halting. He stopped while they were still yards apart. "Carl Petersen wears a beard. I don't."

She wished it wasn't true. She had washed the beard and felt its soft, seductive attractions. More disturbing, though, was the change its absence made. He seemed both more austere and more ruthless, now. More the fugitive, less the man she had tried to heal. "So Simon Vandergriff is clean-shaven."

"Then you got my machine."

"I got more than that. I got tapped—or rather, your phone did." She told him everything that had happened.

He cursed softly, and his face settled into rigid planes.

Tate stared at him. The beard had disguised more than his identity. It had disguised his very essence. Now there was no mistaking what the man facing her was: a knight errant who could face down a prison full of criminals—on both sides of the bars—and still come out of it alive.

She had thought him handsome. Now she knew that handsome had no relevance. Dangerous? Yes, if you weren't on his side. Attractive? The term was too anemic. Compelling was closer, and so was desirable, although, like the man himself, that was too dangerous to consider closely.

"Did you hang up as soon as you heard voices?" Simon asked.

"It surprised me so much that I . . ." Tate saw his eyes narrow. "I didn't," she admitted. "I held the phone for a few seconds afterward. Then, when I finally realized what was happening, I hung up."

He didn't criticize. For someone without training, she had done well just to realize what was happening. "They sound like bunglers, anyway. Maybe they didn't get the trace. Not everyone in the agency is Gallagher's caliber."

"How's your leg?"

"How's your state of mind?"

He hadn't smiled since he'd come into the room. Tate realized he was waiting for her to tell him if she believed his story. "If I was sane, I wouldn't even give you a head start on an escape."

"Do you believe what I've told you?" he asked, getting straight to the point and moving closer.

"I do." The two words freed her in a way she hadn't expected. They were a commitment, just as the same two words signified a lifetime commitment in a wedding ceremony. Now that she'd said them, her decision was made.

She wasn't going to indulge in any more doubts or confusion.

Simon knew the words for what they were. "Thank you."

Tate guessed he was a man to whom gratitude didn't come easily. Gratitude or illness or . . . bonding.

As she stood close enough to him to feel the heat of his body, she realized that the last had more to do with her decision about the truth of his story than anything she had heard over the telephone.

She cared about this man. She had watched over him when he was delirious with fever, used all her limited skill to guide him toward recovery, protected him when anyone else would have turned him in. From the beginning there had been a bond between them, pulling her toward decisions she shouldn't have made.

The bond was stronger now, and unlike the chain that had kept him bound, she doubted that he would be able to discard it easily. She had tried and failed. Even the lies he had told hadn't destroyed the link she felt with him.

"You're welcome, Simon Vandergriff."

"You may wish you'd never heard that name."

"I'm finished wishing. I think I'm stuck with you."

He smiled then, and without the beard she saw that his smile was more dazzling and dangerous, still. "Well, at least you won't be stuck with a grimy-around-the-edges ex-con. Primitive bath facilities you have here, but I made do while you were gone."

She tried to imagine him hauling water off the back porch and heating it. "You're really not well enough to push yourself that hard."

"There were parts you never seemed to get to when you bathed me."

The blush that tinged her cheeks was unfamiliar. She couldn't remember it happening before. "You were lucky I even bothered with the G-rated parts."

"I *know* how lucky I was. And am." He stretched his hand toward her, almost hesitantly. "You didn't know me. You had no reason to trust me, and lots of reasons not to. Even now, my story could be a lie." He told himself to move away, but he touched her cheek instead. His fingers weren't quite steady. "Maybe you should tell me why."

"Some people took a chance on me once, when they didn't have to. I was a pretty hard case, but they didn't care. They were there through all the bad parts, and they never gave up on me. Maybe I learned something."

"There're a lot of creeps out there who aren't worth taking a chance on."

"I've met up with my share."

"And learned to tell the difference?"

She shook her head. "Learned to try."

He started to drop his hand, but it lifted again to brush a lock of hair behind her ear. His voice was low; the words seemed to be wrung from some place deep inside him. "You fascinate me."

She had been admired and desired by men. But no one had ever told her that she fascinated him before. To herself she seemed the most straightforward of women. There was nothing mysterious or exotic about her. Yet she saw he wasn't lying, and she suspected Simon didn't fascinate easily.

She tried to make light of it. "If fascinate means I've been forced to think about you constantly, I suppose you fascinate me, too."

She wasn't transparent like many women he'd known, but right now there was no doubt in Simon's mind that she was uncomfortable. He had never been intrigued by innocence. He had lived too long on the edge to take the time to gently woo a woman. Now, for the first time in his life, he wished he had the time. She was a woman who wasn't quite sure of her effect on men, and he was a man who would be obscenely pleased to show her. His lips curved slowly into a smile that was all heat and feelings repressed.

"You find me funny?" she asked.

"I find you anything but. Shall I tell you what I find you?"

She was afraid to know. "I don't think so."

He stepped back to give her room—another inch or two. He was only too aware that it ought to be miles. Safe subjects seemed suddenly few and far between. He settled on food. "I can put together something for dinner."

"You're going to destroy all the good we've done for your leg if you don't get off it."

"You can stop mothering me. We're beyond that now."

Her cheeks heated for the second time. "Is that what I was doing?"

"It's easier to act like a mother than the alternative."

Again she didn't want to know what he meant.

"Friend," he explained, without prompting. "Shall we be friends, Tate?"

"How long are you planning to stay around and act friendly?"

"That depends on you...and the men searching for me."

"You can stay as long as you need to. I don't want you leaving until it's safe." She didn't add the idea that had been forming since she had begun to believe his story. She wasn't sure Simon was willing to accept more from her than a place to stay.

"You have a foolproof place to hide me in the cellar."

She had completely forgotten his story about the "museum." Now seemed like the time to explore it. "I'd like to go down there."

"The doors are hinged from below. They fold back like shutters so they'll open under the bed. When I went down it was very dark, even when there was light coming from the room above. When I closed the door, it was black as night. Now that it's dark in the bedroom, you'll have to take a lantern."

"I'll go down after we eat."

"Go now, while I get everything together."

"You don't want to come?"

He wanted some time away from her to purge himself of feelings he could never act on. "I think you should see it by yourself."

Tate realized this was a final test of faith in Simon. Once she was in the cellar, he could weight the door and she could be there until her bones were found by the cabin's next resident.

"I won't be long."

He smiled a little. "Is that a question?"

"If you want me out of the way, shutting me down there would be an easy way to accomplish it."

"But I don't want you out of the way. . . ." He stopped. What had he been about to say? That he would never want her out of the way? And what did that mean, exactly?

Tate didn't ask him to say more. Their relationship was already complex to the point of absurdity. "If you wanted to get rid of me, you've had plenty of opportunities. I guess I'll take my chances."

Simon limped to the fireplace and took down one of the lanterns from the mantel. He took a match from the canister on the hearth and followed Tate into the bedroom.

At the bedside she frowned. "Shouldn't we just push the bed to the wall so the entrance is easier to get to? We could push it back after I come up."

"If this was a normal situation, yes. But if anyone comes in here looking for me again, I'd rather they didn't find scuff marks on the floor."

She started to protest, until she remembered that his career demanded attention to details such as that. The men searching for him would have the same keen eye. "You can hand me the lantern after I've dropped like a sack of potatoes to the floor and wiggled under the bed on my belly."

"I'll stand here and enjoy the sight."

Which was exactly what he did. He had proof of how far his recovery had come when he felt each sensuous twist and turn of her bottom in the place where she had never bathed him.

"Ready for the lantern?" he asked after she had disappeared.

"I don't see anything under here."

He struggled to the floor. "You're right on top of it. Slide back. See where all the planks line up? Midway along that line you'll find a depression along the side of one of the planks. It looks almost like a defect in the wood." He waited until she was out of the way; then he pointed. "There."

"I feel like an idiot." Despite that, though, she slid her hand along the plank he had singled out, until she found the depression.

"Push it toward me," Simon instructed.

She did, although it wasn't easy. Just as Simon had said, the section gave under pressure, folding like an accordion until a space was revealed. The other side did the same. Now a hole loomed in front of her. An unappealing, black-as-midnight, musty, suspicious hole.

"You never said what you found down here," she said slowly.

"No, I never did."

"I don't know much about my father."

"No?"

"He wasn't an ax murderer, was he?"

"I don't want to spoil your surprise."

"I'd be comfortable with a little spoiling."

Simon slid the lantern toward her, then handed her the match. "There's nothing to be afraid of."

"How long will this kerosene last, do you think?"

"Certainly long enough to get you down to light the lanterns that are already there. Turn around and lower one foot until you find the ladder. It's sturdy, maybe eight feet long. Feel your way down, a step or two, before you light the lantern."

"I'm planning to work up an appetite."

"I'll be ready."

Tate inched into position. Then, with hands grasping the edges of the folding doors, she started down the ladder.

Making a meal out of the meager supplies in Tate's kitchen was a challenge, but Simon liked challenges. He had cooked meals with the entire city of Paris as his pantry. He had cooked others, when the vegetation and creatures of the Brazilian rain forest had been his only ingredients.

Either challenge paled next to the possibilities present in this remote Arkansas cabin. In one cabinet there were a can of tuna fish, six cans of chicken broth, a jar of cheese spread, half a loaf of stale bread, and salt but no pepper.

Two eggs nestled in what remained of a bag of ice in the icebox, along with a stick of butter and a bottle of luke-warm white wine. In canisters on a counter behind the stove he found flour, powdered milk, coffee, tea and rice. Beneath the sink there was a year's supply of graham crackers, marshmallows and chocolate bars.

He assembled cheese-and-tuna sandwiches and dipped them in a mixture of egg and powdered milk before he sautéed them in butter. He whipped the other egg and threaded it into boiling chicken broth for egg-drop soup, setting it on the side of the stove to stay warm after it was finished.

Tate still hadn't reappeared by the time the meal was ready. Simon hobbled to the back porch to get the wine that he had immersed in what was left of the water Tate had hauled earlier that day. The bottle was cold against his cheek. It was an Ohio vintage, cheap and probably too sweet for his taste, but after three months with nothing to drink but mud-black—and thick—coffee and watered-down tea, he wasn't about to criticize.

He opened the bottle and set it to the side of the fireplace before he went looking for Tate. There was no answer when he called her name in the bedroom. Thoughts of the dangers she might have encountered in the cellar—rats, hibernating copperheads—pushed aside the memory of going down the ladder with one good leg. He was under the bed and hopping from rung to rung in seconds.

He found her standing in the middle of the room, her head bent over a leather-bound volume. When she lifted her face to his, her cheeks were wet with tears.

Simon didn't know what to say. He cursed himself for sending her down here alone. All the objectivity he had struggled for disappeared.

"My father wanted me," she said. Her voice was steady, but the tears were there, shading each word. "All the years when I thought nobody did, my father wanted me."

Simon was at a loss how to answer her. "He left you this place, didn't he?"

"I didn't know why. Not till now." She smiled a little, and Simon felt something inside him twist at the sight. Knowing he shouldn't, he put his arms around her and pulled her close. Her body, soft and warm against him, seemed only an extension of his.

"Tell me about it." He felt her shudder, as if all the tears she still hadn't cried were battling inside her.

She tried to move away. "I can't."

He heard "not yet." "Then tell me about the book you're holding."

Tate knew she should push him away. Instead, she stopped struggling and circled his waist with her arms. Being held felt right. If it also felt confusing, even dangerous, that somehow didn't matter. "One of my father's journals. I didn't know it was here. There's a whole shelf of them in the corner, dating thirty years back. I never would have found them if you hadn't—"

"Hidden here?" He laughed a little. "Strange blessings."

"Your leg!" She tilted her face to his. "Coming down those steps must have—"

He hadn't intended to hold her. And now he didn't intend to kiss her. So much, he thought, for good intentions.

Her lips were soft under his, soft and pliable and young. She felt the same way against him. He had to bend his head to meet her; he had to bring her closer to arch her body against his. In the confused seconds that followed his senses seemed to expand, filled with the woodsmoke and fresh-air fragrance of her hair, the warmth and velvet texture of her skin, the tiny moan she uttered when his lips took hers.

He let her go the moment he felt her stiffen. No matter what happened between them, no matter what he felt, he never wanted her to be frightened of him again.

"That's not why I came down," he said.

Her eyes showed just how vulnerable she felt, though her words were determinedly casual. "For a man who's been in prison for three months, you haven't forgotten how to kiss."

"It's like riding a bicycle."

"I just begin to think I know who you are and something changes."

"I've never changed. The only thing that's changed is that I'm not lying anymore."

"What kind of truth is a kiss?"

"We could analyze it and find out."

"Let's not." Tate turned away from him. By wavering lantern light, the room seemed as much of a mystery as what had just happened.

The room was an airtight historical vault. For most of his life Millard had apparently zealously collected Ozark memorabilia, along with important records documenting the area's folklore. Then he had sealed off this section of the old root cellar and fashioned it into a crypt for a dying culture. The room was proof it hadn't been Millard's style to trust his records to the Smithsonian or a university collection.

Tate slid her father's journal back in place and forced herself to ignore the desire to turn and kiss Simon again.

He rested his hands on her shoulders. "What do you think of this room?"

Tate felt his warmth and support behind her. She wanted to lean against him, but held herself rigid. "I don't understand it."

"Shall I tell you what I think?"

"Why not?"

"I think the cabin's older than your father could have been. It's built from chestnut logs, and the chestnut forests died out in the early part of the century from blight. This room was designed as a place to store bootleg whiskey. White lightning. That's why it's so well-hidden."

"Well, that explains the jugs." Tate stepped away from Simon's gentle hold and started toward the far corner. She moved as much to put some distance between them as to explore. A dozen pottery jugs stood together in a neat row along the wall.

Simon followed and watched her lift a jug for his inspection. Carefully he pried the hand-carved cork from the jug's neck and sniffed. He was instantly racked with coughs. "This stuff defines rotgut," he managed.

She was glad to be talking about something so far removed from them. "You mean it's full?"

"Full and probably nearly as old as the cabin." He held it out for Tate to smell.

She waved it away after a quick whiff. "You think this was my father's secret stash?"

"I think your father was either a historian or one of those people who can't throw anything away."

She defended the man she hadn't known. "A historian."

"Then 'museum' was the right word."

"I'll have more of the answer after I've read his journals." Tate walked along the shelves lining the walls. Everything was almost compulsively neat, except for a thin layer of dust. The room was so well constructed and sealed that the air was surprisingly dry, though cool.

There were three shelves of books other than Millard's journals, which she had instantly recognized because of the one she had found in the loft. The titles indicated that most of the books were works of Ozark folklore. Some of them looked very old; some looked as if they had been bound by hand. She opened one and ran her finger down the page, aware, without looking, that Simon was beside her. "Did you know it's bad luck to change a horse's name?"

"How about a man's?"

She turned the page. "Don't know, but it is bad luck to wear another person's clothes—so you're in trouble, anyway." She replaced the book and chose another. She turned to a page at random and read for a moment. "It says here that Jesse James went undercover somewhere in the Ozarks and died a natural death."

"Definitely the best kind."

She hadn't met Simon's gaze since he's kissed her. Now she did. The flickering lantern light made it hard to tell what he was thinking, but she knew, even without visual proof. He was thinking about her and how odd it was that they had come together so easily. She knew, because she was thinking the same.

She turned back to the shelf and replaced the second book before she moved on to a shelf of carefully labeled tools. There were cast-iron kitchen gadgets that Simon examined with interest. "This peels apples. This pits cherries." He

balanced one in each hand. Tate noticed that his injured leg
was propped so that it didn't have to bear his weight.

"We ought to look for remedies for your leg. Everything
else is here." She moved down the row a little farther, to a
collection of handmade musical instruments, including a
dulcimer that looked as if it might have been crafted from
native woods.

Simon lifted a zinc-lidded Mason jar from a row of
glassware and antique bottles. "This still has something in
it. What do you suppose your father was preserving?"

"Botulism?" Tate could hardly absorb the impact of the
cellar museum, not to mention the entries in her father's
journal.

And then there was Simon's kiss.

Simon saw her bewilderment. She had the look of someone who had just discovered that nothing was the way it had
always seemed.

He wondered if he did, too.

He stretched out his hand to her. She knew better than to
take it. She was too vulnerable, too easy to hurt. From the
beginning she had found his hands oddly compelling. Like
the man.

Exactly like the man.

Unbidden, her hand lifted slowly until he had captured it
in his. His eyes were shadowed. "We'll go back up, and I'll
feed you dinner and ply you with wine. You'll tell me about
your father, and I'll tell you that you have nothing to worry
about from me."

"And will you be lying this time?" she asked softly.

He shook his head, answering his own silent questions,
too. "I guess that remains to be seen."

Chapter 9

Tate spread a quilt over the rag rug in front of the fireplace. "I'm not trying to mother you," she told Simon, "but if you don't get off that leg you'll probably end up back in bed, and I'm tired of taking care of you."

She heard the deep rumble of his laugh somewhere behind her. It had taken him some time to climb the ladder, and she knew how his leg must be throbbing. "Go ahead and laugh," she said, "but see how funny it is, if your leg doesn't heal. Try hopping to Memphis and see how far you get."

"Do I detect a note of personal concern?" Simon lowered himself gingerly to the quilt. Once down, he knew he wasn't going to get up again for a while.

"For me or you? I'm sharing my cabin with a wanted man."

"That might not be bad, depending on *who* wants me."

"At this point, who doesn't? The state, the feds, the prison," she listed, ignoring the double entendre. "Tell me what I'm supposed to get for supper."

"There're soup and sandwiches on the stove."

"The man works miracles."

"The man would have to be a miracle worker to feed anyone with what he found in your kitchen."

"Next time break into a cabin with a larger pantry."

"And miss the fun I've had here?"

She risked a glance at him. He was watching her intently. Even when he was engaging in light banter, he never lost his intensity. She had the feeling that if someone broke down her front door at that moment, he would be ready for them before the door crashed to the floor.

"You stay put. I'll bring the food over."

"Start with the wine." He hiked a thumb over his shoulder in the direction of the fireplace.

"You just get one glass. It has to be rationed."

"*That* has to be rationed?"

"Do you know what I had to go through to get *that*?"

"Whatever it was, it wasn't worth it."

"This is a dry county. I had to drive to the next. They have one liquor store and it's on the worst dirt road you've ever seen, miles from anywhere."

"And you did that for Ohio wine? One bottle of Ohio wine?"

"Their selection left something to be desired. Wine's not their big seller." Tate got the bottle and the two glasses he had set beside it. "Oh, good—you left it to breathe. All the alcohol probably evaporated."

"Let's try it and see."

"Let me guess, you haven't had a drink in three months."

"They don't serve wine with meals at High Ridge."

He was trying to keep his voice light, but Tate heard the anger under his words. "It must be an awful place," she said, and both of them knew she wasn't talking about the beverages that were served there.

"No one deserves to live that way."

"You didn't know anything about the conditions before you were sent?" she asked as she poured the wine.

"Not enough." He held out his glass in toast. "To Tate, who saved my life."

Their eyes met, and she couldn't look away. They sipped their wine, still gazing at each other.

"Grape juice," Simon said at last. "But it's the best damn grape juice I've ever had."

"And you thought I wasn't a connoisseur."

"I think you're not a lot of things."

"Such as?"

"Half as cynical as you like to pretend, half as tough."

"So I cried a few tears down there. It's been quite a week."

He smiled, and there was no edge to it. "Get the soup and sandwiches, then tell me why you were crying."

"It might bore you."

"I don't think so."

Tate found that Simon had already mastered the wood stove, while she still routinely burned anything she tried to bake. "How did you manage to figure the stove out?" she asked, as she carried the bowls of steaming soup across the room.

Simon took his bowl and watched her go back for the sandwiches. He waited until she was seated to answer. "We had a wood stove in our country house when I was growing up. As a boy, I helped our cook stoke it. And when my mother and father weren't looking, she taught me to use it."

"Country house?" She whistled softly. "Somehow I don't think we're talking about a cabin like this one."

"Let's talk about you."

Tate understood secretive. For years she'd thought she had invented it. "Not if we're not going to talk about you, too."

"I've told you my life story."

"You forgot a part or two."

Simon stretched out, so that his injured leg was as comfortable as it could be. "You first."

She was halfway through her soup before she started. "I'm not sure where I was born. My mother worked in a carnival when she got pregnant. She had me on the road somewhere, and didn't stop to file any papers. I guess it was lucky for me that a couple of stops later she ended up in her hometown long enough to hand me over to *her* mother to name and raise. I didn't see her again until I was ten and my grandmother died. A neighbor found my mother's address in Grandma's papers and got hold of her. She came after the funeral and took me to live with her.''

Simon kept his voice neutral. He knew that the slightest show of sympathy would halt her flow of words. "Was she still in the carnival?"

"She was a cocktail waitress, by then. I think she took two drinks for every one she served. By the time she got home she could barely make it into bed. I wouldn't see her in the mornings. I'd get myself off to school alone, but in the afternoons she'd be waiting for me." She finished her soup. These were memories she'd tried to put behind her. Now she was discovering that the feelings were still there.

"She hated me." She waited for Simon to jump in and tell her that was impossible, as so many others had tried before. She was grateful when he didn't. "I know now that she was a sick woman. But back then I never understood what was wrong with her, other than the alcohol and whatever pills she could get hold of. I thought it was me, that something was wrong with me."

"And now you know that's not true?"

She smiled at him, but she didn't answer right away. She set down her soup bowl and started on her sandwich, talking between bites.

"I've known that for some time. Kids don't make parents crazy. It works the other way, and that's what was happening to me before I decided to run away. When I was thirteen, I took off. I got caught and sent back, but I took off again. I was caught twice more and assigned new places to live, first a foster home, then a lockup for juvenile offenders. They weren't bad places, but by then I couldn't trust anyone, so I ran."

He was losing his struggle to sound objective. "You were young to be on your own."

She smiled sadly. "It was safer and better than living at home, but not safe and not good. I might not have made it, but I met a woman named Krista Jensen. I thought she was a runaway, too, at least at first. She was pretending to be one, so she could find her sister. She had teamed up with

Jess Cantrell, who was out on the streets getting stories for a book he was working on.''

Simon was beginning to understand. ''They adopted you?''

''They couldn't find Anna, Kris's sister. At first I thought Kris wanted me as a substitute, but I discovered later that she and Jess really cared about *me*. They got married and started a shelter for runaways in Virginia, called Stagecoach Inn. I ran away from them, too, but I always came back. And one day I came back to stay. After that they started proceedings to have my mother's rights terminated. It was a nasty battle. My mother didn't want me, but she didn't want anyone else to love me, either. After a lot of expense, Jess and Kris won and adopted me. I never saw my mother again. She died about six months ago in a shelter for women.''

''How does your father fit into all this?''

''I never knew who he was. Neither did my grandmother. My mother refused to tell anybody. When I'd ask, she'd say that he was a bastard and I was just like him.''

Simon wondered how she had survived such abuse to become the bright, articulate, risk taker she was.

''I only lived with my mother for three years,'' Tate said, reading his expression. ''My grandmother was a good woman. She was old and sick, but she never made me think the full-time burden of a grandchild was too much. If I hadn't had that, I'd be a different person.'' She held up her empty plate. ''The cook taught you well.''

''Someday you'll have to see what I can do when I have something to work with.''

She got to her feet and reached for his dishes, waving him back down to the quilt when he tried to get up. ''Next course. Don't go away.''

He watched her journey to the kitchen. Her shoulders were thrown back, her chin tilted high. Her mother's hatred hadn't defeated her, but he knew that the pain of it would be with her always. That she had moved beyond it to come so far, was a tribute to her strength and intelligence.

She took her time returning. Talking about her child-hood was never easy. And talking to Simon about some-thing so personal put them on a new footing, although everything had changed when he'd kissed her, anyway.

When she finally crossed the room, she was carrying the ingredients for dessert. "Did your cook teach you how to make s'mores?"

"Apparently not."

"Then you've been deprived." She moved close to the fire and lowered herself to the rug, crossing her legs campfire-style. "A s'more is like a sandwich. You break a graham cracker in half—" She demonstrated. "Then you cover one half with a chocolate square." She stripped the wrapper off a chocolate bar and broke the bar into pieces, putting a square on her cracker. Then she did one for him. "Next you have to toast a marshmallow. You have to do this part yourself. There are two skewers here, one for each of us."

Simon moved closer, taking the metal skewer that she of-fered him. He followed her example and slid a marshmal-low over its tip.

"Have you ever toasted a marshmallow?" she asked.

He shook his head, and she frowned. "You have so much to learn. What else haven't you done?"

His eyes traveled the length of her body, and his lips turned up in a slow smile.

"Never mind," she said, turning toward the fire. She wasn't sure whether the color rising in her cheeks was a blush or the impact of heat from the flames. "This is an ex-act science, so pay attention."

Simon could have told her that nothing was going to dis-tract him from watching her, but he didn't.

"If your marshmallow catches on fire, the inside will still be cold and your chocolate won't melt," she instructed.

"Sounds serious."

She nodded, not looking at him. "And the chocolate won't melt, if you don't toast the marshmallow long enough."

"I don't know if I'm up to this."

She stopped trying to ignore him and shot him a high-voltage smile. "Just hold the marshmallow a few inches from the coals and keep turning it. When it starts to droop, you'll know it's ready."

"Droop?"

"You'll know. Trust me."

He had. With his life. But he didn't remind her. He moved closer, until their shoulders were almost touching. Together they thrust their skewers into the fireplace.

"How long does this take?" he asked.

"You have to have patience."

"I'm noticeably short on patience."

He shifted, and they were touching. "So tell me how you found out about Millard and this cabin."

She felt his hip and shoulder against hers, and wondered if he was trying to tell her he was there if she needed him. The effect, however, was only vaguely comforting and considerably disturbing.

"My mother told the whole story to a shelter worker, a Mrs. Phillips, before she died. I'd like to think she was sorry for the way she'd treated me, but I think she was probably just scared."

"Judgment Day?"

She rotated her marshmallow, and he did the same. "Something like that."

"What story did she tell?"

"Brenda, that was my mother's name, met Millard at the Arkansas State Fair in Little Rock. She was running a game on the midway, and Millard was telling folktales in one of the tents. Apparently they fell in love and conceived me. Millard wanted to marry her. He brought her here, but Brenda was appalled at the way Millard lived. I guess I'll find out more as I read his journals, but according to the story my mother told Mrs. Phillips, she wanted Millard to move to Little Rock, and he wouldn't."

"Not a big-city boy."

"I'm guessing he knew he'd be miserable in Little Rock. According to what I read today, he did promise to put electricity and plumbing in here and build another wing."

Simon pulled his marshmallow toward him to examine it. "But that wasn't enough for Brenda?"

"Nothing would have been enough." Tate reached for Simon's skewer, and her hand brushed his. She let it go immediately. "That's not ready. It has to cook some more."

Simon turned to watch her. She was young; he still didn't know how young. She was reciting the events of her life, as though they were an interesting story—perhaps she had more of Millard's talents than she had even guessed—but he knew the pain that must be associated with all she told him. He was not a nurturer, not a comfort giver. He had moved too fast, seen too much, too often, to have comfort to give. But now he wanted that to be different.

They finished toasting their marshmallows to a golden brown. "They're done," Tate announced at last. She pulled her skewer from the fire and lowered the marshmallow to the cracker and chocolate, sliding it off with the other half of the cracker. Simon followed suit. "Now you have to eat it while it's still hot."

Simon watched as she took her first bite. Chocolate and marshmallow oozed around the edges of the cracker. Her small white teeth closed over it, and her tongue licked its edges to catch the soft insides.

His reaction was visceral.

"Hurry and eat yours," she prodded.

He didn't tell her that watching her eat was more of a sensual delight than the s'more could ever be. He took a bite, but his eyes never left her.

"What do you think?"

For a moment he wasn't sure what she was asking. What did he think about her life story? He wasn't a vengeful man, but he wanted to resurrect Brenda and wreak vengeance on her for what she had done to her daughter. What did he think about Tate herself? He thought she had shown more courage in her short life than almost anyone he'd ever known. What did he think of the sweep of her tongue as she licked melted chocolate off her bottom lip?

"The s'more. What do you think of it?" she clarified.

"It tastes like more."

She nodded. "Exactly."

They finished without speaking, although somehow neither of them could stop watching the other. Simon finished first. When Tate had finished hers, he rested his hands on her shoulders and gently tugged her toward him. "Come here."

She was wary. "Why?"

"Because you need this." Before she could pull away he turned her and framed the top of her spine with his thumbs. Gently he began to knead. "You're as tense as a High Ridge lifer before his first appeal."

"If I'm tense, it's because you're doing that."

"Liar."

"The pot calling the kettle black." Despite her best judgment, Tate flopped into place in front of him.

Simon slid his fingers under her collar to get a better grip. Her skin was as soft as he had imagined. "This is like giving an anvil a massage."

"You can't insult an anvil."

"What did Brenda do, after she realized she couldn't get Millard to Little Rock?"

"She took off." Tate let her head drop forward so Simon could knead the muscles in the back of her neck. His fingers stroked along her skin as if he knew just where her tension lay. "She left one morning when Millard was busy somewhere else. She didn't leave him a note, or even an address where he could find her. She just disappeared, and she never contacted him again."

"So he had no way to find you?"

"Millard never knew if Brenda had given birth to his child or had an abortion. Apparently he tried to find her, but she hid herself well."

"And she never told anyone who the father of her baby was?"

"No one. Including the baby. I guess she believed the greatest punishment for Millard would be keeping me from him. He valued family. Every time she was cruel to me, it was almost as good as being cruel to him."

She managed to say the words dispassionately, but she was suddenly feeling anything but. She had been fine until Simon had touched her. Now she felt under siege. She didn't care about her mother. It was old news. She had long ago overcome the problems her mother had left her. Long ago...

Simon felt her shoulders tremble. He wrapped his arms around her and pulled her to rest against him. "Go ahead and cry," he said softly, his lips against her ear.

"There's no reason to cry! Just because I never knew my father...I'm sure he didn't sit around and wonder about me. He was busy—happy, as far as I can tell. He didn't even know if I was alive. He didn't know—"

He held her tighter. "Go ahead."

"This isn't a therapy group, damn it!"

"No, it's something private between two people who care about each other." He kissed her hair. Then, again, "Go ahead."

She felt as if she were strangling. The tears she had shed in the cellar were nothing compared to the torrent threatening now. She tried to shake off Simon's arms, but he held her easily.

"I'd cry for you if I could," he said.

The tears came then. Not a child's tears. Not the hurt tears of the young teen who'd been rejected over and over by a hate-filled mother. The tears were the tears of a woman who had only begun to count the things she had lost.

Simon turned her so that she was crying against his chest. Each of her tears seemed to wash something from him until the defenses that were as much a part of him as his arms and legs were gone. The man beneath was someone he didn't know.

"I don't want to cry!" Tate cried harder.

"I don't want you to. But you have to. And we'll get through it." Simon rested his cheek against her hair and felt her body shake against his. She seemed unbearably precious to him at that moment. She was everything that he'd almost forgotten existed. Courage and vulnerability. Strength and passion. Fire and tears. In his months at High

Ridge he had forgotten. Perhaps before those months. Perhaps a long time before.

"I dreamed of my father," she said finally, choking back what was left of her sobs. "I dreamed he would come and take me away. It was a child's dream, but I gave it up once I began living on the streets. If I had only known..."

"How did you find out he left you this cabin?"

"Accidentally." She paused until she was able to speak more easily. "Someone from Mountain Glade ran across Brenda before she died. My father was dead, by then, but this man told her Millard had left his place in trust to me—if I existed."

She took a deep breath. Simon's hand was stroking her hair, and she began to relax against him. "My mother told him that she had given birth to Millard's daughter, but she wouldn't help anybody find me. I guess she thought she would make everything as complicated as possible. Will, my father's cousin, was set to inherit this place if I didn't appear sometime in the next ten years. If she'd denied my existence, he would have inherited it right away. As it was, he couldn't inherit, and neither could I, because I didn't know."

"It was too bad your mother couldn't turn her talents to better use."

"Well, at the end she repented. I suppose some might say that counted for something."

"Some might." From his tone it was clear that he wasn't one of them.

"She told Mrs. Phillips that I'd been adopted by Jess Cantrell. Jess is easy to find. The woman wrote him, in care of his publisher, and told him the whole story."

"And here you are." Simon understood so much more than he had before. Tate's story explained her willingness to live a Spartan life-style, but it also explained why she hadn't turned him in to the sheriff at the first opportunity. She had suffered. She knew what it meant not to be given the benefit of the doubt, and in her own way she knew what it was like to be behind bars. Some of her life had been lived outside the law. She had seen firsthand that trust was something to give those who deserved it, not those in positions of authority.

Tate moved far enough back to use the hem of Simon's shirt to wipe her eyes, then she pushed herself away. Reluctantly, he let her go.

"I'll bet you can't wait to get out of here, after that," she said, not meeting his eyes. "You escaped from prison right into a puddle of tears."

"I think I'd take this over High Ridge." He slid his hand under her chin and lifted it. "How old are you?"

"Twenty-one."

"Going on a hundred."

"Thereabouts."

"I'm ten years older than you are."

"Going on two hundred."

He smiled. "Thereabouts."

"The last time I cried like that was the day I asked my mother if I could come home. I was fourteen, and I'd been out on the streets for most of a year."

"Now you've evened it out. You've cried for your father, too."

"Living here had made a difference to me." Her gaze met his. "Of course, then you came along."

She was trying to look cynical, but she only managed wounded. "I came along." He told himself not to reach for her again. Kissing her would be like taking candy from a baby. She needed to be kissed, needed to know how desirable she was, but he wasn't the one to do it. He had nothing to give her. His life was barely worth the few cents' value of the minerals in his body.

He kissed her, anyway. The kiss was neither impulse nor compulsion. He kissed her because nothing was ever certain, and because sometimes more damage came from denial than acceptance. She didn't protest. She moved into the kiss with the passion of a novitiate pleading for grace.

His hands settled at her waist, and his fingers stroked the flesh under her shirt. She pressed closer to him, draping her arms over his shoulders, and her lips parted. Desire, so intense it had no name, knifed through him. He clutched her tighter, and his hands slid higher.

Tate felt the warmth of their bodies fuse, until they no longer seemed separate but became two souls entwined by passion and compassion. Simon was no longer a stranger, no longer someone to be feared. He was part of her, in some way she didn't understand. His struggle was hers; her sadness, his. She explored the taste of him, the heat of him, without fear, and she exulted in the feel of his fingers moving against her skin.

Simon knew the exact moment when choice would no longer be theirs. There was a small part of him that watched, whose voice counseled him to pull back, to protect himself and the woman in his arms. That voice had saved his life more than once, but it only whispered now.

A whisper was enough. He pulled his mouth from hers and pushed her head to his shoulder. "We're asking for more than we can handle."

She felt as if he was asking her to return to a place she could never go again. "I wasn't asking for anything."

He cupped her face in his hands. "We were *both* asking. I want you. I feel like lightning just struck. But I've still got half the state of Arkansas on my tail. I'll go down fighting, but I'll probably go down, anyway. I don't want to be worrying about you when I do."

She stared at him, trying to find a way behind the shield he had erected. "You can't hide from me," she said finally. "You heard my life story. I live in the same shadows you do. Even if you weren't a wanted man, you wouldn't want this."

"This?"

"You walk alone. So do I. You act like you're not afraid of anything, but walking with me would scare you to death."

"I don't walk. I run, even when no one is after me."

She knew how many of his defenses he had breached to admit that. "You're afraid because I might keep up with you."

"I'm afraid for both of us."

She took a deep breath and released it slowly. "You know why I run, but you haven't told me why you do."

He smoothed back her hair and wished this could be easier. "My story's not as straightforward as yours."

"Nothing about you is straightforward."

He admired her. With the firelight flickering over her features and her lips still moist from his kiss, he thought her the most intriguing woman he had ever seen. But more than her physical beauty intrigued him. He was taken with her courage, her determination to make sense of a senseless situation, her commitment to him, despite all the reasons why she should push him away.

He could fall in love with her. He, who had believed that love was something a fugitive never found.

He tried to explain. "I always knew who *my* parents were. They're dead now, but not a day went by in childhood that I wasn't reminded of exactly who I was. I was born on the Hudson, on an estate established before the Revolution. Like all my ancestors, I was educated in England and the Netherlands. My blood's bluer than your jeans, and I'm on the charts of two royal families."

"That explains your accent."

He smiled briefly, and said a silent thanks that she was not easy to impress. "I speak five languages, four of them fluently. I had to be able to do the royal honors, just in case dozens of people were wiped out simultaneously and I was suddenly sitting on a throne somewhere."

"King Simon?" She considered. "Hard to imagine."

"Do you like this story better than my others?"

"Let's hear the rest of it."

"There's not much to it. I was expected to be someone I couldn't be, someone quietly, absurdly aristocratic. Instead I nourished myself on stories of my grandfather. He was a hero during the Second World War, responsible for rescuing hundreds of Jews and smuggling them from the Netherlands safely to Sweden, right under Nazi noses. He died for it, but that didn't worry me. I wanted to be my grandfather. So when I was approached at Oxford to do some espionage for a European government, I accepted."

"And your parents?"

"Didn't know. I'm not sure they ever suspected. They only knew I wasn't the son they'd wanted."

"Did you become a hero?"

He brooded over the question for a moment. "I've done some things I'm proud of, and I've never taken an assignment I didn't believe in. But I suppose somewhere along the way I discovered that you can't work at being a hero. Heroes don't get paid."

There were so many thing he hadn't said, but Tate understood them, anyway. She could picture the little boy of diluted royal blood, who could never please his ambitious parents. She could picture the young man who had chosen his own destiny, but could never please himself. And still he ran, a fugitive from the ordinary, with no place to go.

"Will you keep trying to be a hero until you die of it?" she asked, leaning closer to him, as if to hear his answer.

"I'm about to die of it, now! I could have died already if I'd detoured one cabin or two."

"Don't feed me that line about how your life was saved by coming here. You're much too ruthless to die and much too determined to live. Maybe you don't feel like a hero, but you don't hate what you do, either. You're scared I might get in your way."

His fingers threaded through her hair, but not gently. He wanted to hold her there, to make her face the truth. "I would hurt you. You're much more vulnerable than you think. Just let go of this now. We feel something for each other, but it ends here. I'm leaving tomorrow for Memphis."

"You heard the dogs today. You'll be caught if you try."

"I can't stay here forever!"

"Then let me take you to Memphis myself." She covered his lips with a finger, when he began to protest. Her eyes sparkled angrily. "No, hear me out. Give me a chance, Simon! I've thought this over carefully. Tomorrow night, after dark, we'll leave in my Bronco. I'll load the back with stuff from the barn, and we'll pack you in between so nobody can see you. It won't be comfortable, but it'll be safe.

When we get to Memphis, I'll make contact with Aaron. I'll do it any way you say, but any way I do it will be safer than if you go alone.''

He covered her hands and pulled them to his lap. "I won't involve you any more."

"Any more is right! You've already involved me up to my earlobes. Do you think I'm just going to let you hop out the back door, while I suffer here never knowing if you made it to Memphis alive? You picked my cabin to break into. It was my head you almost shot off, and my bed you handcuffed me to. Now you've got to let me help you one more time."

"Did you hear what you just said?"

"Simon!"

He wondered if he had already fallen in love with her. He wanted nothing more than to take her back in his arms and overwhelm her with the feelings erupting inside him.

It would be safer for them both if she drove him to Memphis, instead.

"I'll have Cooney's gun with me. If I'm found in your car you can say you were forced to drive me," he said.

She nodded. "There's a condition attached. After this has ended, when you're safe again, you'll come back here so I'll know."

"And if I don't?"

"Then I suppose I'll worry for the rest of my life." She hesitated for just a moment. "Or else I'll have to find Josiah Gallagher and see what he can tell me."

"Don't ever go to Gallagher! Do you understand?"

"I'd go to the devil himself, if I had to!"

He groaned and pulled her toward him for one more kiss. It tasted like desperation and regret. Then, before they could mire themselves more deeply, he pushed her away and got to his feet.

Tate watched the bedroom door close behind him.

Chapter 10

The next morning the hounds were closer. Tate knew the precise moment they began to bay, if not their precise location.

The night had seemed eternal, each minute gaining seconds until she was sure the sun would never rise again. And now it had, to light the forests and fields of the sleepy Ozark countryside, so that the men hunting Simon could close in on their prey.

She sat up in bed, pushing the quilt around her waist as she peered out the window behind her. From this perch in the loft she could see far into the surrounding hills. But not far enough. It was still too dark, and perhaps—if they were lucky—the dogs were still too distant.

"So you heard them, too."

Startled, she gasped, turning to find Simon materializing out of the shadows at the top of the steps. She reached for the blanket and tucked it under her arms.

"Sorry, if I startled you." He limped across the loft and dropped to the bed beside her. "Have you seen anything?"

He sat casually, as if he weren't the same man who had haunted her thoughts and dreams through the long night.

He was wearing a pair of her father's jeans and a shirt, but-toned just partway, as if covering himself had been an af-terthought. His hair was rumpled and his face shadowed with the night's growth of beard.

He shouldn't have looked so desirable. The clothes were too large, and he seemed paler than he had the day before. Yet everything about him called out to something long dor-mant inside her. And newly awakened, the feeling refused to be silenced.

She turned back to the window. Whatever she felt was less important than reality, and reality dictated reason and ob-jectivity. Simon's life was in danger. Everything had to be that simple, and that complex. She spoke, without looking at him again. "I haven't seen anything. But they sound like they're coming closer."

"Do you always sleep bundled up like an Eskimo, or is that because I'm in the house?"

She was wearing nothing more than a knit undershirt with lacy straps and a pair of bikini pants. His voice had dripped with irony. "You give yourself too much credit," she said, still not facing him.

The sight of her, tousled and rosy from the cool morning air, was quickly heating Simon's blood. He wanted to reach for her, but even as his hands lifted he heard the baying of the hounds. His hands fell to his lap, and he knotted them into fists. "I think if I was going to be in the house much longer, we'd find another way for you to sleep."

She turned from the window. "Promises, promises."

Simon watched her hair glide across her cheek as she tossed her head. Her sensuality was as natural as some women's was rehearsed. He doubted she knew what she was doing to him. Reluctantly, he turned to the window. "They are getting closer. If they continue in this direction, they'll be here before noon."

"How can you tell?"

"Wind velocity, sound waves bouncing off the moun-tainsides, the number of dogs multiplied by the number of trees between here and the river."

"You're making that up."

"Right."

It was surprisingly easy to discuss Simon's situation, much easier than talking about themselves and their relationship had been the night before. Especially when he wasn't gazing at her. "What if the dogs catch your scent once they're on this property? Even if you're in the cellar, someone might know enough about the cabin to look there. I'm surprised the sheriff didn't find it yesterday."

"You may be able to keep them from catching my scent."

"How?"

"What do you clean house with?"

The question seemed irrelevant, but Tate knew enough about Simon to answer. "Something cheap that was here when I came."

"Know what's in it?"

"Ammonia, mostly. It burns my eyes when I use it."

"Perfect."

"What are you talking about?"

"About ammonia. Those bloodhounds are mostly for show, right now. They haven't picked up my scent because the trail's too old, and it's rained since I've been in the woods."

"But you have been outside. You've been on the back porch."

"I've been farther. I've taken the trail to the outhouse."

"I knew I'd find a sterling excuse to get indoor plumbing."

"Both porches and the outhouse entrance could use a good swabbing down this morning." He turned back to her. "Ammonia will ruin a dog's nose faster than anything. Mix up a bucket ten times stronger than you usually clean with, pour some on the porches and the ground around the outhouse. One sniff and the dogs won't be much good for a while."

She smiled a little. "How do you learn these things?"

"What do you think the men at High Ridge talk about at night?"

"Women?"

"And escape."

"You must be their hero."

"Let's see if we can keep it that way." Simon stood, forcing himself to ignore the pain shooting through his leg. He wasn't going to tell Tate that he had awakened earlier to find the bandage covering his wound wet with blood. Until he was safely in Memphis, his leg was the least of his worries.

She stood, too, draping the blanket sari-style around her. Simon thought any other woman would have looked silly, but she somehow managed it with grace.

From her shoulders to her toes Tate was covered against the cold, but the blanket didn't provide the barrier she wished for. She had slept little that night, knowing Simon was only a cabin's length away. Early this morning, she had begun to believe she had imagined the pleasure of his kisses.

Now she knew imagination had nothing to do with it. She had only rarely indulged in romantic fantasies; now she knew she had outgrown them completely. Simon was no fantasy. He was a man she never could have conjured up from a dream, because he was altogether too human and desirable.

She wanted to comb her fingers through his morning-rumpled hair, button his flannel shirt against the cold, stroke his beard-roughened cheeks. She wanted to kiss him, to savor the warmth of his lips and body against hers.

But there would be no savoring. As a child she had sometimes glimpsed the lives that others led: the special bond between mothers and daughters, the joy of piggyback rides on daddies' broad backs, the jokes and laughter of families around dinner tables. Now she felt as if she was once again being given a glimpse of what others had, the satisfaction of reaching for a man and finding his arms reaching out in return, the fulfillment of sharing lives, the ecstasy of sharing bodies.

Once again those simple human pleasure were out of her reach.

"I have a head start," Simon said. "I could be out of here in five minutes. You don't have to do another thing for me."

She realized he had no idea what she was really thinking. How could he believe she wanted him gone, wanted the complication of him out of her life, when the opposite was true? "Don't you know I'd do almost anything to keep you safe?"

"You looked so sad."

She risked just a little of what she was feeling. "Sometimes I think I'm on a carousel. I see everything I want, only it's standing just out of my reach on the ground, watching, while I go round and round...." She smiled to take the sadness from her words. "Someday I think I'm going to throw myself off, no matter how fast it's going. It might be worth the risk."

He groaned and pulled her against him, although every bit of caution he possessed told him not to. "You're too young to know what you want. You don't need a man like me in your life."

"I haven't been that young in a long time." Tate lifted her face to his. "I'm not asking you for anything, not to stop the carousel or even to catch me."

"You want me to remember you."

"You will."

As his lips took hers, hungrily, possessively, he knew she was right.

The dogs searched around the edges of Tate's property for most of the morning. She could gauge their location by their occasional blood-curdling howls. Once she heard a car on the road to her cabin, but either it turned or stopped midway, because no one appeared.

With Simon relegated to the cellar after a quick breakfast, she began her "chores." She had thoroughly mopped both back and front porches and deluged the path to the outhouse with cleaning solution, when she caught sight of two men on the hill above her house. They had three dogs between them. She dumped her bucket down the front steps and began to mop, watching them zigzag closer.

When they were close enough to see her, she waved.

One of the men waved back, then, leading two of the dogs, he came down the hill.

Even from a distance Tate could see that one of the dogs was a real bloodhound. The other was a mutt that resembled Cinn. As if he were aware of the kinship, Cinn—who had deserted the house the moment Simon disappeared into the cellar—dragged himself out from under her Bronco to investigate.

"I just hope their IQs are on a par with yours," Tate muttered as Cinn ambled past. The dog didn't spare her a glance.

"Mornin', miss." The young man leading the dogs waved again as he moved closer. His moon-shaped face wasn't familiar to her, but his uniform was. She wondered how High Ridge was keeping the rest of its inmates from escaping, when all the prison personnel were out searching for Simon.

"Morning. The sheriff said you might be stopping by today or tomorrow. I guess you haven't found your man yet." Tate leaned on her mop and watched Cinn introduce himself to the other dogs.

"Not yet. Found some more evidence he's been nearby, though."

"Oh? I didn't think anything exciting ever happened around here."

"You haven't seen anything?"

"Not a thing."

The young man's gaze was openly admiring. "You don't live here alone, do you?"

"I like it that way," she said pointedly.

"Mind if I check around the house?"

"Be my guest." Tate watched men and dogs approach. Both dogs had their noses to the ground. The man on the other end of their leashes was too busy gaping at her to pay them much attention. He looked up, though, when the bloodhound began to howl.

"What the . . . ?" He watched the dogs dance around the edges of the puddle at the bottom of the steps; then he knelt and scooped up a handful of mud. "Jeez, what's this?"

Tate attempted to look perplexed. "What's the problem?"

"This smells like pure ammonia!"

"I've been mopping, getting ready for the winter. I had birds nesting in the eaves of both porches, and you know what a mess they can make."

The man stood and jerked both dogs backward. "Well, if we were going to find anything around here, we sure can't now."

She continued to look perplexed. "Just because I've been cleaning? I didn't wash the whole outdoors."

"Ammonia'll wipe out a dog's sense of smell!"

"No…" She changed her expression to stunned. "I never knew that. Listen, don't take them down behind the house, then. I was scrubbing up around the outhouse, too."

The young man was obviously disgusted. "It's too late to worry. These two couldn't find a skunk in a toolshed, now. It'll be tomorrow before they're good for much."

Stunned progressed to contrite. "What a shame. I'm sorry. Really."

"We'll keep the other dog away from the house."

She shrugged. "Hope you have some luck. I don't like the idea of a convict hanging around here."

"Oh, if he's around, we'll find him. We've even set up roadblocks on some of the major routes out of here."

She made a mental note not to take any major roads tonight. "We're all glad you're working so hard." As she watched, he pulled the dogs around and started back toward the hill.

He called over his shoulder, "You hear anything or see anything, you give the sheriff a call. Don't take any chances."

She thought of all the chances she had already taken. The young man would be amazed.

She found more outdoor chores to do until the men were out of sight. Then she went inside and tapped on the bedroom floor. In a few moments Simon was beside her.

"They were here. They've gone." She told him about the ammonia.

He didn't spare a smile. "They'll be back."

"Why? They didn't find anything. I think you're safe now, safer than you'd be out on the roads, anyway. He said they're setting up roadblocks on the major routes out of here. If you stay for a few more days, they'll move on and it'll be safer to leave."

"Those guys were just the beginning. Gallagher's going to be along right behind them. And Gallagher's immune to tricks."

A shudder passed through Tate. "I'm going to put more wood on the fire. You'd better stay out of sight until it's dark and I can draw the curtains."

"I need Cooney's gun and holster."

"What for?"

"I'm going to make a shoulder holster to wear under my jacket."

She stared at him, but she knew nothing she could say would change his mind. "I'm sure you know where they are."

"I just didn't want you to be surprised when you found them gone."

"Nothing surprises me anymore." She watched him limp to the closet and dig under a pile of her father's clothing. "Simon, is your leg worse?"

"Don't worry about my leg."

"How are you going to fight off the bad guys . . . ?" She paused. "Or is it the good guys?"

He straightened, the gun and holster in hand. "I don't want you worrying about me. Understand?"

"Fine. Great. I'll just pretend you were never here."

"That would be best for both of us." He stared at her and allowed not a flicker of feeling to show. "I never *was* here. You never saw me, never took care of me. You never kissed me. I'm nothing to you, because I never existed."

"Then why am I driving to Memphis tonight?"

"It's not too late to change your mind."

She was frustrated and hurt. Perhaps he could forget everything that had passed between them, but she couldn't. Not that easily. "Of course I'm not going to change my mind. But while you're still here, can't we at least be honest about our feelings?"

"It won't do either of us any good. You won't see me again after tonight."

"You said you'd come back when this was over!"

"No, you said you wanted me to." Simon looked up from the gun, which he had unloaded. "This was a dream. I'm not real. You can't call a dream back, Tate. It turns into a nightmare."

She wanted to curse him; she wanted to beg. Worse than either, she wanted to tell him she knew he was right. What reason was there to believe that something could come of their time together? It had been built on isolation and danger. What chance would they have in the real world, where day followed day and what to have for supper assumed paramount importance? No woman could hold a man such as Simon. No woman should want to.

"How will I know if you're all right?" she asked at last, trying not to sound as if she was pleading. "I deserve to know that much."

"I'll be sure you know."

Her face was as carefully blank as his. "Thanks." She had one foot over the threshold before she added, "You'll need some sandwiches to take with you, and some money. I'll get them together. I think we should leave as soon as the sun goes down, in case we have to take back roads the whole way to Memphis."

"I'll be ready."

"I'm going to make a run into town in a little while and see if I can discover which roads are blocked and which aren't. I've got some things to buy for the garden that'll make good cover for you tonight. I'll buy you some sturdy boots, if you give me your size."

Simon stared after her when she had gone. He believed everything he had told her. So why did he feel the same way he had the day he realized that Josiah Gallagher was never going to spring him from High Ridge?

By six the sky was dark. Tate fixed sandwiches to eat on the road, as well as some for Simon to take with him. She had seen little of him until sunset, but when she came in from hauling water to the back porch, he was dressed and ready to go. The gun was nowhere in sight, but she imagined it was close at hand in case he needed it.

He was wearing a clean flannel shirt topped with a blue, much-mended sweater and a khaki windbreaker. He was a tall man, but he still had been forced to roll up the cuffs on a pair of her father's jeans. Luckily, that never seemed to go out of style.

"I found these in a drawer." Tate handed Simon a pair of wire-rimmed spectacles. "They're not strong. They shouldn't bother your eyes." She watched as he slipped them on. He really didn't resemble the trial photographs of Carl Petersen, any more—if he ever had. But then, Josiah Gallagher wasn't looking for Carl Petersen.

"Where's your car?" he asked.

"I parked it out front. I thought I should go out first, then if it looks safe, I'll start to whistle. You can come out and get right in the back. I'll pack sacks around you."

"Sacks?"

"I told you I was going to the feed store. I bought some things to work into the garden to get it ready for next spring. And I got corn for the geese, birdseed for the winter."

"You sound like you're staying."

"I'm a long way from knowing what I'll be doing." She hadn't really looked at him as they'd talked. Now she did. "But I'll be here a while. Drop me a postcard."

"So you and everyone in town will know I'm all right?"

"Then make it a letter. They did teach you to write at Oxford, didn't they?"

Despite himself, he smiled. "I could probably piece together a sentence or two."

"We'd better get going." She started toward the door, but he caught her arm before she'd gone more than a few feet.

Her eyes fell to the fingers gripping her. They were long and tapered, almost deceptively slender. They were also as powerful as the handcuffs he had once forced her to wear. She stared at them and, finally, at him.

Their eyes said everything their voices couldn't. He pulled her close, like a man who had just lost a battle with himself. His hands framed her face, and his thumbs traced her eyelids, her nose, her cheekbones, before dipping lower. He caressed her bottom lip. She felt tears rising, and it was all she could do not to plead with him to stay.

He lowered his head and took her mouth with his. She circled his neck with her arms and rose to press herself against him. His lips demanded everything, as if he were absorbing the very essence of her to take with him.

How could something that felt so gloriously simple be so hideously complicated? The kiss should be a prelude, not a postlude. She struggled to get closer to him, to let her body, her lips, her hands, tell him what he had come to mean to her. For just a moment she believed he knew and that somehow, someday, he would find a way to come back to her. Then, abruptly, he pushed her away. His eyes glittered, but somehow, his feelings were still masked. Slowly he shook his head.

Tate stared at him, all too aware that her heart was exposed for him to see. "Go with God," she said at last. Then she started toward the front door.

The moon glowed behind angel-hair clouds. The night was a perfect one for secrets. Tate slammed down the backseat and juggled sacks in the rear of the Bronco. If Simon had to leave, it was best to get it over with quickly. When the wagon was ready and she was as sure as she could be that no one was watching, she swallowed hard and began to whistle.

She didn't even know that Simon had left the house, until he was climbing in the back of her car. The moment he was stretched out, she pushed a blanket toward him. He covered himself, and she began to pile sacks around him. When she was finished, the back of the wagon looked as if it belonged to a farmer, and nothing more. Unless it was closely scrutinized, no one would suspect that she carried a fugitive under the sacks of bonemeal and dried blood, sand and peat moss.

"Can you breathe?" she asked softly.

"Enough to keep me alive."

That was hardly reassuring, but Tate knew it would have to do. "Then we're off."

"Stay on the back roads."

She fought down her fear for him. "No kidding." She slammed the back door and started around the car. In a minute she was pulling up the drive toward the main road.

There were a variety of routes into Mountain Glade, although only one, Kalix Road, was well traveled. The others were variations of cow paths. Tate chose a meandering dirt road that followed the twists and turns of the river. She had taken it before, when she was in the mood for a scenic drive. Once—in a rainstorm—she had needed every bit of power and four-wheel-drive agility her wagon possessed, to make it over the mud-slick ruts. There was no storm tonight, however, not unless she counted the one raging inside her. There was only a hazy night sky and the light of a three-quarter moon.

There had been no one on the road earlier that day. The route was little used and little known. She had found it, by accident, because it cut across a corner of her land. Only later, where it joined another more-traveled road, would they be in any danger of detection.

Tate winced every time she hit a bump. The road was bad enough from the front seat, but she could imagine Simon's discomfort with fifty-pound sacks bouncing on top of him. She navigated carefully, particularly where the road began to edge up the mountainside. The road twisted and curled, a red clay gash in the midst of a pine-and-poplar forest. She shifted into second gear as she climbed higher.

Around one corner she could see the sparse lights of Mountain Glade. The view was to be her excuse, if she was stopped and questioned about why she was out on this road at night. Of course, an excuse wouldn't do her any good if the car was searched. Simon had told her to say he had threatened to kill her if she didn't cooperate with his es-

cape. She wondered if anyone would believe that a man en-
cased in fifty-pound sacks was dangerous.

The road wrapped around the mountainside once more,
and she followed it slowly, the lights of Mountain Glade
disappearing behind her. The lights appearing just beyond
the next bend were a sobering surprise. So was the barking
piercing the clear night air.

She began to whistle ferociously, and she took her foot off
the accelerator so that the car, which had already been
nearly crawling, almost came to a halt. From the rear of the
car she heard a muffled, "Roadblock?"

"Yes."

"Don't hit your brakes. They'll know something is
wrong."

She couldn't turn to see what Simon was doing. She was
whistling and praying silently, until each shrill note seemed
to be aimed straight for heaven. She was close enough now
that she could see lanterns in the hands of the men standing
on each side of a wooden barricade. They were waving them
up and down to warn her to stop.

From behind her she heard a click. Nothing more. She
knew the sound. Simon had gone out the rear door. On one
side of her was a cliff, almost a sheer drop-off. On the other
was the bleak wall of a mountain. She knew which side he
must have chosen.

She prayed that he hadn't been seen, hadn't been injured, hadn't been killed. She prayed the wind wouldn't turn
and blow his scent in the direction of the dogs. She prayed
she would find a story good enough to explain why the dogs
went wild when they smelled the inside of her car. If she
didn't, the dogs could be turned loose—she would be turned
in to the sheriff.

She reached the barricade much quicker than she wished,
but she wasted time by rolling down the window at a lei-
surely pace. "Tell me you haven't stopped me for speed-
ing." She gave the good-looking young officer at her door
a tooth-jarring smile. He was not in High Ridge uniform.
She guessed he was a state trooper.

He ignored the smile and the joke. "License."

She reached for her purse and pulled out her wallet, handing it over to him. "Is there a problem, officer?"

He didn't answer. "This says Virginia. You're a long way from Virginia, lady."

"I'm here temporarily, living just off the river. That way." She pointed over the mountainside.

He handed back the wallet, after making notes. "Registration?"

She got it from the glove compartment and gave it to him.

"What are you doin' out here tonight?" he asked, as he handed it back.

"I'm on my way into town. I like this road because the view is so pretty just around that bend back there. I come up here sometimes at night, just to see the lights."

"Do you know there's an inmate from High Ridge on the loose?"

"I know he's on the loose somewhere. He's probably in Timbuktu by now, don't you think?"

"What do you have back there?"

Tate wanted badly to swallow, but the trooper was watching everything she did. "Birdseed, fertilizer for my garden."

"I thought you said you were here temporarily."

"I haven't decided for sure. My father died. I'm here settling his estate."

"You won't mind if we check what you have?"

"Of course not. But would you mind telling me why?"

"You a lawyer or something?"

She was beginning to get angry, and anger might distort her good sense. She was about to need all the sense she had. "No, just a citizen," she said, with forced calm. "One who believes in the Bill of Rights and the Constitution."

"I told you, there's an inmate loose. We think he might be tryin' to escape by car, maybe with help. Now, are you gonna let us check, or are you gonna make us get a warrant, all official-like?"

"I said you could check. I just asked why."

The trooper said something to his partner on the other side of the car. Then Tate's heart dropped as the man gave a shrill whistle. From just beyond the barricade she saw another trooper leading a pack of dogs.

"The back locked?" the first trooper asked.

"I'm not sure." Tate turned around and saw that the lock wasn't engaged. "No. You can get in without the key."

"How about steppin' outside while we do?"

"There's not much room over there."

"Then slide on over and get out the other door."

Tate knew protesting was no use. Awkwardly she hitched her legs over the gearshift and moved to the next seat. Then she got out and stood beside the door.

The dogs might be the same basic species as Cinn, but they snarled and snapped as they passed her. If Cinn had possessed even a drop of their temper, he would have eaten Simon before he had broken into her cabin.

"Stay out of their way," the second trooper said unnecessarily.

"Good advice." Tate watched the trooper who had interviewed her start toward the back of the car. He opened the door and peered inside, while the trooper with the dogs held them several yards away. But at the first whiff of the car's interior, the dogs began to emit ear-splitting howls.

Tate widened her eyes innocently. "What a racket."

The trooper moved closer to her. "Any reason they should be barking?"

She shrugged. "They're your dogs. I don't know anything about them."

"They bark when they smell what they're trained to smell."

"They're dogs. Dogs bark at everything."

"Mind if we rearrange your load?" the trooper in the back asked.

"Just don't make it too hard for me to get everything out."

He was already piling sacks toward the front of the Bronco. The dogs were going wild. Tate prayed that Simon had left nothing behind to incriminate her. As it was, she was certain she had a long night of questioning ahead.

"Damn!"

Tate closed her eyes briefly, and wondered what Krista would say when she got to make her one phone call.

"Well, that's why they're barkin'." The trooper waved the man with the dogs back. Then he slammed the door and started around the car. "You got a sack of dried blood back there's been ripped open. Smells like a damned slaughter-house to those dogs. Probably thought they were in for a feast."

For a minute Tate had nothing to say. She knew the sack hadn't been ripped when she covered Simon with it. In the few seconds he'd had to escape, he had thought of every-thing.

Where was he now?

"You go on ahead," the trooper continued. "Just stay off the roads for the next couple of days unless you want to be searched again. We're gonna get this no-good and get him soon, if we have to stop every car in the county."

Tate bit back every incriminating reply that came to mind. "Hope it warms up a bit for you," she said instead. Then, with a careless wave, she walked around to the other side of the car, forcing herself not to look over the mountainside, and slid carefully into her seat, rolling up her window once she was settled.

She started the engine and waited for the barricade to be pushed aside. When the road was clear she began to creep forward, but at the last minute the trooper who had checked her license waved her to a stop again. She felt ill. She had almost pulled off the deception.

He strolled around to her side and motioned for her to roll down her window once more. Her hand trembled, but she forced herself to take as long as possible.

"You stay in Arkansas," he said, when they were eye-to-eye once more, "and you'd better get an Arkansas license. You hear? Next time, somebody's gonna write you a ticket. And it might just be me."

Chapter 11

There were no more roadblocks on the road into Mountain Glade. Tate's intention had never been to visit town, but now she didn't want to arouse suspicion by turning around and going right back home. Simon was somewhere on a mountainside, struggling to make his way to Memphis. She had to protect him in the only way she could, even if that meant spending an agonizing hour in Mountain Glade.

She parked in front of the café and momentarily rested her forehead on the steering wheel. Where was Simon right now? Had he survived the dive from her wagon? She was helpless to do anything more than stay in town and look busy for a little while. There was no one she could safely alert, no way she could search for him.

No one she could safely alert.

She straightened and turned to stare at the sign in front of Allen's Pharmacy. There *was* someone she could alert. She had Aaron Reynolds's phone number. She could call him and tell him that Simon was on his way. His phone might be tapped, but if she only stayed on the line a moment, if she asked him to go to another phone where she could call him right back, they could safely have a conversation, couldn't they?

She knew her head wasn't as clear as it could be. She was worried sick about Simon and suffering the aftereffects of the encounter at the roadblock. But she couldn't just sit back and do nothing. Simon was alone somewhere in these mountains, fighting to stay alive. She had to do what she could, *anything* she could.

And besides, what difference did it make now if someone traced the call to Mountain Glade? Obviously the authorities believed Simon was in this area, anyway. What was one more piece of evidence?

Convinced that calling Aaron was the right thing to do, she got out of the car and headed into the pharmacy. Allen's was surprisingly busy, with half a dozen customers blocking the aisle leading to the telephone. Tate hoped they would entertain each other and Wally, and leave her to have her conversation with Aaron in privacy.

She knew so little about how a telephone was tapped or a call traced that she wasn't even sure how to take precautions. She did suspect, though, that using the Stagecoach Inn credit card might make Josiah Gallagher's job easier. So she bought a candy bar with a ten-dollar bill and begged the high-school student at the pharmacy counter for some of her change in coins. Then, after a few words of greeting to a harried Wally, she went to the telephone.

She couldn't seem to stop shaking, and lecturing her body to halt its flood of adrenaline didn't make any difference. She settled for dialing Aaron's number with an icy, trembling hand.

The number rang once. She remembered the last call she had made for Simon. Then she hadn't been sure that she wasn't being taken in by an expert liar. *The number rang twice.* She remembered how surprised she had been to hear Simon's recorded voice. *The number rang a third time.* She remembered how surprised she had been when she had realized that call was being traced.

And what if that trace had been completed? What if one of the people crowding Allen's Pharmacy, even now, was a buddy of Josiah Gallagher's? What if he or she was watching her at this moment—had been watching a moment ago, as she dialed?

As the number continued to ring she turned to investigate the people closest to her. None of them was familiar, but all looked as if they belonged there. One old man was bent, as if with arthritis, and his hands were leather-tough and stained. A young woman had a toddler in a stroller beside her. Another man had the baby-soft cheeks of a recent high-school graduate.

The number rang again. She had lost count by now. What would she do if Aaron wasn't home? Allen's would be closing soon. Should she drive to the next town and call again? What if Simon found his way back to her cabin and she wasn't there?

Hysteria was as foreign to her as waking in a lover's arms, but she recognized the feeling as it welled inside her. She took a deep breath and tried to force the hysteria away. The number rang again.

And then a voice spoke.

"Hello."

Tate was not so overwrought that she couldn't tell the difference between a man and a woman. "Hello," she answered, as softly as she dared. "I'd like to speak to Aaron Reynolds, please. This is an emergency."

There was a short silence. "Who is this?" the woman asked.

"I can't say. Please, may I just speak to Mr. Reynolds? It's very important."

Tate thought she heard a sigh, and then, "I don't know who you are, but obviously you haven't heard."

Tate waited, counting the seconds that ticked by, seconds that would make tracing her call easier.

The woman spoke again. "I'm Sylvie Reynolds, Aaron's wife. Aaron was killed several months ago," the woman said at last. There was no sorrow in her voice, just acceptance. "In a break-in at the store."

"No!"

"I'm sorry, but it's true. It's lucky that you got me at all. I'm in the middle of a move, and the telephone is going to be disconnected tomorrow."

Tate tried to hang on to her good sense. "You're moving?" She imagined Simon making his way to Memphis, only to be greeted by an empty house and the ghost of the one man he could have trusted.

"The van comes tomorrow." Sylvie paused. "Who is this?" she asked gently. "Are you a friend of Aaron's? Someone he worked with?"

"No." Tate wished she could say more, but she knew it wasn't safe. "I'm sorry to hear about your husband. I'm sorry I troubled you." She hung up before the other woman could answer.

Aaron was dead. Dead, and Simon was blindly seeking his help.

She wanted to cry. Instead, for the benefit of anyone watching, she casually flipped open the coin return on the telephone, as if hoping to find change, then strolled out of the store, stopping twice to price items on the shelves.

Outside, she debated heading straight to her cabin or wasting time at the Sassafras. She settled for ordering coffee and pie at the café counter, forcing herself to linger over a second cup to lessen her chances of looking suspicious.

"Cold out there, ain't it?"

Tate had been so deep in thought that she hadn't even realized the stool next to hers was now occupied. She turned to find the baby-faced man from the pharmacy. Coffee turned to acid in her throat. The man's words were down-home Southern, but to her suspicious ear, his accent was distinctly East Coast.

She swallowed more than the coffee. She swallowed fear. "It's usually cold in the fall."

"You're not from around here, are you?"

She raised one brow. "Are you?"

"I been here a while."

"I've been here a while, too."

"Do you like it?"

"What's not to like?"

"My name's Ben Kinney."

She'd just bet it was. Tate fished around in her purse for a couple of dollars and anchored them under her plate. "It's been nice talking to you, Ken."

"Ben. Ben Kinney."

"Right."

"You never told me yours."

"Right." She stood. "See you around." She was gone before he had a chance to answer.

There was no time in Tate's memory when she had felt so helpless. Even as a runaway, she had felt some sense of control over her own life. And in the worst moment of that life, Jess and Krista had been there to turn to when she could no longer handle her problems alone. Now there was no one to help her, and nothing she could do. She was compelled to wait for events to unfold by themselves. And she knew that she might never know what that unfolding would bring.

Simon was as good as dead to her.

She had taken a different way home from her involuntary trip to town, only to find her cabin empty and the ashes in her fireplace cold. She had busied herself making a new fire, hauling wood and water, coaxing a reluctant Cinn indoors to keep her company, but nothing had taken her mind off Simon.

She had lived almost twenty-two years. The days they had spent together were few in number, only a speck on the time line of her life, but she wasn't going to be able to fool herself into believing that the number of days mattered. She and Simon had lived an adventure together, but that was only a small part of what she felt for him.

She had never expected to fall in love. Love was for warmly nurturing women such as Krista and her sister, Anna. Love was for those who threw themselves into life, not for those who stood along its borders, watching and waiting.

And longing. Hadn't she learned that longing for something was the same as chasing it away?

Now, close to midnight, she sat in front of the fireplace, Cinn an arm's length to her left, and wondered how she could have failed to stop herself from falling in love with a man such as Simon. Perhaps she had even done it on purpose. She had never lived her life the normal way. Why shouldn't it follow that she would fall in love with a man she could never have and shouldn't even want?

Except that she did want him. And in the first hours of the life she would live without him, that knowledge was a jolting pain in the region of her heart.

She was about to bank the fire and crawl in bed for another sleepless night, when she heard a noise outside. If she hadn't been so ready to hear it, so attuned to every sweep of the wind and brushing branch, she never would have noticed. As it was, the shout, quickly chopped off, sounded like an explosion.

She was out on the porch in seconds.

The cobweb clouds that had hidden the stars earlier had solidified as night deepened. The moon, which should have illuminated the woods beyond her house, had been snuffed out. Her eyes adjusted slowly, but even when her pupils were at their widest, she still could see nothing out of the ordinary. Dried leaves blew in widening circles as the wind increased. A nighthawk rose from the limb of a nearby oak and soared overhead, disappearing in a graceful swoop to feast on some unseen forest creature.

She listened intently. From the pond behind the cabin she heard the honking of geese. The wind and trees moaned an atonal duet, but there was no countermelody of a human voice. She wanted to shout Simon's name, but she knew she could not. There were others who could be waiting in the woods.

She thought of her father's shotgun. Millard had shown a definite talent for hiding relics under beds. During her first week in the cabin she had found the ancient shotgun in the top of an old army trunk under the bed in the loft. She had left it there, since she hadn't known any safer place to keep it. Now she was glad she hadn't followed her first inclination and gotten rid of it. If Millard had kept ancient shotgun pellets to go with the gun, she had never found them. But now just the sight of the weapon might be good for something.

A few moments later she stood in the same spot on the porch, Millard's shotgun by her side. Nothing appeared to have changed, yet she sensed a change, anyway. The geese were quiet, and this time Cinn had followed her. He stood beside her, listening.

Just as she was beginning to believe her instincts were playing tricks on her, she heard another shout. She raised the shotgun to her shoulder and braced her leg against the porch railing. "Who's out there?" she shouted.

A figure condensed from the shadows. At first she wasn't even sure it was human. Then, as she watched, she realized it was a man. "Simon," she said softly. She dropped the butt of the gun to the porch and stepped forward.

It was then that she realized the man was not Simon. The man coming toward her, his arms stretched over his head, was Will. The man behind *him* was Simon, and Simon was armed.

Cinn barked in happy recognition. Tate stopped where she was and watched. She didn't know what to say, but she wasn't given a chance to speak, anyway.

"Drop the gun, miss," Simon shouted to her. "Drop it or I'll blow this man's head off."

She was surprised enough to do as he asked. *Miss?*

"Now put your hands over your head."

She did that, too. Beside her, Cinn's tail thumped rhythmically against the porch.

She watched, in silence, as Will came toward her. Simon was limping badly, but he managed to keep pace. The two men were climbing the porch steps before she spoke.

"Will, what's going on?"

Simon answered. "Your friend here was in the wrong place at the wrong time."

"This has gotta be the man who escaped from High Ridge," Will told her. "I saw him crossin' a field when I was out checkin' on my horses."

"And I saw *him* before he saw me." Simon motioned Tate against the porch wall. Then Will. "Now I've seen you both first."

Tate stared at him. Simon's face was covered with scratches, but his expression was as stiff as if it were cast in bronze. He hadn't once looked her in the eye.

"Be careful," Will said softly. "He's desperate."

"Is anybody else home?" Simon asked Tate. He ignored the dog rubbing back and forth against his good leg.

She just stared at him. Then, suddenly, she understood. She would have understood sooner, if she hadn't been so stunned. Simon had not changed into a desperate criminal; he was just putting on a good act. Once again. Only this time, it was for her protection.

"Dog sure likes him," Will observed.

Tate ignored him and spoke to Simon. "Nobody's home but me," she said.

Simon tried to nudge the dog away, but Cinn wouldn't budge. "Is that your car out front, then?"

She knew just what he was leading up to, and she knew she had to stop him. Simon was going to pretend to steal her car and drive to Memphis. Only Memphis was no longer the haven he had hoped for. Aaron was dead, and she was going to have to find a way to tell him.

"You won't get more than a mile down the road in it," she said.

"I'll take my chances."

"There's no place safe for you to go," she said pointedly. "There's no place you could drive it, where you'd be safe."

"I'll take my chances."

"Your record's stuck," she said angrily. "And you're not listening!"

"I don't have time to listen to you, sweetheart. I'm getting out of here right now." Simon motioned Will toward the door. "You go on in. The young lady and I will be right behind you."

For a moment Tate thought that Simon was going to hold her back for a brief conversation, but as soon as Will's back was turned, he motioned for her to follow him. She tried to catch his eye, but he was concentrating on Will.

"You're hurt," she said as she turned. "You won't make it anywhere. Next big city's Memphis, and they'll be looking for you there. You won't get any farther with that leg."

"Move it, sweetheart."

She felt such a surge of frustration that she lost all perspective. Whirling, she almost spat her words at him. "Simon, for God's sake, listen to me! You can't go to Memphis. Aaron's dead. I called there to tell him you were coming, and I talked to his wife. He was killed months ago when somebody broke into his store!"

The pain that twisted his features sent her into his embrace. She pushed his gun aside and wrapped her arms around his waist. "I'm sorry I had to tell you like that," she said, near tears. "But you weren't listening to me. I couldn't let you leave, knowing what I do about Aaron."

He put his arms around her and leaned heavily against her. Somehow she knew that he never cried, and that right now he was as close to breaking down as he would ever be.

"What the hell's goin' on?" Will demanded from behind her.

"Tate, you little fool," Simon said in a shaky voice. "You should have kept quiet!"

"And let you put yourself in danger?"

His arms tightened around her. "It would have been better than this."

"I'm not taking any chances with your life!" She turned to face her cousin. Simon kept his hands around her waist. "Listen, Will, this man is not who you think he is. He's not Carl Petersen, and he's innocent of any crime. He's proved it to me. Now you've just got to take my word for it."

"I don't take nobody's word for nuthin'."

Tate admired his courage. After all, he was the one being held at gunpoint. Despite herself, she also admired his stubbornness. It reminded her of her own.

"That's good thinking," Simon said. "There's not much I can tell you except that I was working for the Justice Department, undercover at High Ridge. I escaped, because something went wrong.''

''What do you mean, somethin' went wrong?''

''They left me there too long and I'd learned too much. It was either escape or be killed.''

''Killed, at High Ridge?''

Simon gave a curt nod.

''It's true, Will,'' Tate said. ''He was half dead when he found his way here. He's been here since the escape until tonight.'' She told him of the attempt to get Simon to Memphis. She felt Simon's weight sag against her and knew that whatever reserves of energy he'd had were all used up. ''Right now I've got to get him to bed and try to treat his leg.''

''No. I've got to get out of here,'' Simon answered. ''Can you keep your cousin here long enough to give me a head start?''

''You can't go anywhere!''

''I don't have a choice. Somebody's going to miss Will. And there'll be a search for him that will lead right here.''

Will humphed. ''Nobody's gonna miss me, 'cause I'm goin' right back home to get Dovey. She'll fix yer leg. She's a nurse, does most of the fixin' in this part of the county. Good as Dr. Monson. You think I'm too much of a hick to know the difference between a story and the truth? I've got kin workin' at High Ridge. I *know* what goes on there. If the Feds didn't send someone in to investigate, then *that*'d be the crime.''

He dismissed Simon with a wave of his hand and turned his attention to Tate. ''Now you, girl, I've had some doubts about you, make no mistake about it. You look like yer pa, but I haven't seen no sign of Millard in you. I reckon yer his kid, though. Only a Carter would do anythin' as stupid as this!''

Tate just stared at him, but that didn't deter Will.

''What were you thinkin', keepin' this man here with no help from us?'' he demanded. ''We're yer family, even if you don't seem to want to claim any of us. Millard was a hermit, but Millard asked for help when he needed it, and gave it back, too. He was family. You better be more like yer pa if yer plannin' to stay, 'cause if you don't start actin' like a Carter, I'm gonna have to turn you over my knee!''

"Nobody turns me over their knee."

"Which might be half o' what's wrong with you!"

The events of the night had been too much for Tate. She blinked and realized her eyes were wet. "It wasn't that I didn't want to claim you, Will," she said tightly. "It's just that I didn't know how. And I didn't know you wanted me."

"Yer Millard's kid, aren't ya?"

Could it really be that simple? Was that all it took? All the years when she hadn't really felt a part of anything or anyone, she'd had a home and a family waiting for her, just because of one act of passion between her parents?

"I guess you didn't know," Will said gently, when she didn't answer. "But now you do."

She nodded, unable to speak.

"As for you," Will said, turning his attention back to Simon. "Go ahead and shoot me, if you think it'll help, but I'm leavin' now. And I'll be back with my wife, if you don't kill me first. Get off that leg while yer waitin'. Tate, girl, get him ready for Dovey. She'll fix him up, but I doubt it'll be much fun. You might want to give him some of Millard's home brew first."

"*Millard's* home brew?"

"I never did know where he kept it, but I know he always had a supply."

"My father made whiskey?"

"Oh, Millard practiced all kinds of old-time skills." He winked. "A real folklorist, our Millard."

Tate watched Will stroll toward the door. Only a brave man would turn his back on a gun-wielding Simon. Tate reached for Simon's gun and took it from his hand. The door slammed behind Will.

"You're safe with him," she said, turning to face Simon. "He's not going to turn you in."

"I guess I can trust him or I can trust him." A pale Simon lifted her face to his. "I didn't plan on seeing you again."

She rubbed her cheek against his hand. It was icy cold, and she could feel a slight tremor. "I didn't know if you'd survived your dive out of the wagon. I was so worried! And if the wind had been blowing in the other direction, the dogs would have picked up your scent."

"I've been up and down every hillside and hollow between here and the roadblock."

She covered his hands with her own. "I'm so sorry about Aaron."

"Gallagher had him killed."

"No!"

"He ran a security business. No ordinary two-bit burglar could have gotten the drop on Aaron. It had to have been Gallagher's men."

Tate watched him grow paler. The night had taken a terrible toll on his strength. She didn't even want to think what it had done to his leg. She slid his hands to her lips and kissed them. "Let's get you to bed. Lean on me, Simon."

She guided his arm over her shoulder until his hand dangled over her breast. He didn't protest; he was too exhausted to pretend he didn't need her. They moved slowly toward the bedroom. Tate guessed the trip would take them practically as long as it would take Will to reach his house.

"My leg's worse," Simon said unnecessarily.

He was leaning heavily on her, but she welcomed his weight. "I can tell."

"I've got to get away from here. It's only a matter of time until they close in on this cabin."

"Where will you go?"

"North. I'll find a place to stay, until I've got my strength back. Then I'm going after Gallagher."

"But if he's as dangerous as you say he is—"

"I'm just as dangerous!"

Tate had no reason to doubt him.

In the bedroom, Simon lowered himself to the bed. He squeezed her hand, and she knew the simple gesture took most of his remaining strength.

She sat beside him. "Unsnap your jeans, and I'll help you slide them off."

"I can do it myself."

"Don't get modest on me. You were practically naked the first days I took care of you," she reminded him.

"Out!"

Tate knew he needed a moment of privacy. He had to have some time to assimilate everything that had happened. "Then I'll get you something to drink. I don't want you to get dehydrated again." She wrapped her arms around him and gave him a fierce hug before she left the room and closed the door behind her. Ten minutes later she knocked and entered, carrying a glass of tea.

Simon had done as she'd ordered, managing the jeans alone. She lit the bedside lantern. His legs were bare, except for the blood-soaked bandage on his calf. She felt a shudder of foreboding as she gently stripped that off, too. As she'd been afraid, whatever healing had taken place was a thing of the past.

"It's got to be stitched," she said, pressing a clean towel against it. "If it's not, it's just not going to heal. There's nothing else I can do for you. You've got to see a doctor."

"I'm all the doctor we use in these parts, unless he's dyin'." Dovey bustled into the room, followed by Will. "Lord!" She stopped and stared at Simon. Tate wasn't sure it was his leg that interested her so much.

Tate conferred briefly with Dovey, telling her everything she had done. Will lifted the tea Tate had put by the bedside and sniffed, wrinkling his nose in distaste. He left for his car and reappeared a few minutes later with a bottle of Jack Daniels. "Didn't take me seriously, did you, girl?" he chided Tate as Dovey finished her exam. He held out the bottle to Simon. "Drink."

Simon assessed Dovey, who was rummaging through a well-equipped black bag. His gaze settled on Tate, whose face was paler than his own. With a nod to Will, he held out his hand.

Chapter 12

Tate added more logs to the fireplace and watched sparks scatter in iridescent spirals. There seemed little she could do for Simon tonight, other than keep the cabin warm and stay nearby if he needed her. Dovey had tsk-tsked and mumbled over his leg for the better part of an hour, but when she'd finished, the wound was cleaned and stitched, and Simon shot full of antibiotics.

Backbone, and more than a few slugs of whiskey, had gotten him through the operation. Now he was sleeping off the effects.

Or so she'd thought.

"Aaron!"

Tate hurried toward the bedroom. Simon hadn't shouted, but his voice had been loud enough to be heard if anyone was outside his window. She was apprehensive enough, by now, to believe that anything was possible.

She found him tossing restlessly. Memories of the fever and delirium he had suffered in his first days at the cabin came flooding back, and she was horrified. She lit the kerosene lamp by the bedside with trembling hands, then dropped to the bed beside him and touched his shoulder. "Simon," she called softly, "Simon, wake up!"

His hand gripped hers, and before she could brace herself, he had jerked her to the bed beside him. He rose above her and his eyelids snapped open, but his eyes stared right through her.

Tate rested her hand on his shoulder. "It's just me. You're safe. You must have been having a bad dream."

Little by little he seemed to focus. Tate's heart beat faster. At last he fell back against the pillow to stare at the ceiling. His free arm lifted as if to shade his eyes, but not from the moonlight filtering through the window. From the truth. He gripped Tate's hand harder, although she doubted he was aware of it. "Aaron's dead, isn't he?"

"I'm so sorry." Tate rolled to her side so she could watch him. "But you can't think of Aaron now. You've got to think of yourself."

He was silent for a while, but when he spoke it was clear who had filled his thoughts. "Aaron taught me to fish when we were up in Oregon working on the case I told you about. I hadn't fished since I was a little boy, but Aaron bought me enough equipment to catch a whale."

"Simon—"

"He was going to sell his business when he turned sixty and buy a house on a lake somewhere, so he could fish every day. Sylvie was going to weave, and they were both going to entertain their grandkids. He didn't see much of his own kids when they were growing up. He was hoping to make it up to them by being a perfect grandfather."

"It's hard to lose a friend, especially after what Gallagher's done."

"Gallagher." The three syllables were heavy with bitterness. "Aaron made Gallagher fish, too. Gallagher was like a son to him."

"Gallagher's a young man?"

"Not much older than I am."

"Simon, you're not going to..." She paused. She wanted to find a prettier word than avenge—or its soul mate, revenge. ''You're not going to go after Gallagher, are you? Your only priority right now has to be your own safety.''

''I'll never be safe, until Gallagher's been taken care of.''

''What do you mean 'taken care of'?''

He shook off her hand. ''It's late. You'd better go to bed.''

''Look at me!'' Tate held his face in her hands. ''This has to stop somewhere, doesn't it? Aaron's dead, and you came a lot too close to death for comfort, yourself. Dovey says your leg's going to be fine now, but if the bullet had passed just inches to the left, the bone would have been shattered. You might have died out in the woods somewhere, trying to drag yourself to safety. At the least, you would have been caught.''

He covered her hands and dragged them down to his chest. His eyes were the color of smoke. ''This doesn't concern you.''

''No?'' Slowly she lowered her mouth to his until she was only a whisper away and showed him why it did.

''Go to bed, Tate.''

''You concern me.'' She brushed her lips across his, then back again. ''I was terrified all evening, wondering what was happening to you. I don't want to be terrified, and I don't want to be concerned. But I am.''

''If you keep that up,'' he said harshly, ''you'll be in this so deep you can never turn back.''

''I'm already there.'' This time her lips lingered.

His hands dropped hers, and he reached for her shoulders to push her away. His fingers dug into her flesh, but he couldn't find the strength.

''I don't want to be terrified or concerned or in love with you,'' she said softly. ''But I am.''

''No, you're not!''

''No?'' She brushed his hair back from his forehead. In the flickering lamplight, his face was a kaleidoscope of expression. Each changing nuance made it harder to read his feelings. ''I don't want to love you. I don't want to love anybody, because I don't think I'll be very good at it. But I don't think I have any choice.''

"You can get up from here and walk away. When I leave tomorrow, you can tell yourself it doesn't matter." He slid his hands under her hair. "And it doesn't, because I don't have anything to give you. I'm a walking dead man."

"You've stayed alive this long!"

Her hair slipped through his fingers. It was fine and silky, the color of night against her pale, worried face. He thought of all she had done for him, and all she still wanted to do. And he thought of all he could never do for her.

When he spoke, his voice denied his feelings. "I'm only alive because of luck, and because I've had nobody else to think about."

"You need to think about someone else," she said fiercely. "You need to remember that avenging Aaron's death is going to get you killed, and that someone will be left here to mourn you! If you go after Gallagher and he kills you, it will kill me!"

He gripped her head and forced her to look into his eyes. "You're acting like a little fool! I'm nothing to you. Nothing. And when I leave tomorrow, I'll still be nothing."

"Tell me again this is nothing!" Simon's fingers were tangled in her hair, holding her back, but Tate found his mouth, anyway. His lips were warm, but they didn't yield under hers.

He turned his head. "Stop it!" This time he found the strength to push her away. "You're not in love with me! You're still a kid, damn it. You've got a kid's fantasies, that's all. I'm some lousy fairy-tale knight to you. I brought excitement into a dull existence. But that's all I've brought, Tate. Maybe you want me—maybe you've never really wanted a man before. But wanting's a hell of a leap from loving."

"You're not a knight. I don't want you because you've spent your life running from human warmth and being a hero." She sat up. Her hair swung across one cheek, but she didn't shake it back. "And I'm not a kid. But maybe I am a fool."

Behind the veil of hair, he saw her pain. "You're also lovely and desirable, but that passion belongs to a man who can give you what I can't."

"Then maybe I'm more of a kid than I thought. I didn't know passion was a request to share the rest of your life. I didn't know that asking you to work at staying alive was the same as asking for a commitment."

"You're asking me to think of you!"

"I'd ask you for the moon and stars, if I thought it would keep you alive."

"Go to bed." Simon almost choked on the words. His voice was not as aloof as he had intended.

Tate stood and turned to face him. She knew more about rejection than most people learned in a lifetime. She also knew more about the horrors of running from it. She examined Simon as dispassionately as she could and wondered whether the pain would multiply if he continued to reject her—or if that was impossible.

Her hands rose to the top button of her shirt. "You've told me *my* feelings. You haven't told me yours." She pushed the button through the buttonhole and slid her hands lower to the next. "Have I just imagined that you want me?"

He gave a harsh laugh. "I'm a man."

The third button was unfastened, then the fourth. "Am I supposed to believe that all men want me?"

Simon sat up and grabbed her hand. "Cut this out!"

"This, Simon?" She didn't smile. "Am I asking you for something, again? Something you can't give me?"

"Damn it, Tate, you may be a kid, but I'm not!"

"A grown man driven wild by the sight of a child?" Her free hand unfastened the next button.

Simon jerked her back down beside him. "You're asking for sex, is that it? Nothing else?"

"I'm asking for whatever you can give me, and not one thing more." She stared into his eyes.

"That's not asking for much."

"Maybe it doesn't seem like it. But I've never asked a man for anything before."

Her message was unmistakable. Simon's breath caught, and for a moment he couldn't find words. Then he did. "Find someone who'll appreciate what you're offering. You're wasting it on me."

"I guess that's my right." Tate slipped her hand out of his and pulled the last button free. She shrugged, and the shirt glided down her back and arms. In the lamplight, her bra was only a shade whiter than her skin.

Simon stifled a groan. He hadn't remembered seeing more of her body than wrists and hands. But there had been one tormented dream where he had seen her naked, bathing in the firelight. Since that moment, he had wanted her—and now he knew it had not been a dream.

He was a strong man, a man for whom weakness was a deadly sin. But he wasn't strong enough to resist her. He wouldn't, couldn't, name his feelings, but he knew they had little to do with the absence of women from his life, or even the acute danger he was in.

He knew he should reach behind her and pull the shirt back over her shoulders. Instead, he watched silently as it fell to the floor.

Tate reached behind her for the clasp of her bra. Her fingers trembled, but the clasp fell free. She shrugged once more.

Her breasts were small and rose-tipped. They tilted up, as if in supplication. "Warm me," she said softly.

He tried once more. "You don't know what you're doing."

"No? Then you can show me." She moved closer. "Show me." She reached for his hand and hoped he didn't feel her trembling as she guided it to her breast.

He had never felt anything as soft. It seemed like forever since he had touched a woman. It *was* forever since he had touched a woman such as Tate. He didn't want to draw her close, but he did. He didn't want to circle her with his arms as she unbuttoned his shirt. But he did.

She lingered over every button. Simon's hands moved slowly over her back. He pressed his face into her hair, and she felt him shudder. She didn't know whether it was passion or regret.

Under her fingertips, his chest was hard with muscle. She had bathed him; he was not a mystery, but the things she felt as she touched him now were mysterious to her. Her hands glided from his waist to his neck, savoring each separate texture, savoring the heat of his skin. She lifted the shirt from his shoulders and pushed it down over his arms. Then she pressed herself against him.

He held her there, although he knew he should force her away. He felt her nipples harden, and he knew he was lost. "I don't want to hurt you," he said, swaying against her in unconscious caress.

"Then don't." Tate arched her back to be closer, still. "Don't. Just love me. Just for now. Just for tonight."

He wanted to warn her again. He wanted to make her understand that even this exposed them both to a danger she couldn't conceive of. But his lips wouldn't form a warning. Instead they moved over her hair, stroked the petal-soft skin of her forehead, grazed her cheeks and drew a shimmering welcome from hers.

He stroked her breasts as he kissed her. She lifted herself against his hands in invitation. Her lips moved, then parted against his. His tongue touched hers, and she sighed with pleasure and relaxed against him.

He knew she had been afraid he would continue to resist her. She had no idea of how powerfully he was drawn to her. She believed her feelings were her own; she didn't know that he shared them. Yet she had risked humiliation to come to him, to offer herself.

Beneath his wandering hands her frame was delicate, almost fragile. But he knew better. She was held together by steel. Perhaps she wouldn't break apart when he left her. She had more courage, real courage, than anyone he had even known.

"I just want to protect you," he murmured against her lips. "But I've wanted you since I first saw you."

She kneaded the muscles of his back and shut her eyes as he kissed her again. Sensation ran hot and liquid through her. Simon ran his thumbs along her spine until his hands cupped her bottom. He guided her against him, and even through the heavy denim of her jeans, she could feel his arousal. She flung one leg over him as he leaned back against the iron headboard.

His eyes were half closed, his lips pressed together as he fought for restraint. He was always a patient lover, able to keep enough distance to give pleasure as well as to take it. Now he wondered if there would be any distance between them tonight. He felt himself moving toward fulfillment, and they weren't even fully undressed yet.

She was so slight he could hardly feel the burden of her weight. But he could feel every heated inch of her skin, as she pressed against him; feel every silken hair that brushed his face. Perhaps she had never had a lover, but she was no tremulous virgin. She was sharing herself, her warmth, her emotion, with a generosity of body and spirit he had never known.

He turned her so they were on their sides, but she kept one leg thrown over his, afraid he would move away. She was drifting, drowning in the river flowing through her. When his hand caught in the waistband of her jeans, she leaned away to give him room to unsnap them.

"This is happening fast enough." Simon's hand dipped lower and unfastened her jeans, but he left them on. Instead, his lips began a slow journey. He found the drumroll pulse in her neck, and savored its wild rhythm. He found the hollow at her throat with his tongue, and heard her moan.

Her skin was so pale he could trace the fine network of veins beneath it. She tasted like warm cream and wild-flower honey. He was wrapped in the scents of autumn, of sweet forest air tinged with pine and the fragrance of burning applewood.

She moaned again, when he drew the tip of her breast into his mouth. He buried his face against her, and for a moment the pleasure was too intense to bear. She moved against his hand, against his mouth, silently begging him for more.

He found her other breast with his lips. As sensation jolted through her, Tate wondered if she could die of such ecstasy. She hadn't known what she was asking of him. She had only yearned for something that couldn't be explained.

He lifted his head to look at her. Her lashes were dark shadows against her flushed cheeks. Her hair was a thundercloud against the white pillowcase. He was flooded with emotion that gave wings to his passion. She was no ordinary woman, and he was not just a man trying to hold on to a life that was rapidly slipping away. She was *his* woman, by her own words and by the emotions suffusing him. And she would always be his woman, whether he lived to see tomorrow or not.

She moaned his name and lifted her hips to meet his. There was so little he could give her, and nothing he could say. But he knew he could give her this night.

He pushed her jeans down, caressing her stomach, her hips, as he eased them off. She attempted to help him, but he captured her hands in one of his and kissed her. "Let me," he said.

"Your leg?"

"Was hurting like hell, and now I don't even feel it." He stretched half across her, pushing down the jeans just inches at a time and caressing the long, sleek length of her legs as he did. He brushed his hand over the dark triangle of her hair that was now his to touch. And then his hand settled there to caress her.

The sound she made was almost a whimper. Every touch of his hands trailed heat into new parts of her body. She pulled her hands from his grasp and wove them through his hair as his lips followed the path of his hands. Her body no longer seemed earthbound, and thought didn't exist. She floated, tossed from wave to wave of sensation. Simon had undressed her, before she realized it. Her hands were at the waist of his briefs before she knew she was undressing him.

Nothing had prepared her for the overwhelming perfection of their bodies together. She felt the beat of his heart, the heat of his skin, the rasp of his hair, all as if they were part of her. His chest was firm against the soft pressure of her breasts, his arms rigid with muscle. Her hands slipped lower. And stopped.

Simon's laugh was a harsh rumble. "Where's your courage, now?" He covered her hands and moved them lower still to cover the place she hadn't yet touched. Tate opened her eyes and stared into his, as she began to explore him. She watched his expression change by slow degrees. She felt suddenly, powerfully female. She was not the recipient of Simon's lovemaking, but a willing, eager partner. And perhaps what she didn't know, she would soon learn.

As he captured her hands again and moved them above her head, she arched her back, seeking, craving, the feel of his body against hers. Then she lifted her hips to meet his first ecstatic thrust.

The fire had almost died by the time Tate got out of bed to bank it. Simon was sleeping, and she had pulled on his shirt as a robe. She shivered in the cold air, and debated whether to throw more logs on the fire or to crawl back into bed and the warmth of his arms.

She compromised, using kindling and several small logs to revive the fire while she washed with water from the kettle hanging in front of the fireplace. But by the time she was ready to add hardwood that would burn all night, she found she had little desire to do so. Instead she pulled an afghan from the sofa and sat on the rug, staring into the flames.

She was Simon's woman now, although she knew he would never claim her. She had given herself to him, given everything she knew how to give. But what would Simon remember of tonight? Certainly not her prowess as a lover. She had been so bombarded by sensation that she had been at a loss to focus it, to use it to give him pleasure.

He hadn't complained, but she had seen the regret in his eyes afterward. She might be a kid, and she might be a fool. But she wasn't enough of one to believe that what they had shared had been enough for him. He had made love to her because she had begged for it. The most she had given him was sexual release after months of imprisonment.

There was no doubt in her mind that he expected more from a liaison. She had never asked him about his personal life, but there had to have been women in the past. And there would be more in his future—if he had a future.

She was left with a body that still throbbed from his lovemaking and a heart that was filled with despair.

Hands settled on her shoulders. "Is this a private party? Or can I join you?"

She had been so deep in thought that she hadn't heard him get up. "I . . . I was just warming the cabin a little before I banked the fire for the night."

"I missed you beside me." Simon lowered himself to the rug. He had felt Tate grow tense under his hands, and he was careful not to touch her now.

Tate glanced at him. He was wearing jeans and a blanket, Indian-style, around his shoulders. She turned back to stare at the flames, the picture of his broad, blanket-clad shoulders flickering brightly with them. "You need your sleep. You shouldn't be up."

He tried to fathom what she could be thinking. She sounded like the woman who had been his nurse, not the woman who had just been his lover. "You shouldn't be up, either. You could rekindle the fire in the morning."

She was silent for a long time, and he was silent beside her. When she spoke at last, there was little emotion in her voice. "Simon, I'm sorry."

He quelled the urge to shake an explanation out of her. "Are you?"

"I pushed you to make love to me. And I kept pushing."

He doubted that she was really apologizing for being too bold.

"I . . . you were right. It was a bad idea," she finished.

One minute she was staring into the flames, the next she was lying half across him, staring into his eyes. Simon's fingers dug into her upper arms. "All right," he said coldly, "let's hear you say that again."

"It was a bad idea! I know you regret it. I know I wasn't much good. I don't know what to do, what to feel. I was the kid you accused me of being!"

He stared at her. "Kid?"

"Kid. I'm not experienced. You know that now. I . . . I thought it didn't matter, but it did."

He struggled to make sense of what she was saying. "Are we talking about what you felt or what I did?"

"What you felt. I—"

He touched her lips with his fingertips. "How do you know what I felt? Let's forget that for a moment, anyway. Let's talk about what you felt."

She couldn't look at him, and she couldn't speak.

"It wasn't much fun, was it?" Simon cradled her face and brought it back to his. "I hurt you. I tried to be gentle, but I wasn't. I lost control before I could give you much pleasure."

"It wasn't your fault. It was mine. I thought I'd know what to do. I was sure—"

"You did everything just right." He caressed her hair and felt himself growing hard again. The conversation was an aphrodisiac; touching her was a reminder of how she'd felt, naked and soft against him.

"Look, I don't need to be reassured. I mean, I'm not some vulnerable—"

"Yes, you are. And yes, you need reassurance. So let me tell you what I felt."

"You were sorry you made love to me! I saw it in your eyes afterward. It can't be much fun to make love to a virgin. And not what you're used to."

Gently he pushed her to the rug and pinned her there with the weight of his body. Her insecurities were legion. He hoped he didn't neglect any of them. "I did feel regret. You're right. But not because we'd made love. Because I can't make love to you every day for the rest of your life. We didn't even hit the highlights tonight, and I didn't give you the pleasure you were entitled to, and I regretted that, too."

He kissed away her reply, until there wasn't even a rumble. "And yes, making love to a virgin has some drawbacks, but do you know how sweet it was to be your lover, anyway? To be the man to share that with you?"

He kissed her again. He knew she wanted to believe him, but she couldn't yet. "You gave me more pleasure tonight than I knew I could have," he said softly. "I'll never forget this. Never. And I'll never forget you." He began to unbutton her shirt, even though she tried to still his hand.

"You don't have to—"

"Don't I?" He raised one aristocratic brow. "You're not a virgin, now. And I'm not going to lose control again. We've got the rest of the night together. Let's see if we can rid you of your doubts, one...by...one."

The fire died, and the cabin grew cold. But it was only later, much, much later, that they found their way back to bed. Replete and satisfied with her ability to please Simon, Tate fell asleep immediately, wrapped tightly in Simon's arms. He lay against her, stroking her hair, and wondered if a hero could learn to be an ordinary man and a fugitive could learn to stop running.

Chapter 13

In the hour just before dawn, Simon eased his body from Tate's. She hadn't awakened during the night; he had hardly slept. Now she still lay sleeping, her body curved like a graceful willow branch, her hair a midnight cloud against the pillow they had shared.

Monitoring the deep, even rhythm of her breathing, he got up slowly, careful not to shake the bed. She slept with one arm outstretched. Who or what was she reaching for? Even in sleep, did she somehow sense he was leaving her?

He remembered the last words she'd spoken before falling asleep. "Let me help you escape," she'd murmured. "Let me try again. Promise you'll let Will and me find a way to get you to safety."

He had whispered that she wasn't to worry; she had been too exhausted to realize that he hadn't made a promise. She would know when she awoke, though; he just hoped she would also know why he had left without her help.

He had already put her in too much danger. Once, he had believed Josiah Gallagher was an honorable man. Now he knew that if Gallagher suspected Tate's involvement in his escape, he would stop at nothing to silence her. The only way Simon could keep her safe was to disappear. From her house, from Arkansas, from her life.

He didn't want to. He wasn't a man who lied to himself. He didn't want to disappear. Even now, with his life nearly a thing of the past, he wanted to slip back into bed beside her, to caress and kiss her into wakefulness, to merge with her so totally that nothing else—not danger, not fear—was real.

Instead, he stepped away from the bed, taking one long last look at her. Then he turned and carried his clothes into the living area to dress. His leg throbbed unmercifully, but for the first time he had faith it would heal. It bore his weight, and that was all he could ask for. Luckily he had found a way to leave that didn't require much walking.

Last night, as he'd painfully hobbled through fields and forest, making his way back to the cabin, he had encountered a boat shed at the river's edge. Gauging what he knew of Tate's property lines, he had suspected the shed was hers. The task of picking the lock and investigating had been a simple one.

Inside, he'd found a rowboat upended on sawhorses and a sturdy pair of oars. In the moonlight, the boat looked as if it had seen some use, but he hadn't been able to gauge its seaworthiness. Now he was going to take a gamble. Millard Carter had been a man to keep and care for everything that crossed his path. Even if Millard had never used the boat, he would have kept it in good repair.

He had probably used the boat often, though. The walls of the shed had been lined with fishing gear, including a collection of rods and lures, a fishing vest and a battered rain hat sporting a feathered fly on the brim. All testified to Millard's enthusiasm for the sport.

Simon planned to make good use of all that gear today as he drifted down the river to freedom. He was going to pose as an Ozark angler, an ordinary man taking one final fishing trip before winter set in.

He knew if he waited until dark to launch the boat his chance of escaping detection was better, but he didn't want to spend even one móre day putting Tate at risk. He also knew enough about the river to realize that somewhere up ahead there was white water and waterfalls. People came from all over the country to raft the river rapids. Shooting them in a rowboat after dark was a wet, cold way to commit suicide.

He had no illusions that his pretense of fishing would be foolproof. His chances of escaping were fifty-fifty, perhaps even less, but he had no other choices. He was not staying in Mountain Glade even a day longer.

He dressed quickly, easing the jeans he'd worn yesterday over his bandaged leg. When he finished, he strapped the ersatz shoulder holster in place and checked his gun.

The sandwiches Tate had slapped together yesterday were still in the pocket of his parka. They were worse for wear, but they would have to do. He wanted to have the boat in the water before the sun rose.

The front door closed behind him, and he pressed his back to the log wall of the cabin, letting his eyes adjust. The silence of night was broken only once by the call of a wakening bird. Beyond him the forest was still, as if all its nocturnal prowlers were already in hiding and its day creatures not yet about. He listened hard, all senses alert, but only silence greeted him.

When he was satisfied, he crossed the porch and took the steps as quickly as he could, edging along the front of the cabin until he reached the corner. He knew he would be at his most vulnerable as he crossed the clearing to the grove of Christmas trees. He considered doing it on hands and knees, but decided against it. His leg wouldn't cope well with the strain.

He crossed the clearing as quickly as he could, leaning heavily on a large pine when he'd reached the safety of the trees. The silence still held as he gauged the best path to the boat house. He had two choices. One was shorter; one, under cover of the forest, was safer.

He chose the second. When he had rested, he wove his way through the Christmas-tree grove. There was another clearing to cross, and then, if he was judging correctly, he could stay in the woods until just before he reached the shed.

The journey took most of thirty minutes. As he traveled, the darkness seemed too quiet. Dawn was fast approaching, yet all he heard were intermittent bursts of birdsong. The forest seemed to be holding its breath, as if waiting for something.

As he drew closer to the river, he could taste its presence on the misty air, hear its subtle cadences. Days before, it had carried him to this place, to a woman he would wish for every day of his life, to a time of learning to share himself.

He was all too aware there was no guarantee it would carry him anywhere else.

Minutes later, he stood at the edge of the forest and stared at the boat shed. It was fifty yards away, bordered by brush and a grove of tulip poplars. A path had been cleared from another direction, obviously Millard's chosen route. Simon's only choice now was to make his own path. He stood quietly for a minute first, watching the river, watching the trees beyond him for any movement. Satisfied at last, he started through the brush.

At the shed he pulled the unlocked door toward him. The door opened with a rusty creak until he could prop it with a rock. Inside, the boat was just as he'd left it. He ran his hands over the keel, searching again, both with his eyes and fingers, for reasons to scrap his plan.

He managed to swing the boat off the first sawhorse without incident, although the increased pressure on his leg was agonizing. Before he swung it off the second, he gathered the supplies he would need: vest, hat, rods and tackle box. The vest fit neatly under his parka, the hat brim sank low enough on his forehead to help disguise his face.

When he was ready, he pulled the boat to the doorway and turned it on its side. Then, backing out, he slid it through.

A man's voice sounded behind him. "That'll do, Vandergriff. Just keep your hands on the boat, and don't move."

Simon didn't recognize the voice, but he recognized his own situation. It was a breath away from hopeless. He stood absolutely still, waiting for a gunshot. "At least let me see who you are," he said, buying time.

"Don't you know?" The man's voice sounded almost jovial. "I'm surprised."

"Let me turn around, and maybe we'll both be surprised."

"Put your hands over your head. Clasp them. That's right. Then turn slowly. No funny stuff, okay?"

It was more of a request than an order. Simon turned as slowly as he could. The voice hadn't been familiar, but the man it belonged to was. The last time Simon had seen him, the smiling young man had been in the company of Josiah Gallagher. He was chubby-cheeked and shiny-faced—and altogether deadly. "Barker," he acknowledged. "Where's your boss?"

Barker shook his head. "The name's Kinney today. Ben Kinney. Didn't the little brunette mention me?"

Simon never got a chance to answer. A figure materialized from the grove of trees behind Barker. The butt of a shotgun arabesqued through the air and descended across his skull. Barker crumpled and hit the ground before the shotgun had made a full arc.

"Thought you could sneak out on me?" Tate knelt over Barker, lifting his wrist to take his pulse, but her words were addressed to Simon.

"You could have gotten yourself killed!" Simon was beside her, lifting her up again before the words were out of his mouth.

"Your friend's going to have a heck of a headache."

"What do you mean, following me?" He shook her once for emphasis.

"You didn't even know, did you? That's how good you are at what you do. I could give you some lessons."

He didn't know whether to kiss her or shake her again. He pushed her away instead. "We've got to get out of here." Stooping, he grasped Barker under the arms and painfully began to drag him toward the boat shed. "Can you finish sliding the boat out? It's not heavy."

Tate beat him to the doorway and managed to move the boat. Then she watched dispassionately as Simon dragged Barker inside and left him there.

"Who is that guy?" she asked, as he slammed and locked the door.

Simon picked up the shotgun and tossed it into a patch of mountain laurel before he spoke. "Gallagher's right-hand man." He retrieved Barker's gun, which had fallen to the ground after Tate's attack, checked it, then handed it to her. "Do you know how to use this?"

She nodded. "Then Gallagher—"

"Isn't far behind." Simon drew his own gun and pulled her behind him. He started toward the woods, turning once to be sure she was with him.

"You were going to float down the river, weren't you?" she asked accusingly.

"Quiet!"

"You would have been a sitting duck!"

In the relative safety of the woods, he turned and jerked her against him. "Have you got any better ideas? I'm trying to get out of here. I'm trying to save your life."

"And what about your life? What good is mine, if you go and get yourself killed?"

"It's a life, which is more than I can give you if I stay around here."

"I told you, Will and I can get you to safety."

"You don't know who you're fooling with!" Simon dropped his arms. He was furious at her for risking her life for him, and he was furious with himself for ever involving her.

"I know your life's at stake. That's all I need to know." She stretched out a hand pleadingly, touching his cheek. "Let me help!"

"It's probably too damn late to help either of us." He shook off her hand and turned, limping through the forest as fast as he was able. His head turned from side to side, scanning the trees that bordered their trail. His gun was at his hip, ready to fire.

Tate stayed close behind him, Barker's gun dangling by her side. There was nothing she could do now, except shoot if she were forced to. She had probably just saved Simon's life, but if his words were true, she had also just delayed the inevitable. He was sure Gallagher was somewhere nearby, waiting to finish what his youthful sidekick had started.

She didn't dare speak, although she had a thousand questions, first and foremost why he hadn't said goodbye. Not that she really needed to ask. She already knew what Simon would say. The passion they had shared was over. She had willingly agreed to one night; he had never promised her more. Now all his energy was focused on escape, as it should be. Their time together had ended; no goodbye had been necessary.

Simon was moving as swiftly as he could, but it was still taking them too long to get back to the cabin. At one point she touched his shoulder and forced him to stop. "There's a better way," she whispered, pointing to a hollow to their left.

"You're sure?" he mouthed.

"When I was a runaway, my life depended on shortcuts and quick getaways." She took the lead, walking silently with a skill she'd acquired years before. Behind her, leaves and twigs crunched under Simon's halting steps.

The sun was rising, as they reached the last stand of trees before the clearing that led to the Christmas-tree grove. They waited, watching together.

"It looks okay," Tate said doubtfully.

"Okay is hardly good enough." Simon scanned the tree line and the clearing repeatedly, but his task was hopeless. There were more places to hide than there were people searching for him. "It looks like we're going to have to make a run for it. We'll do it in stages. Let's just get to the thickest part of the grove, then we'll do the last leg. I'm going first. You follow, if nobody starts shooting, but count to ten."

She held him back. "Let me go first. Nobody wants me. I'll just stroll out, like I've been for a walk in the woods. Then you can follow, if it looks all right."

He shook off her hand. "Nobody who's traced me here would be stupid enough to think you were out for fresh air." Before she could argue, Simon, bending low, started through the clearing. It was light enough now that he made a clear target, but no one seemed to care.

Tate counted to ten and started after him. He waited for her in the thickest patch of white pines. There was one more clearing to cross. From their vantage point it seemed a mile wide. "We'll do this the same way," Simon told her. "Wait until I'm almost to the porch."

She grabbed his arm. "Be careful."

"I've never needed anybody to tell me that," he said coldly.

"Somebody should have told you that before you let yourself get put behind bars in the first place!"

He wanted to be angry at her. Anger was the quickest way to sever the bond between them. But it wasn't anger that threatened to explode inside him. He was so worried about her that he couldn't concentrate. And he had never needed to concentrate more than he did now.

Anger wasn't going to work. Arrogance wasn't, either. Nothing was going to work. He could tell himself all the lies in the world, and when he was done, she would still fill his mind and heart. He covered her hand with his own and raised it to his lips. "Damn you," he said against her palm. "Just don't go getting yourself killed. Watch closely, and don't move if you suspect anything is wrong. Anything! Understand?"

"I've never needed anybody to tell me that!"

"Somebody should have told you that before you let a fugitive into your life, love." He dropped her hand. In a moment he was running low, zigzagging through the clearing.

She knew the meaning of "her heart in her throat" as she watched him cover the distance as quickly as he could. She couldn't breathe, and the pulse in her neck had the doomsday meter of a time bomb.

He was on the first porch step, when she began to follow. She imitated his crooked route, aware that it would make her a more difficult target if someone was going to fire.

The decision was a good one. She heard the unmistakable whine of a bullet as the ground her foot had just deserted exploded in a spray of rocky soil.

She didn't have time for fear, nor did she have time to trade fire. Instinctively, she knew that her best chance was to keep running. She put on a burst of speed. She heard another shot and realized Simon was firing from the porch. She ran faster, the ground beside her exploding once more.

She took the steps two at a time. Simon was behind one of the massive pillars supporting the porch roof. "Get inside!" he shouted.

There was no time to argue. She reached the door and flung it open, ducking behind it to wait for Simon.

"Don't even think about firing at me."

She heard the voice coming from the direction of the window behind her. Turning slowly, she saw a man, gun in hand, at the window's far edge.

"Simon, run!" she shouted, but it was too late. Simon was already inside, barring the door before the words were out of her mouth.

"I've got my gun on the woman, Simon," the man said. "Drop yours. You do the same," he said, motioning to Tate.

"Do it," Simon said from behind her.

She considered aiming at the man and firing.

"Do it, Tate!" Simon ordered.

She heard Simon's gun thud as it hit the floor. Reluctantly she dropped hers, too.

"Kick them this way."

Simon moved forward and kicked both guns toward the man. "Nice work, Gallagher. But you've got me now. There's no reason to hurt her." He continued to move, as he spoke, until he could rest his hands on Tate's shoulders. She felt the firm pressure and knew he was going to push her out of the way if Gallagher fired.

Gallagher, long awaited and finally here. Tate examined him with an objectivity that said everything about shock. He was Simon's height, but stockier. His hair was a mop of tamed chestnut curls, his cheekbones broad and strong, his mouth wide and unsmiling. He looked more like a tough Irish cop than a man who could betray his two best friends.

"Just what do you think I'm here for?" Gallagher asked. He looked more irritated than murderous.

"To finish what you started at High Ridge."

A shot rang out from the woods along the far side of the cabin. For a moment Tate didn't understand. Gallagher had the gun. But Gallagher wasn't shooting.

"Go ahead and call off your boys," Simon said. "We'll wait."

Gallagher's eyes flicked to the window. "I hate to break good glass," he said with distaste. "Old glass, too. That's the worst." In a minute, the pane was fragments on the porch floor and Gallagher was firing through the resulting hole.

There was another shot from the woods, then silence.

Gallagher spoke. "Not my boys, Simon. If I'm right, they're friends of yours. Hired killers. They've been after you for months."

"You've been after him!" Tate said.

"Shush, Tate." Simon moved her to one side, then behind him. Gallagher didn't seem to care. His gaze darted back and forth between them and the woods.

"What are you talking about?" Simon asked.

"The Knapp family. There's been a contract out on you for months now. One of the Knapps managed to arrange it from prison. There's one out on Aaron, too."

"Aaron's dead."

"Wrong. Aaron's in Hawaii, probably on a deep-sea fishing boat catching mahimahi at the taxpayers' expense. We'll never get him back to the mainland."

Gallagher turned his full attention to Simon. "Aaron's a lot smarter than you are. I could go to him, once I knew about the Knapps, and I could tell him we were going to protect him. You? You were a different story. You've never let anybody help you. I knew you'd refuse. The Petersen thing came up just about the same time. We decided you'd be safer in High Ridge than anywhere else we could think of, so we hired you to go in undercover. Only nothing went like we wanted it to. These guys kept slipping through our fingers. I couldn't tell you. I knew you'd make us release you, and you'd have been dead the minute you stepped out on the streets.''

"You expect me to believe this?" Simon asked.

"I expect you to use your head!" Another shot scudded along the ground, splintering a porch step. "You got a better explanation? Some reason I don't know about, why I'd want you and Aaron dead? I saved your neck once, remember? Why would I want to kill you, now?"

"You left me at High Ridge to rot! I'd have been dead in another month."

"I didn't know about Shaw, when we put you in! I knew he was harsh, but not corrupt. But I know now. We put Cooney on our payroll after you'd been there less than a week. He was watching over you all the time. With his help we would have gotten you out of there before anything happened."

"Why didn't he tell me, then?"

"He was under orders not to reveal anything. And you took him by surprise the night you ran." Two more shots were fired, and Gallagher fired one in return before he turned back to them.

Tate couldn't keep silent another moment. "Who are the Knapps?"

Simon didn't look at her. "The last case Gallagher hired me to help him with. A bunch of thugs in the Northwest."

"It looks like Aaron's fishing lessons took," Gallagher said, gesturing toward the hat Simon still wore. "But you look ridiculous." He stared at Simon for a moment, then, as if his assessment was positive, bent over and lifted both guns from the floor. He tossed one to Simon. "How well does she shoot?"

Simon caught the gun. "Ask her."

"Well enough to worry *you*," Tate said, holding out her hand.

"Can I trust her?" Gallagher asked Simon.

"Ask her."

"Simon, if he's telling the truth," Tate said, "Shaw's looking for you, and all the cops and troopers in Arkansas are looking for you, and the rest of Gallagher's men are probably still looking for you, and these Knapp characters are—"

"That's what it means to be wanted." Simon jerked his head toward Tate. Gallagher sighed and tossed the other gun in her direction.

She caught it and released the safety.

"Every bullet's going to count," Gallagher said, turning his back to both of them. "We tried to get to you before they did, and if you hadn't made it so damn hard, we might have. My men are combing the hills north of here. I've only got Barker with me, and I don't know where he disappeared to."

"He's taking a little nap," Simon said.

"Thanks a lot."

Simon grabbed Tate's hand, and then, bending low they ducked beneath the windows on the other side of the door. "Listen," he said, not sparing her a glance. "I want you to get in the cellar. The gun's to defend yourself, if somebody finds you who shouldn't."

"Dream on." Expertly she snapped it open and checked her ammunition. "I'm not leaving."

"Where did you learn to use a gun?" he demanded.

"Jess made sure both Kris and I learned, when he was afraid her crazy stepfather, the senator, was stalking us." She shot him a smile as she stationed herself at the side of the window. "My life's never been dull. And I'm still here. Breathing, too."

Simon knew they had no time to argue. "Just stay away from the window."

"I will. When I'm not shooting." She punctuated the last by shattering the glass on her side.

He finished the job, and the cabin sported another gaping hole. "You take any chances, and I'll throw you in the cellar!"

"We both know how easy that would be!"

"I do believe King Simon's met his match," Gallagher said from across the room. "If we get out of here in one piece, I want to hear this story."

"If we get out of here in one piece, you're not going to *stay* that way for long," Simon threatened.

"Hey, I only aimed to please." Gallagher gave one derisive laugh. "And right now I'm going to be pleased to aim."

Chapter 14

By the full light of morning it became obvious that three men, armed with semiautomatic weapons, were in the woods. If they were caught, neither they nor the imprisoned members of the Knapp crime family would ever see the light of day again as free men. But somehow, as bullets plowed into the cabin's thick log walls, that seemed a small compensation.

As he reloaded for the third and final time, Gallagher spoke. "How many bullets do you have left?"

"Enough to put two in every man out there," Simon said.

"Tate?"

"Three."

"Then we're going to stop firing. Let's draw them out."

"They won't fall for that, if they've watched even one old Western," Tate said, moving back against the wall.

"Put yourself in their shoes. They've got to make a run for us, sometime. They'll be most tempted, if we're not shooting at them. They're sure to be dressed for business. No bullet's going to get through the armor they're probably wearing." Simon lounged indolently against his portion of cabin wall, like a teenage thug on his favorite street corner.

"Then why have we been shooting at them?"

"We've been pretending. When they come for us, we'll be serious," Gallagher said.

"And you'll be in the cellar," Simon added, nodding to Tate.

She ignored him. "Where do I shoot? If they're wearing vests, do I aim for their heads?"

"She's good at heads," Simon told Gallagher. "She used the wrong side of a shotgun on Barker's."

Gallagher flashed Tate a smile. "Ever think about a career in law enforcement?"

"The two of *you* ought to think of a career in something else," she retorted. "You've botched this from the beginning."

"Tactful, too." Gallagher came to attention beside his window and pointed. "They're moving closer."

Simon peered out his corner, and Tate, hers. She saw several unnaturally swaying tree branches where Gallagher was pointing. "Will they rush us?"

"Most likely."

If they did, she wondered what the chances of survival were for anyone in the cabin. The three hit men were dressed and armed for deadly assault. She, Simon and Gallagher had only a handful of bullets between them.

She was still contemplating what seemed like the inevitable, when she realized Simon was at her side. No one seemed to be shooting at anyone anymore. She doubted that was a good sign.

"Will you stop being a tough guy for a minute?" Simon asked softly.

Tate's eyes flashed to Gallagher. He was pointedly looking away. She concentrated on Simon again. "I'm not going downstairs."

"Don't you get it? If you're up here, I'll be worrying about you. You'll be putting us both in danger."

She wanted to tell him to take a flying leap, but his concern was so obvious that the words died on her lips. "Maybe you're better at your job than I thought. You know exactly what to say, don't you?''

He brushed her hair back from her cheek and cleared his throat. ''Maybe I haven't said enough. I'll say it now, even if it doesn't change a damn thing. I love you.''

She was so caught off guard she could only stare. ''Do things look that bad?'' she asked at last.

''They don't look good.''

''Most people say a prayer before they die.''

''I just did.''

She tried to smile. ''I should have known it would take something like this to make you admit you loved me.''

He tried to smile, too. ''This or the apocalypse.''

''I'll be a lot more frightened downstairs than I would be up here with you.''

''If you're down there, I'll be a lot less frightened and a lot better shot.''

She moved into his arms, and he kissed her with all the passion that had been missing from his voice. Then he pushed her away. ''Don't disturb anything. Don't leave any clues where you've gone.''

''We could all go down and make them crazy.''

''If we all disappear, they won't stop looking until they've found us.''

''Simon—''

He didn't let her finish. ''Go!''

She held out her gun. ''Take this.''

''You might need it.''

''If they found me, I wouldn't have time to get off a shot.''

He accepted the weapon. ''Now go.''

''I love you, too.'' She turned and started toward the bedroom.

Simon watched her until she was out of sight.

''I hope you're not feeling quite as desperate as you sounded,'' Gallagher said dryly.

''Don't worry about your stinking neck, Josiah. I plan to pick off every last one of those bastards.''

''She's something else.''

"You always did have a way with words."

"Did I hear you say you loved her?"

"Only if you were eavesdropping."

"I was."

"Then you heard what you heard."

"Is it true?"

Simon answered with one of his most austere looks.

"She'd make a lovely queen, if they ever make you king of somewhere," Gallagher said with a laugh. "You've been on an emotional roller coaster, haven't you?"

"One of the first intelligent things you've said since our touching reunion."

"I never would have betrayed you." Gallagher wasn't laughing now.

Simon's eyes narrowed. "What you did was almost as bad."

"What I did, you made necessary."

"You could have come to me."

"And what would you have done?" Simon didn't answer, but Gallagher continued as if he had. "If I hadn't cared what happened to you, I could have let them kill you. You're good, Simon, but not good enough to have handled the Knapps on your own. You're not infallible. Never have been, never will be."

"I know."

"Do you?"

"I know." Simon bit off the words.

"Then that woman's taught you something." Gallagher turned all his attention back to the woods, and both men fell silent.

The cellar blocked all light and sound. With the trapdoor closed, Tate felt like the last person in the world—which, she suspected, was just the way Millard had wanted it.

Why else was the cellar so completely sealed and insulated? It was as impervious as a bomb shelter, a time capsule filled with all the life-enriching traditions of one mountain man's unique heritage.

Now, for good measure, crazy old Millard's museum might accidentally save the life of the daughter he had never been sure he had. Except that as Tate lit the one lantern she planned to allow herself, she felt anything but gratitude.

Nothing here could save the life of the two men above her. Nothing here could stop three hit men intent on earning their living. What good were dulcimers and carefully kept journals against the violence of semiautomatic weapons? She could sing every chorus and verse in the yellow shape-note hymnal lying on top of the pump organ in the corner, but it wouldn't keep Simon from dying.

Simon had said he loved her. Maybe he did, or maybe he had just said it to get her down to the cellar, but no matter which it was, Tate knew she had to find a way to help him. The last time she had sat quietly by and waited for someone to take care of her, she had been in a playpen.

Resolutely she began to investigate the shelves, one by one. Maybe dulcimers and hymnals weren't going to do the trick, but there had to be something here that could help. And with the age-old partners, imagination and desperation, she was going to find it.

"I think they're about to make their move." Gallagher squatted beside the window for better aim and protection.

"They're going to be coming from different directions."

"Damn! We need something to make them take notice!"

"How about a blonde?"

"How about an Uzi?"

"How about this?" Tate joined Simon at his window. It was a measure of the two men's concentration that they hadn't heard her coming back up.

"I told you—"

"To be a good girl. I was. I've been downstairs saving your lives." Tate thrust an antique bottle that she had filled with her father's homemade whiskey toward him. The neck had been plugged with a pair of her bikini panties taken from the bedroom dresser. "You'd prefer a blonde?" she asked, as Simon stared at her invention.

"What the hell is this?"

"Apparently you haven't been to any of the world's hot spots."

"You think this thing is a Molotov cocktail?"

"It's a bomb. Primitive, maybe, but useful. I didn't have time to split any atoms down there."

"What is it?" Gallagher asked.

Tate answered before Simon could. "Pure grain alcohol, as flammable as gasoline. The wick's one-hundred-percent cotton."

"The wick's a pair of your panties!" Simon said.

She shrugged. "I can buy more."

"You have one for me?" Gallagher asked.

"I've got one for each of us. I only had time to make three."

"Can you get it over here?"

"If Simon will let go of me." Tate shook the arm Simon had wrapped his fingers around.

"Let her go," Gallagher ordered. "There's not much chance they'll work, but we haven't lost a thing if they don't."

"You don't have time to drag me down to the cellar." Tate covered Simon's hand with hers. "I'm here. I'm going to stay long enough to throw my bottle."

"Then you'll go back down?"

"I promise." She didn't add that she'd be returning with another round of cocktails. He wouldn't be amused.

The moment he dropped her arm, she bent low and took one of the bottles to Gallagher. Then she returned to Simon's window, standing on the side that had recently been hers.

"I doused all the pants with some of Millard's mountain dew," she said. "They'll burn fast."

Gallagher sniffed his bottle. He spoke when he'd finished coughing. "What a waste of good corn whiskey."

Simon ignored him. "The trick's going to be throwing them at the right moment. Too soon, and the wick'll go out in midair. Too late, and it could go off in your hand. I'll say when to light and throw. When they're close enough, aim for the ground at their feet."

Tate looked at him with horror.

"They'll be rushing us any second," he affirmed.

"Then I was just in time."

"That's one way to look at it."

"Don't be mad."

"Then don't be stupid."

"I'll be careful."

"I'll bet."

A movement in the woods cut the conversation short. There was a burst of gunfire, and one by one the three men appeared.

"Get down."

"I'm down." Tate squatted beside the window, as Gallagher and Simon were doing. She prayed the chestnut timbers would continue to stop the killers' bullets.

"How far do you think you can throw?" Simon asked.

Her tongue felt like cotton, but she tried to sound brave. "I was pitcher on the Stagecoach Inn softball team."

"Why don't I feel better?"

"Because you never saw me pitch." Tate slid a pack of matches toward him. She didn't dare look out the window. Simon was keeping to one side, but he still managed a view.

"Damn, these guys are dressed like a SWAT team," he muttered.

"What are they doing?"

"Running for the Christmas trees."

There was another round of fire. "How close are they?" she asked.

"Almost there."

"I planted some of those seedlings myself!"

"I'll yell at them, if they step on any."

"You can be a real jerk, sometimes." Tate tore off a match. She knew the men would have to be almost halfway to the porch before she could throw. But she was going to be ready.

Simon slid the gun she had been using back to her. "Here. Just in case."

She waited, and refused to think that everyone in the cabin could be dead in minutes. She had to believe her homemade bottle bombs would buy them time, maybe even put one or two of the men stalking them out of commission.

Gallagher was first to predict the final rush. He shouted over the next round of shots, "Okay, get ready."

Simon needed no more direction than that. He struck a match, holding it well away from the wick, and waited. Tate did the same. She watched his face and knew the moment the killers began their last dash.

"Light," he said gruffly.

The panties flared like a sparkler on the Fourth of July. In less than a second, they were engulfed in flame.

"Throw!"

Tate rose and with one graceful movement swept her hand parallel with her shoulder. Then, with every bit of her strength, she heaved the flaming bottle out of the window. Ducking to the side she listened to the joyful music of three explosions. Like a burst of jubilant percussion, it could have been the central theme of a symphony.

Simon reported results. "One man's down. He won't be getting up."

Tate marveled at his calm voice.

"Second man's running. Third man's . . ." He raised his gun and fired.

Gallagher began shooting, too. Tate could hear shots being returned. She peeked out the window, gun in hand. One man was almost to the porch, face down on the blackened ground. It took her longer to find the others. She finally located them in the Christmas-tree grove.

"How long will they stay there?" she asked.

"Until we're out of ammunition . . . and whiskey."

"This isn't the Alamo! Somebody's going to hear the shots and come."

"It's deer season. Nobody'll give shots a second thought."

"Will will."

"That's quite a stutter." Simon aimed a terse smile in her direction. "You bought us some time," he said, before she could explode like one of her bombs. "Somebody might come."

Tate knew she was being placated. "What about you?" she said, spinning to face Gallagher. "You're supposed to have walkie-talkies or something. Can't you send for backup?"

"My radio doesn't work worth—" He stopped himself. "It doesn't work in the mountains."

"Bunglers, both of you!"

"Go see what else you can find in the cellar," Simon said. "We'll bungle better up here without you." There was another round of gunfire.

"Don't bother," Gallagher said. "By the mole on my sainted grandmother's nose." He pointed out the window. "That was the sound of shotguns. Will you look who's come calling?"

"I'll be damned." Simon lowered his gun slowly. "Will-will came through."

Tate knew better than to ask what was happening. One look was worth a thousand of Simon's explanations. The risk seemed minor compared to not knowing.

At first she thought nothing had changed. Two of the men were still in the Christmas-tree grove; one man was on the ground. She glanced away from them, her gaze darting toward the horizon. As she watched shadows began to move slowly toward the cabin.

Shadows with guns.

"Will..." She leaned back against the wall.

"Will and about ten of his friends." Simon leaned back, too. "Do you want to break the news, or shall I?" he asked Gallagher.

"Let me." Gallagher moved out of all range of fire. "This is Josiah Gallagher of the Justice Department. Throw down your weapons," he shouted. "You're surrounded."

The cracks of ten rifles from the forest beyond strengthened his words.

"We know who you are and who sent you," Gallagher shouted, in case the message hadn't been clear. "You won't get out of here alive, unless you put your guns down and your hands up.''

The silence was as loud as the previous rounds of fire.

"This is going to take a while," Simon said, after a tense minute. "They were walking arsenals."

"Were? They're dropping their guns?" Tate abandoned caution and peered out the window. "They're dropping their guns!"

"They don't know who's shooting at them. They probably think it's cops or some more of Gallagher's men."

"They'd be better off with cops. Cops have some sense. I'm not sure my family does, but they do have guts, don't they?" Tate said proudly.

"Hillbilly justice."

"It saved your life."

"I've been lucky, from the start, to know the Carters, haven't I?" He didn't wait for a response. "Ready, Josiah?"

"I don't think they're bluffing, but let's be ready to shoot, anyway." Gallagher moved to the door and met Simon there. "Stay low, Tate. At least until we've got their weapons."

Simon and Gallagher hit the front porch at the same moment, their guns aimed at the men at the edge of the Christmas-tree grove. Like surrealistic sugar-plum fairies, the Knapps' hired killers swayed against the trees, hands over their heads and their feet wide apart.

The rest was over in minutes. Both men were efficiently searched as Tate's family, both male and female, swarmed out of the woods. Tate recognized Will and Dovey, Andy and the preacher of their church. She left the cabin and found herself in the embrace of people she hadn't even met. She ended up in Will's arms for a final hug.

"You saved our lives," she told him.

"You're Millard's girl. He'd a' done the same thing for one of mine."

"Would he?"

"Darn right."

"Maybe you can tell me some more about Millard?"

"Just been waitin' for you to ask."

She gave him one more long hug before he went to help Dovey, who was monitoring the pulse of the fallen hit man. Tate looked for Simon and found him off to one side talking to Gallagher. Before she could reach him, the wail of a siren silenced the excited, self-selected posse.

The siren grew louder, bouncing off the surrounding hills until siren and echoes were indistinguishable. Tate made her way to Simon's side just as the sheriff arrived.

"No one's ever going to believe this," she said, grabbing Simon's arm. "What if he tries to take you back to High Ridge?"

"You don't have to worry about that." He covered her hand, but he didn't look at her.

Monroe Howard eased himself out of his car and squinted at the crowd surrounding the men lying on their backs, hands folded as if in prayer. He muttered something to the deputy, who had gotten out, too. Both men looked distinctly disappointed that all the fun was over.

"Somebody gonna tell me what's going on?" Monroe asked.

Will strolled to the front. "Took you long enough to get here, Howard. That radio of yours still workin'?"

"We been down south of here..." His voice trailed off as he saw Simon.

Gallagher moved away from the others and reached in his pocket, flashing his badge at the sheriff.

Monroe nodded curtly. "I know who you are. You can put that thing away. We're informal-like 'round here. Just tell me he's not who he looks like." He inclined his head toward Simon.

"He works for me."

Monroe rolled his eyes. They were still rolling minutes later, when Gallagher had finished a short explanation. "Why the you-know-what didn't someone tell me what was goin' on? You Feds ever think about workin' with us locals, for a change? This top-secret stuff makes about as much sense as a pig in a penthouse."

"We didn't want any of this to get back to Shaw. With Simon's testimony, we've got a strong case against him. We didn't want him getting rid of any more evidence than he probably already has."

Monroe still looked disgruntled. "I'm no friend of Shaw's. He won't hear about it from me."

"We need your help to get Vandergriff out of here. I could drive him out in the trunk of my car, but his leg's been injured, and I'd rather not."

"Well now, that's something I can do. Not hard a'tall. When do you want to leave?"

"I've got a man lying around here somewhere with a bad headache. And these three have to be dealt with." Gallagher gestured to the men on the ground. "One of them's got some burns, but the woman over there tells me he's not hurt bad." He nodded toward Dovey.

"We'll load 'em up in my car." Monroe signaled to his deputy, who along with several Carter family members began the process of reading the men their rights and moving them.

"I sent somebody down to the boat shed to get Barker as soon as the shooting stopped," Tate said. "He'll take the short way, so he should be back in a minute." She followed Simon forward to join Gallagher and the sheriff. His hand was still clasped over hers.

Monroe gave her a long assessing look. "Carter through and through," he pronounced at last, shaking his head.

"Thank you."

"Don't thank me. It's a mighty heavy cross to bear."

She smiled. "I guess I'll manage."

"I guess you'll have to."

"Looks like the other problem's solved." Gallagher nodded to the forest break. Barker and a young man were coming through the trees. Barker looked like a freshman quarterback who had just suffered his first defeat.

They waited for him to join them. "If you'd held off bashing in my head just a minute more," Barker told Simon, once he was standing in the circle, "I would have explained what was going on."

"I held off," Simon pointed out. "She didn't." His hand still covered Tate's.

She felt the warm pressure all through her. Simon hadn't looked at her, but neither had he been able to drop her hand. She wondered just what he was feeling. "I'm sorry I hit you," she told Barker. "At the time, it seemed the thing to do."

He rubbed the back of his head, but he shot her a rueful grin.

"Barker'll go with you into town," Gallagher told the sheriff. "We'd appreciate you keeping our friends here in jail until we can get all the paperwork done."

"My pleasure." Monroe extended his hand, and the two men shook.

"You never said just how you were going to help me get Vandergriff out of here," Gallagher said.

Monroe nodded. "That's right. I didn't." He still didn't. Instead, he strolled over to his car and reached through the open window for his radio. He made brief official chitchat, then turned so that everyone could hear him.

"Listen, connect me to the search command center. I think we've finally got Petersen cornered. Yeah, Petersen." He lounged against the car while the connection was made. "Search command center's nuthin' but Glenn Austin's garage in town," he told Gallagher. "We had to call it that, to keep you Feds happy."

Another voice came over the radio, and he waited until it had finished. "Yeah, Sheriff Howard here. We've got the break we needed. Right." He listened to the static-laden voice, then cut it short. "Stop flappin' your gums, woman. Petersen's been spotted twice in the last ten minutes, down in the old stone quarry south of here. Yeah, the one down by Two Chimneys. He's done some shooting, too. Looks like it's gonna take everybody to get him."

He waited until the disembodied voice on the other end was silent once more. "That's right. Get everybody down there. All our boys, the troopers, the prison folks. Tell 'em to clear the roadblocks. No sense in anybody missin' out on the fun." He signed off and switched off the radio.

"The roads'll be safe in ten minutes," he predicted. "I just hope nobody gets killed racin' down to Two Chimneys."

"How far is it?"

"Fifty miles south. You'd better go north."

Gallagher nodded. "My car's parked down the road. I'm going to go get it. Then I'll come back and get Vandergriff."

The sheriff nodded. "The timing should be just about right."

Tate realized her neighbors were drifting back the way they had come. She pulled her hand from Simon's to say a final thank-you and goodbye to each of them, promising over and over again that she would come visit just as soon as things returned to normal. Last of all, she kissed Will's cheek and hugged Dovey. "I can't remember everybody's name," she admitted. "All those people are really related to me?"

"Some more than others. Kissin' kin, some of them," Dovey said. "You and Simon, you gonna be kissin' kin, too?"

"I...I don't—"

"Don't go nosin' where you're not wanted," Will warned his wife.

"If I hadn't gone nosin' this morning, this girl'd still be gettin' shot at."

"Dovey was the first one to hear shootin'," Will explained. "She'd picked up the phone and called everybody for a mile around before she even woke me up."

"We take care of our own." Dovey nodded toward Simon. "But there's nothing to do about that one, is there?"

"He takes care of himself. Usually," Tate added.

"C'mon. Shootin' makes me hungry." Will took Dovey's arm and gave Tate an exaggerated wink.

She watched them head through the woods toward their home.

Behind her an engine coughed and sputtered, then roared to life. She turned to see Monroe, his deputy, Barker and a backseat full of subdued bad guys crowded into the sheriff's car. She didn't envy any of them the trip into town.

Only Simon was left standing nearby, and she knew that was only for a few minutes. She joined him as the car pulled away.

"Gallagher's gone to get his car." He didn't touch her.

"Then you'll be leaving." She hesitated. It seemed so odd to be talking like two people who hardly knew each other. But she didn't know what to say in the short time left to them. "Do you have everything you need?"

"The only thing I need is the diskette." He fished it out of his shirt pocket and held it up. "You can keep the cuffs, but Cooney would probably like his gun back."

Her gaze met his and held. "There's something I want to know," she said softly. "What you said to me this morning. Was it true?"

"Tate—"

"No stories, Simon. And no promises. I just want to know."

"This wasn't real. Nothing that happened here was real."

"What you said wasn't real?" She watched him struggle—with himself, with his answer, with the seconds left to them.

"You have your whole life ahead of you," he said finally.

"We always have our lives ahead of us. Until the second we die. I'm asking you if you love me. You owe me an answer."

"What good are answers? If I said yes, you'd be waiting for me to come back."

"I haven't asked you to come back."

"You're a beautiful woman, everything a man could want."

"Spare me the compliments." She folded her arms and turned toward the cabin. "You're right about nothing being real this last week, Simon. I didn't even know who you were, not for a long time. Maybe I still don't."

She felt hands on her shoulders. Strong hands with strong, slender fingers. "You know who I am. You told me yourself once. I'm a man who lives in shadows."

"No, you told me the real answer. You're a man who plays at being a hero. I'll tell you about real heroes, Simon. They don't go off seeking adventure. They're men and women who can be honest about what they feel, who make commitments and share themselves, who deal with life's problems whenever they come up against them. They're men like Will and men like Jess."

She turned to face him. "You know, I never thought about it before, but you and Millard have a lot in common. He thought he was some kind of hero, too. He lived in his log monument to the past, telling folktales and cataloging bits and pieces of Ozark culture. He made a halfhearted effort to love my mother and even to find her when she vanished. But if he hadn't been so busy trying to be a folk hero, he would have found her and he would have known for sure about me. Then he really might have made a difference in the world!"

"I'm not your father."

"Maybe not. But you're like him. You're living proof that my mother and I had something in common, after all."

He thrust his hands in his pockets; his eyes were smoky and filled with secrets.

"I wanted to know if you loved me," she said, when he didn't answer. "I guess that's asking too much. But if my life's ever threatened again, if I need somebody who'll hijack an airplane or start a revolution, I'll be sure to look you up."

A nondescript blue sedan rolled over the last hill of her drive and pulled to a stop on the road beside them. Tate watched Gallagher get out and approach. It was better than watching Simon.

"Ready?" Gallagher clapped his hand on Simon's back. "We've got to get you out of here fast."

"I'm ready." Simon didn't take his eyes from Tate.

She looked at Gallagher as she spoke. "Have a safe journey."

"I'll take good care of him."

"If he'll let you." Her eyes flicked back to Simon, and she saw he was still watching her.

"For whatever it's worth," he said, "I meant it."

She stared at him, then shook her head slowly. "You're the only one who knows what it's worth, Simon."

He buried one hand in her hair and pulled her close. His kiss was hard and quick; then he let her go.

She didn't say a word as he limped to the car. Instead, she turned and started up the slope to the cabin. Cinn, who had survived the hailstorm of bullets from a safe vantage point, gave one mournful howl as Simon was driven away.

Chapter 15

"*W*hen one brilliant star hangs in the midnight sky like God's own night-light, folks hereabouts call it a wise-man star. I can't think of a reason to call it anything else, can you? Even the wisest of us needs help finding his way sometimes.

"There's always been a wise-man star on Christmas Eve as long as I've been alive—and sometimes I think I've been alive forever. The star has always been there, reminding me that there's something out there to search for, something that needs finding.

"The wise men weren't just wise, they were brave. It took courage to go looking for that tiny baby in the manger. Not because they could have gotten lost. No, getting lost was the least of their troubles. It took courage because the baby might just get himself found, and once he was, well, lives were going to be changed forever. The son of God can do that to you.

"The son of man can do that to you, too—or the daughter of man. Go looking for the baby in the manger or the hospital, or in the pitiful, thin arms of a starving mother, and your life is changed forever, too. Some of us can't find

*our camels to make that search. We sit home, and we search
for the star instead. And when it hangs high in a Christmas
Eve sky, then it's just the same thing as being told we're not
all we were meant to be.*

*"But ain't it wonderful the way the wise-man star just
goes ahead and shines on, anyhow? Every Christmas Eve it
shines. Maybe it's God's way of egging us on. Or maybe it's
His way of telling us He loves us, anyway, even if we've put
our camels out to pasture this year.*

"I'd like to think so anyway, wouldn't you?"

Tate stopped reading and closed her father's journal,
setting it on the table at her side. For a moment, only the
crackling of the logs in the fireplace broke the stillness.

Krista, who was sitting beside her on the sofa, covered
Tate's hand. "What a wonderful legacy he left you. Not
many of us ever know what our parents really thought about
anything."

"I've got Millard's journals and Jess's books. I guess I'm
extra lucky." Tate smiled at both Krista and Jess, who was
standing behind his wife. Dark-haired Jess, still tan from his
successful weeks in the Mid-East, was a perfect backdrop
for Krista's pale-skinned, golden-haired beauty.

"Everything about this place is amazing," Jess said.
"The cabin, the land, Millard's cellar. But his journals are
more than amazing. They're priceless. They should be
shared."

"I know. I've had time to study them lately. He had so
much to say about everything. I guess living alone gave him
a lot of time to think. Apparently he was good at it. Will
tells me he could ask Millard a question and he'd be so deep
in thought it would take him a week to hear it and another
week to think of an answer."

Jess laughed. "It sounds like twisting words around runs
in the Carter family."

"I live in fear that one day I'll wake up and start spout-
ing tales."

"Well, the one about Simon Vandergriff wasn't bad for
a start," Krista said, squeezing Tate's hand.

Tate felt a familiar stab of pain. She made her voice purposely light. "And it even had the requisite happy ending, didn't it? Captain Shaw's going on trial, and according to what Jess has been able to find out, Simon's back in Washington playing James Bond."

Krista sent Jess a quick worried glance before she answered. "I guess now the question is…are you happy?" She gestured to the interior of the cabin. Evergreen boughs hung in graceful, ribbon-bedecked swags on the mantel and around the door and windows. A huge pine reached from floor to ceiling in one corner, decorated with popcorn and cranberries and turn-of-the-century ornaments that Tate had unearthed from a box in the cellar.

"This cabin is amazing," she continued. "And the way you've fixed it up for the holidays is wonderful, honey. But is this enough for you? You're so alone here."

"Not as alone as you'd think. Now that the Carters are sure I want to be family, somebody's visiting all the time. I have to shoo kids and dogs out the door on an hourly basis."

She went on, before Krista could say more. "I can't do a lot with the land in the winter, but when spring comes I'll be planting more Christmas trees and making a garden. In the meantime, I'm going to start typing up some of Millard's journal entries to see if anyone is interested in publishing them."

"That's a good idea," Jess said. "I was going to suggest it."

"Then it must be a good idea," Tate said, sending him a grateful smile. "And you'll give me advice?"

"And contacts."

"You could come back to Virginia for the winter, bring the journals with you and work on them there," Krista said, worrying out loud.

"Kris, I'm almost twenty-two. You've got to let go." Tate put her arm around Krista and rested her cheek for a moment against her blond curls. "I'm not that raggedy kid from the New Orleans streets anymore."

"You're not a kid anymore, period," Jess said. He rested one hand on each of their shoulders. "I'm proud of you for living here and making something of this place."

"But all those bullet holes in the logs out front!" Krista shuddered.

"Not a one in me." Tate was glad Krista hadn't seen the condition of the cabin before new glass had been installed and the porch steps rebuilt.

"Kris is feeling a bit overly maternal these days," Jess apologized.

Tate hugged Krista. One day earlier Jess's words would have been a mystery to her. But yesterday, just after their arrival, Jess and Krista had popped the cork on a bottle of champagne to tell her that her status as an only child was about to change.

"I still can't believe I'm going to have even more family," Tate said. "Carters, Cantrells, not to mention the Claytons. When will it end?"

"We're planning at least two children, maybe three, one right after the other," Krista warned. "We're going to inundate you with sisters and brothers, so you'll have a reason to come back and visit."

"And as long as I stay here, you can bring them for an old-fashioned Arkansas Christmas."

Jess glanced at his watch. "Speaking of which, isn't it just about time for the Claytons to get here?"

Tate stood. Krista's sister, Anna, and her husband and son were coming to spend the holiday, too. "Will's supposed to be back from the airport with them anytime, now. Dovey wants us to go over to their house to wait. She's invited some of the rest of the Carters over to meet all of you. She's fixing squirrel dumplings for dinner."

Krista swallowed audibly.

"And chicken for the squeamish," Tate promised.

"It's snowing." Jess went to the window and peered out. "It's a perfect Christmas Eve."

Tate wanted to believe that. Jess and Krista were here, and Anna and her family were coming. With one exception, all the people Tate loved most in the world were going to be with her for the holidays.

With one exception.

"Let's walk over." Jess turned away from the window. "Do you feel like it, Kris?"

"I'd love to." She stood. "Tate, can you guide us?"

Tate tried to shake off the grief that always filled her when she thought about Simon. "Let me tell you how to get there. I'll be along in a little while. I've got some chores to do here first." She waved aside Jess's offer of help. "No, you and Kris go ahead. I want to change my clothes, too. You can have a romantic walk through the woods without me."

She gave them directions and watched as they buttoned themselves into winter coats. Jess wrapped a long yellow scarf around Krista's neck, gently lifting her hair over it. His tenderness tightened the knot in Tate's stomach. Not because Krista and Jess loved each other, but because of what was missing in her own life.

She called goodbye and watched from the porch to be sure they took the right path through the woods, since it was fast getting dark and she didn't want them to get lost.

She wasn't surprised that snow was already powdering the landscape. The smoke from her chimney had been rising in curls since that morning, and according to one of Millard's books, that was a sure sign that snow was expected. According to the same book, she should be able to tell how much snow they were about to get by the size of the snowflakes. She just couldn't remember whether big flakes or little flakes meant a heavy snowfall. Nor did she much care.

When was everything going to stop reminding her of Simon? Less than two months ago, she hadn't even known him. Why couldn't she go back to that time? Then a snowfall would have been just a lovely new way of seeing her surroundings. Now it made her feel lonely for warm arms around her.

She hadn't forgotten how Simon's arms felt, or how his kisses tasted. She hadn't forgotten lying together in front of the fireplace, their bodies entwined.

There were other things about him she hadn't forgotten, couldn't forget even if she had tried. His long, elegantly tapering fingers. The smoky warmth of his eyes. The unconsciously regal way he held his head. The broad, muscular expanse of his back.

Krista would never know how tempted Tate had been to take her up on the offer to go back to Virginia. The cabin was filled with too many memories, but even so, she couldn't bring herself to part with them yet. She wouldn't live here for the rest of her life. Someday the cabin would be nothing more than a summer place, a retreat from the frantic pace of the rest of the world. But now it was a museum to her memories, as well as to Millard's Ozark heirlooms. She wasn't ready to let go of the little part of Simon she still had.

When Krista and Jess were out of sight, Tate turned and went back inside. Just a brief spell on the porch had been enough warning that, heavy snow or light, the night was going to be cold. She had learned to live without central heat, but her guests were going to have enough hardships with outdoor plumbing and a wood cookstove. The least she could do was throw another armful of logs on the fire now and raise the temperature before she went to Will's. Then, with a good bed of coals waiting for her, she could make a fire quickly when she returned.

She threw the last of the logs from the hearth on the fire and drew the screen in front of it. She would need more wood to get comfortably through the night, and she slipped on her jacket and work boots to go out to the woodpile. There was water to haul and geese to ply with corn. And unless Cinn had followed Jess to Will's house, she had one chauvinistic hound dog to feed and bed down in the straw in the barn.

Chores, backbreaking and ever-demanding, had gotten her through the weeks since Simon and Gallagher had driven away. Now she was glad for the hard work ahead of her tonight.

Simon slowly threaded his way through the trees. There had been another night in the not-too-distant past, when he had made his way through these same woods by the light of a giant amber moon. As if to remind him, his leg throbbed. Actually, it was the temperature that caused it. The thermometer was dropping, and although his leg was completely healed, it was still sensitive to both heat and cold. Weeks of physical therapy had helped alleviate his limp, but it would be many more weeks before he could forget he had ever been shot.

Other things wouldn't be so easy to forget.

He wondered if he was on a wild-goose chase. What right did he have to think that Tate might still be here, waiting for him? He hadn't written; he hadn't tried to make contact through Will or the sheriff. He hadn't needed to ensure her of his safety, because he knew it had been obvious that with Gallagher's protection he was no longer in danger.

Six weeks ago he had left her, steeling himself against backward glances. He had told himself it was best that way. He had little to offer any woman, and nothing to offer one as intense and passionate as Tate. She needed commitment, stability and enough love to wipe away all the loneliness and trauma of her childhood. He was more experienced at rescuing people than loving them.

Funny, wasn't it, the things a man could tell himself when he was frightened?

He supposed it was also fear that had made him park on the road, instead of driving straight up to her door. This way he could hike the crazy quilt of forest and field until he had his first view of the cabin. He had no clear idea what clues he was looking for, or what would make him cross that last clearing and knock on her door. Perhaps he had just needed these extra minutes in the icy mountain air to rehearse what he would say. Or even to decide if he would say it.

Whatever the reason, he knew he was nearing the spot where he would be able to glimpse both the cabin and the river far below. Yesterday Aaron had informed him that the river held some of the finest bass and trout in the Ozarks.

He'd even threatened to come and show Simon how to catch them, if Simon stayed a while.

Simon had told him not to pack just yet.

Leaves and finely powdered snow crunched under the soles of his boots. The moon was just peeking through the trees, but it shone with a soft glow put to shame only by one incredible star hanging over the cabin roof. Simon stopped and took in the scene of Christmas-card splendor. The cabin's tin roof was white with snow that glistened like billions of tiny diamonds under the caressing celestial beams. Smoke curled from the chimney, an encouraging sign, but no lights shone from within.

It was Christmas Eve. Tate might be anywhere, at church, in town, with relatives. There was a strange car parked beside the cabin. Perhaps she was showing company the sights. Perhaps her visitor was another man.

His eyes narrowed, as he considered that possibility. What did he know of her, really? Their time together had been so short. They hadn't talked of other loves. She had come to him a virgin, but he wasn't foolish enough to think he was the first man to pursue her. Even Gallagher and Barker mentioned her now, every chance they got, like two love-smitten idiots. Simon was beginning to think both men were envious of where danger had led him, never mind that he had almost died.

The night was too cold for him to stand and make guesses about where she might be and with whom. He could go back the way he had come and write her a letter, or he could continue on to find some answers.

The choice was the first simple one he'd made in six weeks.

Tate lunged for Cinn one more time, only to have him slip out of her grasp. He obviously had plans for the night, and they didn't include sleeping in the barn. He gave her a big-eyed, soulful stare, then turned his nose to the rising moon and howled.

Tate dusted her hands on her jeans and gave up the battle. Cinn hadn't slept inside once since Simon had left, but with Jess, Grady and Ryan sleeping in the cabin tonight, she imagined she could coax him in to the rug in front of the fireplace. Man's dog that he was, he would be in canine ecstasy. As she watched, he trotted off to the front of the cabin, almost as if he had read her mind.

She had hauled water and done what she could for the geese and dog. Now she had only to fill the wagon with firewood. In the first agonizing days after Simon left, she had split enough logs to last the winter. Tonight, everyone would benefit.

When all the wood was loaded, she began to pull the wagon up the slope to her back porch. She welcomed the heavy load as a job almost finished. Before she brought in enough logs to last the night, she would heat a kettle of water, so she could wash after she stacked the wood. Then she would change and drive over to Will's. A walk through the snowy, silent forest on Christmas Eve seemed torturously sentimental.

At the porch she anchored the wagon and began to haul the logs up the steps. When she'd finished, she grabbed one load to carry inside with her and opened the back door to start toward the fireplace.

A man stood in the center of the room, illuminated only by a thin, golden wash of moonlight. She stopped, but the panic she felt was different from what she'd experienced the first time she had seen him.

"Simon!"

"Aren't you supposed to drop the logs . . . or throw them at me?"

The firewood grew heavier in her arms, but she clutched it like a precious burden. His hair was longer now than the regulation High Ridge cut. He was wearing a dark wool overcoat with a subtly striped scarf and pants he hadn't had to roll the cuffs on. He stood even taller, weight easily distributed on both legs, as if he were no longer in pain.

He seemed untouchably elegant, the distant heir to a foreign throne instead of the man she had fallen in love with.

"You do have a way of sneaking up on people," she said at last. She started to cross the room to deposit her logs on the hearth, but he intercepted her, taking part of the burden to lighten her load.

His arms brushed hers, and she stepped away. "I saw a car out front," he said. "Is somebody else here?"

"Jess and Kris, but they're over at Will's right now. I'm expecting more company, but I wasn't expecting you." She dropped her logs on the hearth with a thud. "Damn it, Simon, I wasn't expecting you! You never wrote. You never tried to get in touch with me, at all. And now you just waltz into my house like I should be glad to see you!"

"Are you?" He dropped his logs and turned her to face him.

"I don't know."

"I couldn't stop thinking about you."

"You had a strange way of showing it." She crossed her arms and lifted her chin. "For all I knew, you were off in Europe doing your royal duty, or stealing somebody's computer secrets, or getting shot at again."

"I've been in D.C. You know where I've been, because you had Jess Cantrell check up on me."

Her chin jutted another notch. "I risked my neck more than once for you. I thought I deserved to know if *yours* was still in one piece."

"You had him check because you care about me."

"Never assume anything. Didn't they teach you that in Undercover 101?"

"You'd be surprised what I've learned. For instance..." One hand glided down her sleeve to her elbow. Gently he pried one arm from the other and stripped off her glove. "Your hands are cold."

She tried to shake him loose. "It's snowing outside."

"Yes, but your gloves are fur-lined. And the snow wouldn't explain why your hand isn't quite steady." He clasped it with his own.

She could feel the warmth of his skin flowing right through her, but she tried to ignore it. "It's not steady because you scared me to death."

"I probably do scare you. You scare me. When I'm with you, I don't know who I am."

"You could have solved that problem by not coming back."

He lifted her hand to his lips and kissed her fingers, one by one. She squeezed her eyelids shut and squelched the absurd desire to cry.

"I don't want to be a fugitive, anymore," he said, holding her hand against his cheek.

She swallowed hard. "I had to learn to stop running. Can you? It's not easy, Simon."

"You're running right now. I asked if you were glad to see me, and you ran."

"Yes. I'm glad to see you."

He pulled her into his arms and clasped her against him. "I've wanted to come back. Every day I've been away. I couldn't write, because I didn't know what to say."

"I never asked you to say anything!" She lifted her face to his earnestly. "I never asked you *for* anything. If you're here because you think you owe me—"

"I'm here because I want to be!" He cut off the possibility of an answer with a kiss. Then, for a long moment, there was no possibility of words, at all. Her scarf yielded to his fingers and adorned the floor at their feet until her jacket covered it. She was as greedy to touch him as he was her, and his coat and scarf followed the path of hers.

"I planned to do this with a little more finesse," he said shakily, his fingers tunneling through her hair, his lips against her forehead, her cheeks.

"I don't want finesse. I want you." She arched against him, emphasizing her words.

"I promise you both. Someday." He finished undressing her with the haste of a child tearing the wrapping paper of a Christmas present.

She tried to undress him, but he was too impatient to let her finish alone. The rug in front of the fireplace welcomed them as old friends.

She had wondered if memory had expanded the mystical pleasures of his hands on her body, but now she knew that memory was only a poor substitute. There was no way to recall such exquisite perfection. One moment built inexorably upon another. How could this be remembered—the slow upward climb, the intensifying of unbearable sensation, the yearning for, reaching toward, cataclysm?

She twisted and moved beneath him, above him, like a dancer so immersed in her performance she transcended the steps. Everything about him was familiar, yet altogether new. She absorbed the heat of his body, the smooth slide of his skin, the pressure of his lips against her breast. She felt the muscles in his back ripple against her fingertips as he lost patience completely and turned her back to the rug.

She watched his face as he slowly united them. Memory might capture only a wisp of truth, but at that moment she knew she would never forget what Simon's eyes told her as he began to move against her.

"I didn't know if I would ever see you again," Tate said later, still wrapped in Simon's arms. "But I told myself if I did, I'd be wearing a dress. You've never seen me in anything but flannel and jeans."

"I might have passed you right by and felt guilty I'd noticed you when I already had a woman I loved back in Arkansas."

She shivered and pretended she was cold. "Is that what you would have told yourself?" she asked lightly.

He wasn't fooled by her tone. He turned her to her back again and lay half across her, gazing into her eyes. "Why don't I tell you, instead? I have a woman I love right here in Arkansas. I want to love her forever. Will she let me, do you think?"

"How could she stop you?"

"She couldn't stop me from loving her. But she could stop me from being with her."

"Why would she want to?" Tate lifted her hand and brushed his hair off his forehead.

He took a long time before he answered, and he chose his words carefully. "I'm still the man I was. I'll probably die trying to be a hero. I'm planning for that to happen when I'm an old, old man, but..." He shook his head, and his meaning was clear.

"You're not going to change everything about yourself for me?"

Her tone had been neutral. He wasn't certain what she'd meant. "I want you in my life. It's selfish. I know I'm asking too much. But I finally realized this is your decision to make. I won't run from you again, but I'll leave if you tell me to go."

Her eyes widened. "No nine-to-five? No house in the suburbs?"

He smiled slowly, beginning to understand. "Just a man who loves you. A man who promises he won't take foolish risks."

"No bank president? No Boy Scout leader?"

He considered. "I could lead a unit or two on tying knots."

"And picking locks." She brushed back the same strands of hair once more. "There's not a part of me that expects or even wants life with you to be ordinary, Simon. I wouldn't know what to do if it was. I never want to chain you again. Can't we work out the other details as they come?"

"I want you with me!" He wasn't smiling now. Tate saw how much he meant his words, and how hard it had been to ask her to share his life.

She hugged him hard. "Then I'll come and be with you."

"What about the cabin?"

"Will and Dovey will look out for it. I've asked Will to use whatever portion of the land he wants anyway, so he'll be over here frequently. And we can come back for vacations."

"What will you do in Washington?"

"I'll ask Gallagher for a job."

He stared at her. "Gallagher?"

"He'd hire me in a minute."

He was afraid she was right—and not for office work. She had proven that fieldwork was her forte.

"We'd never be at a loss for something to talk about," she added, when he didn't answer. "Do you think you're the only person in the world who likes adventure?"

"Let's work out the details as they come."

"And if we don't agree?"

"I know how to compromise. Do you?"

"Sure." She smiled. "If I get my way."

"I have a feeling you will, more often than not." He lowered his head the necessary inches to kiss her, and for a long time they were silent.

"Shall we go tell your family we're going to be married?" he asked at last, his lips reading the pulse at her throat.

She pushed him away. "Married? Who said anything about marriage, Simon?"

"What did you think I was talking about?"

"Moving to Washington to be with you."

"Your life hasn't been ordinary, has it?" He cradled her face in his hands. "I'm past needing to try this on for size, love. I want you forever. People marry, when that's what they want. Even would-be heroes and heroines."

"I said I wouldn't chain you."

"Marriage is a bond, not a chain. Don't you know the difference?"

She felt something stirring deep inside her. "Are you sure you do?"

"When I finally stopped running, I began to understand."

As he kissed her again, she pulled him tighter against her. There *would* be time to work out all the details. Most important, there was nothing for either of them to flee again. Without looking over their shoulders, they could journey wherever life called them. Together.

She wondered if that was what Millard had meant about following the wise-man star.

"Millard would have been happy we found each other," she murmured against his cheek.

"Your father was a wise man."

"In a way, he brought us together."

"A very wise man."

She smiled and knew he was right.

Epilogue

"Anna, you anchor her headpiece. I can't get close enough to do it!" Krista stepped back and slapped her hands on her silk-covered hips.

Anna, a smaller, more vibrant version of her older sister, stepped forward to take the wreath of white roses out of Krista's hands. "Does she sound a little irritable to you, Tate?" she asked.

"I feel like a new moon in this dress," Krista said, holding folds of yellow fabric away from her body in distaste.

"You look like a woman about to have a baby any minute," Tate said, holding her head still as Anna began to anchor the wreath with hairpins.

"Not for another six weeks. And why are you so calm?"

"I'm just getting married." Tate watched herself being transformed from ordinary to extraordinary. Her dress was fragile white-tissue silk, cocktail-length and elegantly simple. The sweetheart neckline was adorned with a sapphire locket that Krista had worn at her own wedding. Tate had been her only attendant that day; now Krista would return the favor.

"Just?" Krista lowered herself to the side of the bed. "Just? Have you looked outside, by any chance? There are two hundred people trampling your wildflowers. There is a duchess out there," she said, lowering her voice in emphasis. "And not a bit of indoor plumbing in sight."

"Simon insists his relatives are all terribly stoic. And most of my guests live within a four-mile radius and won't need it, anyway."

"Krista's been reading up on how to be the mother of a bride," Anna said, poking one last pin in place. "Doesn't she do it well? Nerves, and all?"

"Someone has to be nervous. Tate is positively radiant."

Tate stood and adjusted her skirt. In the freestanding mirror that Dovey had donated for the occasion, she did look radiant. In the last five months Simon had frequently seen her dressed up, but she doubted that he realized she could look like this.

She doubted he had any inkling what she was feeling right now, either. Apparently no one did. Simon was probably somewhere outside with Gallagher and Aaron. For all she knew they were behind the barn swilling what was left of Millard's white lightning. Dutch courage was the appropriate phrase.

Simon had never flagged in his determination to marry her. She had given him every out, and he had taken none of them. But what was he feeling now that the event was almost at hand? She wondered if he felt like running; after all, she was bringing something to his life that he had never wanted. Surely this was the moment when the truth would wrap its tentacles around his throat and choke him.

She had spent the past five months trying to let Simon know he could still be free and love her at the same time. She had delayed their wedding, insisting that she wanted to be married when the wildflowers bloomed in the Ozarks. Now she wondered if she should have insisted on falling leaves.

It wasn't that she didn't want to marry him. Their lives had become more entwined, their lovemaking more exquisite. She was enthralled with Washington and her job with the Justice Department working on missing-children cases.

Even Cinn seemed contented in his new Georgetown home—just as long as he got to sleep on the floor next to Simon's side of the bed.

She was happier than she had believed it was possible to be. Still, there was one, tiny nagging voice that eternally questioned whether marriage might kill Simon's love for her.

She turned and saw that she and Krista were alone. "Anna went to signal the musicians," Krista said.

Tate and Simon had compromised on music. She would walk up the flower-strewn hillside overlooking the river to the strains of a string quartet that Simon had imported from Washington. Then, for the reception, they would be entertained by local musicians, including a Carter or two.

"So soon?" she said.

"Are you ready? Jess is just outside." Krista lifted the bouquet of roses and lilies of the valley from the bedside table.

Tate straightened her skirt. She wondered what she would do if Simon weren't there waiting for her when she reached the hilltop. "I'm ready," she said.

"You're beautiful, sweetheart. I love you." Krista leaned over and kissed Tate's cheek. "I'm going to cry all the way up the hill." She sniffed, as if to prove a point.

"Don't you dare. Not one of the kids from Stagecoach Inn will invite you to their wedding if you cry at mine!" Tate sniffed, too.

Krista gave her a watery smile. "Let's go."

They walked to the door, and Krista stepped out first. Will was waiting on the porch to escort her up the hill—and Dovey was standing by, in case Krista went into labor on the way. When they were halfway there, Jess opened the door and held out his arm to Tate. "Come on, daughter."

She almost said no. He took in her suddenly pale face and smiled gently. "He loves you," he said. "Don't worry."

She searched his eyes. "I am worried."

"I know. I've known. You don't need to be."

She looked at the man who had been the only father she had ever known. For a moment her vision blurred and she saw the photograph of the father she'd never know, taken when he was just about Jess's age. For one crazy, heart-stopping moment they seemed to be the same man. "Come on, daughter," Jess repeated.

"Millard?"

He cocked his head in question.

She smiled shakily and shook her head. She extended her hand to Jess and rose on tiptoe to kiss his cheek once she was in place.

The walk took forever. The sun had never shone brighter; the air had never smelled sweeter. The fields were a carpet of gold and pink. As she walked, she understood why Millard had never left his mountains.

The trail took a turn, and Tate looked up to see her guests lining the hillside. Some were wiping their eyes; some were smiling. The group of girls from Stagecoach Inn was gawking at her, as if she had suddenly become a stranger. Gallagher and Barker were, out of long habit, assessing the crowd. Anna and Grady were holding hands, their other hands on a grinning Ryan's shoulders. Krista was waiting at one side, trying not to cry—and failing.

Tate couldn't look at Simon, because she was afraid of what she might see.

She slowed her pace. The music built in intensity; the sun shone even more radiantly. At last she had no choice. She and Jess were close enough that she could no longer avoid Simon's eyes. She knew that if he felt trapped or regretful, she would see it now.

She lifted her gaze and found him next to his best man, sun-wrinkled, balding Aaron. Simon was staring at her. Slowly his smile welcomed her. Then, with no regard for tradition, he strode down the path. One hand reached out, as if he were too impatient to wait for the steps that would bring her to his side. In moments he had pulled her close and swept away all her doubts forever.

"Take care of her," Jess said, leaning over to kiss Tate's cheek. Then he shook Simon's hand and went to stand beside Krista.

Tate gazed up at Simon. As if he knew what she had feared, he shook his head. Then he leaned down and kissed her.

"I think you're supposed to wait until we're married to do that," she said, when everybody laughed.

He tucked her hand under his arm and led her toward the minister. "Then let's get married and do it again."

And they did.

* * * * *

The tradition continues this month as Silhouette
presents its fifth annual
Christmas collection

SILHOUETTE
Christmas
STORIES
1990

The romance of Christmas sparkles in four
enchanting stories written by some of your
favorite Silhouette authors:

Ann Major * SANTA'S SPECIAL MIRACLE
Rita Rainville * LIGHTS OUT!
Lindsay McKenna * ALWAYS AND FOREVER
Kathleen Creighton * THE MYSTERIOUS GIFT

Spend the holidays with Silhouette and discover
the special magic of falling in love in this
heartwarming Christmas collection.

ARE YOU A ROMANCE READER WITH OPINIONS?

Openings are currently available for participation in the 1990-1991 Romance Reader Panel. We are looking for new participants from all regions of the country and from all age ranges.

If selected, you will be polled once a month by mail to comment on new books you have recently purchased, and may occasionally be asked for more in-depth comments. Individual responses will remain confidential and all postage will be prepaid.

Regular purchasers of one favorite series, as well as those who sample a variety of lines each month, are needed, so fill out and return this application today for more detailed information.

1. Please indicate the romance series you purchase from regularly at retail outlets.

Harlequin	Silhouette	
1. ☐ Romance	6. ☐ Romance	10. ☐ Bantam Loveswept
2. ☐ Presents	7. ☐ Special Edition	11. ☐ Other _____
3. ☐ American Romance	8. ☐ Intimate Moments	
4. ☐ Temptation	9. ☐ Desire	
5. ☐ Superromance		

2. Number of romance paperbacks you purchase new in an average month:

12.1 ☐ 1 to 4   .2 ☐ 5 to 10   .3 ☐ 11 to 15   .4 ☐ 16+

3. Do you currently buy romance
series through direct mail?   13.1 ☐ yes   .2 ☐ no

If yes, please indicate series: _____
                                        (14,15)   (16,17)

4. Date of birth: _____ / _____ / _____
                  (Month)   (Day)   (Year)
                   18,19   20,21   22,23

5. Please print:
Name: _____
Address: _____
City: _____ State: _____ Zip: _____
Telephone No. (optional): (_____) _____

MAIL TO: Attention: Romance Reader Panel
          Consumer Opinion Center
          P.O. Box 1395
          Buffalo, NY 14240-9961   ☐☐☐☐☐☐☐☐☐☐☐

                                          Office Use Only   IMDK

Take 4 bestselling love stories FREE

Plus get a FREE surprise gift!

PASSPORT TO ROMANCE
SWEEPSTAKES RULES

1. **HOW TO ENTER:** To enter, you must be the age of majority and complete the official entry form, or print your name, address, telephone number and age on a plain piece of paper and mail to: Passport to Romance, P.O. Box 9056, Buffalo, NY 14269-9056. No mechanically reproduced entries accepted.

2. All entries must be received by the CONTEST CLOSING DATE, DECEMBER 31, 1990 TO BE ELIGIBLE.

3. **THE PRIZES:** There will be ten (10) Grand Prizes awarded, each consisting of a choice of a trip for two people from the following list:
   i) London, England (approximate retail value $5,050 U.S.)
   ii) England, Wales and Scotland (approximate retail value $6,400 U.S.)
   iii) Carribean Cruise (approximate retail value $7,300 U.S.)
   iv) Hawaii (approximate retail value $9,550 U.S.)
   v) Greek Island Cruise in the Mediterranean (approximate retail value $12,250 U.S.)
   vi) France (approximate retail value $7,300 U.S.)

4. Any winner may choose to receive any trip or a cash alternative prize of $5,000.00 U.S. in lieu of the trip.

5. **GENERAL RULES:** Odds of winning depend on number of entries received.

6. A random draw will be made by Nielsen Promotion Services, an independent judging organization, on January 29, 1991, in Buffalo, NY, at 11:30 a.m. from all eligible entries received on or before the Contest Closing Date.

7. Any Canadian entrants who are selected must correctly answer a time-limited, mathematical skill-testing question in order to win.

8. Full contest rules may be obtained by sending a stamped, self-addressed envelope to: "Passport to Romance Rules Request", P.O. Box 9998, Saint John, New Brunswick, Canada E2L 4N4.

9. Quebec residents may submit any litigation respecting the conduct and awarding of a prize in this contest to the Régie des loteries et courses du Québec.

10. Payment of taxes other than air and hotel taxes is the sole responsibility of the winner.

11. Void where prohibited by law.

COUPON BOOKLET OFFER TERMS

To receive your Free travel-savings coupon booklets, complete the mail-in Offer Certificate on the preceeding page, including the necessary number of proofs-of-purchase, and mail to: Passport to Romance, P.O. Box 9057, Buffalo, NY 14269-9057. The coupon booklets include savings on travel-related products such as car rentals, hotels, cruises, flowers and restaurants. Some restrictions apply. The offer is available in the United States and Canada. Requests must be postmarked by January 25, 1991. Only proofs-of-purchase from specially marked "Passport to Romance" Harlequin® or Silhouette® books will be accepted. The offer certificate must accompany your request and may not be reproduced in any manner. Offer void where prohibited or restricted by law. LIMIT FOUR COUPON BOOKLETS PER NAME, FAMILY, GROUP, ORGANIZATION OR ADDRESS. Please allow up to 8 weeks after receipt of order for shipment. Enter quickly as quantities are limited. Unfulfilled mail-in offer requests will receive free Harlequin® or Silhouette® books (not previously available in retail stores), in quantities equal to the number of proofs-of-purchase required for Levels One to Four, as applicable.

OFFICIAL SWEEPSTAKES
ENTRY FORM

Complete and return this Entry Form immediately—the more Entry Forms you submit, the better your chances of winning!
- Entry Forms must be received by **December 31, 1990**
- A random draw will take place on **January 29, 1991**
- Trip must be taken by **December 31, 1991**

3-SIM-3-SW

YES, I want to win a PASSPORT TO ROMANCE vacation for two! I understand the prize includes round-trip air fare, accommodation and a daily spending allowance.

Name_____

Address_____

City_____ State_____ Zip_____

Telephone Number_____ Age_____

Return entries to: **PASSPORT TO ROMANCE**, P.O. Box 9056, Buffalo, NY 14269-9056

COUPON BOOKLET/OFFER CERTIFICATE

Item	LEVEL ONE Booklet 1	LEVEL TWO Booklet 1 & 2	LEVEL THREE Booklet 1, 2 & 3	LEVEL FOUR Booklet 1, 2, 3 & 4
Booklet 1 = $100+	$100+	$100+	$100+	$100+
Booklet 2 = $200+		$200+	$200+	$200+
Booklet 3 = $300+			$300+	$300+
Booklet 4 = $400+	_____	_____	_____	$400+
Approximate Total Value of Savings	$100+	$300+	$600+	$1,000+
# of Proofs of Purchase Required	4	6	12	18
Check One	_____	_____	_____	_____

Name_____

Address_____

City_____ State_____ Zip_____

Return Offer Certificates to: **PASSPORT TO ROMANCE**, P.O. Box 9057, Buffalo, NY 14269-9057

Requests must be postmarked by **January 25, 1991**

✂ -

ONE PROOF OF PURCHASE

3-SIM-3

To collect your free coupon booklet you must include the necessary number of proofs-of-purchase with a properly completed Offer Certificate

- -

See previous page for details